Mick Townsend

A newbie on the paper, and a thorn in Barrie's side from the instant he showed up. For one thing, jobs were scarce enough without extra competition. But that wasn't even the start of it.

There was something almost preternaturally beautiful about him. Dark gold hair and green eyes, cheekbones you could cut glass with. The way he held himself, that casually aristocratic elegance that was the territory of actors and, well, aristocrats... He moved like a cat, strong as a panther and just as lithe.

Mick Townsend stopped right in her path, towering over her in an alarmingly commanding way. "Gryffald."

Barrie put up all her defenses as she coolly replied, "Townsend," and was proud that she didn't blush.

"You're looking very Audrey Hepburn tonight," he said lazily, and looked her over, a direct look that managed to be slow and sexy and aloof all at the same time, which didn't help her state of mind at all.

KEEPER OF THE SHADOWS

ALEXANDRA SOKOLOFF

First published in Great Britain 2013
by Mills & Boon, an imprint of Harlequin (UK) Limited,
Eton House, 18-24 Paradise Road, Richmond, Surrey TW9 1SR

© Alexandra Sokoloff 2013

ISBN: 978 0 263 90406 2
ebook ISBN: 978 1 472 00670 7

089-0713

Harlequin (UK) policy is to use papers that are natural, renewable and recyclable products and made from wood grown in sustainable forests. The logging and manufacturing processes conform to the legal environmental regulations of the country of origin.

Printed and bound in Spain
by Blackprint CPI, Barcelona

Alexandra Sokoloff is a California native and the daughter of scientist and educator parents, which drove her into musical theater at an early age.

At UC Berkeley (a paranormal experience all on its own) she majored in theatre. After college, Alex moved to Los Angeles, where she has made an interesting living writing novel adaptations, and original suspense and horror scripts, for numerous Hollywood studios.

The Harrowing, her debut ghost story, was nominated for both a Bram Stoker Award (horror) and an Anthony Award (mystery) as Best First Novel. She is the author of the paranormal mystery/thrillers *The Price, The Unseen* and *Book of Shadows*, and is the winner of a Thriller Award for her story *The Edge of Seventeen*.

Alex is also the author of *Screenwriting Tricks for Authors*, a workbook based on her internationally acclaimed blog and writing workshops.

This one's for my beautiful and wildly talented co-authors. Sisters, cousins, whatever you are, Heather and Harley, I love you forever.

Chapter 1

There is nothing more beautiful than the city at night, thought Rosalind Barrymore Gryffald as she hit the freeway toward downtown.

Being that the city was Los Angeles, it was easier to feel that way *late* at night, the later at night the better, because traffic did let up eventually, even if it was sometimes well after midnight. But then, oh, then, the city was all hers, in all its shimmering glory.

L.A. Lotus Land. The dream machine, the end of the rainbow. Was there anything in the world more romantic?

And Rosalind Barrymore Gryffald—Barrie for short, which unfortunately she was; pixieish, people tended to say, to her eternal exasperation…a copper-eyed, copper-haired sprite of a girl—loved her town.

Oh, she knew L.A. had its detractors, the ones who

were always joking that there was no *there* there. But those people just didn't know where to look. She knew where to look. In fact it was her job to look.

Not only did she live in the most exciting city in the world, she also knew its most secret excitements: there was a world within the world, even more magical than the movies. And that world was her job.

Her day job...well, her day job was actually a night job, the night shift on the Los Angeles *Courier* where she worked as a crime beat reporter. But her secret job, her all-the-time job, her passion, her *calling,* was Canyon Keeper of the shape-shifters of Los Angeles.

She was startled out of her thoughts when the digital billboard on the Wilshire Grand Building suddenly loomed up in the dark, a twenty-story-high architectural lighting tour de force featuring car-size butterflies flitting across a rainbow landscape. She was at the downtown turnoffs already.

She steered her vintage Peugeot—which she'd wheedled out of her father when he'd left the country—to the right and took the Third Street exit into the island of glittering skyscrapers that was downtown. L.A. was made up of those dense clusters of tall buildings sticking up in the middle of the relatively flat residential neighborhoods around them, a landscape that was never so apparent as at night.

Downtown L.A. was the oldest and most decrepitly grand of those islands, and the *Courier* building was right in the middle of it.

It was always a thrill to drive up to the historic Art Deco building in the heart of downtown, lit up like a wedding cake at night, to drive under the building using her very own official parking card.

Barrie charged up the escalator from the garage and breezed past the huge decorative globe in the center of the domed lobby. Ten-foot-high murals towered above her—her cousins would say everything towered above her, but she had a long history of ignoring them.

She rode the decadent Deco elevator up to the sixth floor and felt her heart lurch a little as the ancient contraption jerked, then settled.

Something was up; she could tell from the second she stepped into the newsroom. The entire floor was buzzing.

Her reporter's mind scrolled through the possibilities. *Terrorist attack? Stock market crash? Assassination?*

Or, seeing as this was L.A.….*Celebrity death?*

She grabbed the sleeve of the nearest scrambling reporter, tall, thin, redheaded Steve from Metro.

"What's going on?"

"Saul Mayo," Steve said breathlessly, and yanked his arm away.

Saul Mayo, head of World International Pictures, one of the town's six major movie studios.

"What about him?" Barrie demanded, turning to yell after him.

"Dead!" he called over his shoulder, and skittered away.

Barrie relaxed, at least as much as she ever relaxed. Not that it wasn't big news; in an industry town, a studio head in his relative prime dying was not just big news, it was huge.

But it wasn't the kind of news that she was in journalism to pursue. There was only one kind of story that interested her, and that was anything concerning the Others and the Otherworld.

Because Barrie, along with her cousins Rhiannon and Sailor Ann Gryffald, was a very new member of a very old tradition. They were Keepers, from a long line of Keepers, charged with an ancestral duty to guard and keep peace among the communities of vampires, shapeshifters, werewolves, Elven and all non-human beings—the Others, who lived all over the world, hiding in plain sight among mortal populations.

As anyone who knows anything about paranormal beings might guess, there was a large population of Others in Los Angeles. Just as mortals were lured by the shining promises of the city, so, too, were Others drawn here, some hoping to exercise their talents and find the spotlight as actors, musicians and other artists, some seeking protective camouflage in this famously eccentric town. There was a saying that "Everyone in California is from somewhere else." *So* not true; Barrie herself was a proud native Californian. But in a community of outsiders, no one looked twice at someone different, and that made Others relatively safe in their conspicuousness.

And almost since the first appearance of an Other, there had also been families born with the mark of certain beings, indicating their potential as Keepers: mortals with some of the powers of the beings they were marked with who could communicate and facilitate between the worlds.

Keepers were sworn to uphold the Code of Silence: to

keep the secret of the existence of the Otherworld. And to that end, if there was trouble or outright crime in the Otherworld that threatened to spill over into the human world and expose the existence of the Others, it was the Keepers' duty to keep the peace—quietly.

Barrie had been waiting to take on that duty all her life. Even so, it had been a shock when it happened so quickly, just months ago, when her father and his two brothers, Keepers of the shifters, vampires and Elven of the L.A. canyon districts, were called to the newly established international Council of Keepers in the Netherlands. Barrie, Rhiannon and Sailor had suddenly been thrust into the Keeping of the Canyon.

Now, instead of the endless waiting and training, it was all real. Rhiannon and Sailor had already been instrumental in solving two recent cases, a series of murders committed by a power-mad vampire and the mystery of a rare blood disease killing off Elven.

Every morning—well, some days more like afternoon—since Barrie had taken the oath in front of the local Keepers' Council, she'd woken up with a fluttery feeling of exhilaration, almost like that feeling you get when you know you're going to meet...*someone.* It wasn't that she wanted trouble, or crime, of course not, but trouble was inevitable, and when it came, she would be ready for it.

Until just recently she'd been struggling along doing "filler" stories on the *Courier,* and in the current journalistic climate, with newspapers shutting down all over the country, she'd felt lucky to get those. But a piece she'd done on the string of vampire murders that her cousin

Rhiannon and Rhiannon's now-fiancé, LAPD homicide detective Brodie McKay, had solved, had not just solidified her job but moved her up to the crime beat.

Barrie's job on the paper perfectly complemented her Keeper duties. As a crime beat reporter—well, actually, crime beat stringer, but she would get there eventually—she was able to get a first look at police reports to scan them for Other-related crimes that needed immediate attention or intervention, to ensure that: 1) humans were not harmed by out-of-control Others, and 2) the Others and the Otherworld remained a secret from the human population of the city.

So, Saul Mayo the movie mogul, being a human, or formerly human, didn't interest her.

Good riddance, anyway, she thought uncharitably. Mayo hadn't been known for his humanitarian efforts.

She steered away from the swarm of her colleagues and was headed for the local crime editor's desk when she saw the one person she didn't want to see coming toward her.

Mick Townsend.

A newbie on the paper, and a thorn in Barrie's side from the instant he'd shown up. For one thing, jobs were scarce enough without extra competition. But that was only the start of it.

Townsend was *waaay* too good-looking to be a journalist, and too stylish, too. In a city of surreally gorgeous people, he was truly heart-stopping, if you liked men who were a combination of all the best parts of young Leo DiCaprio, Russell Crowe and Hugh Jackman.

Only movie stars were supposed to look like that;

there was something almost preternaturally beautiful about him. Dark gold hair and green eyes under perfectly arched eyebrows, cheekbones that could cut glass. The way he held himself, that casually aristocratic elegance that was the territory of actors and, well, aristocrats.... He moved like a cat, strong as a panther and just as lithe. He was tall, too, which made Barrie glad she was wearing some serious heels—tonight, Chanel pumps to go with the little Balenciaga number she'd found in her favorite thrift store in Echo Park. Vintage was a particularly good look for her. People were smaller then, too.

Mick Townsend stopped right in her path, blocking her way and towering over her in an alarmingly commanding way. "Gryffald."

She put up all her defenses as she coolly replied, "Townsend," and was proud that she didn't blush.

"You're looking very Audrey Hepburn tonight," he said lazily, and looked her over, a direct examination that managed to be slow and sexy and aloof all at the same time, which didn't help her state of mind at all.

She sidestepped him and kept walking toward the crime editor's desk. Unfortunately, he turned and walked with her.

"A lady on the scent of a story, if I ever saw one."

"Looks like there's only one story tonight," she said, glancing at their huddled coworkers.

"Ah, yes. The Prince of Darkness. *Requiescat in pace*," Townsend added. *Rest in peace.*

But there was a bitter quality to his voice that belied his words, and made Barrie stop and look at him for a

moment; it seemed more than mere journalistic cyni-
cism, but some deeper feeling.

Interesting, she thought. *I wonder what that's about?*

"But that's not a story you're interested in," he said.

"No point. Even if he was murdered, they're not going
to give it to a rookie like me," she answered innocently.
"Enjoy your night."

She sidestepped him and continued to her boss's desk
where she snagged the police blotter while he paced and
talked on the phone a few desks down. She caught his
eye and held up the blotter, and he nodded at her distractedly. Now that she'd checked in, her time was hers
for the rest of the night.

She had a desk of her own in an anonymous row of
desks, and she settled down at it with the blotter while
her coworkers swarmed on the Mayo story.

Unfortunately, her hormones didn't settle down with
her; her pulse was racing out of control from that brief
encounter with Townsend.

*What kind of name is Mick Townsend for a journal-
ist, anyway?* she thought irritably. It sounded more like
a rock star. And she had a rule: no musicians, no actors.
In L.A., that was simple survival.

But she didn't really think Townsend was an actor.
She had darker suspicions: he was a spy from corporate,
skulking around to find more people to give the ax. The
newspaper would be all of three pages long by the time
the suits were through with the bloodbath; it seemed
never-ending these days, the worst time in the world to
be a journalist. She'd had to fight tooth and nail for the
tiny bit of turf she had on the paper.

Fortunately, as a Keeper, she had more than a passing acquaintance with tooth and nail, or fang and claw, or just about any variation on the above. And bloodbaths, come to that. When a person dealt daily—or at least weekly—with the loves, lives, deaths and turf wars of vampires, werewolves, shape-shifters, Elven and whatever supernatural creatures happened to present themselves, a little backbiting among journalists was small potatoes.

Well, okay, it wasn't the backbiting that was the problem this time, it was Townsend's charm.

Barrie really hated the fact that he made her uncomfortably aware that she hadn't had sex in…she didn't even want to think about it. Except that she was being forced to think of it—*constantly.* With Rhiannon engaged to Brodie McKay and Sailor newly engaged to nightclub owner Declan Wainwright, the House of the Rising Sun was a literal hotbed, licit though it might be. Barrie frowned and thought darkly, *Might as well rename it House of the Rising—*

All right, enough of that, she told herself, and forced herself to stare down at the police blotter.

The list of the night's crimes was already long: Burglary/Theft from Motor Vehicle. Grand Theft. Vandalism. Battery. And the usual collection of oddities: the owner of a La Brea Avenue business reported that someone tipped over a Porta Potty and attempted to break into a storage barn; a Vista Street woman reported a female who had delivered pizza to the address the night before had shown up at 2:00 a.m. with blood dripping from her nose and asking for money; a resident of Orange Grove

Avenue reported an unknown person stole four solar lights and a garden gnome from his yard.

Barrie knew how to scan for potentially Other-related crimes; you developed a kind of sixth sense about it. But tonight it didn't take any special skill to find the case that she would need to look into; it jumped out at her from the reports as if it were lit up in neon:

Dead body in alley off Hollywood and Gower.
Mixed race, late teens, street name Tiger. Suspected OD.

Barrie felt as if she'd been punched in the stomach.

She knew Tiger. *Had* known him. He was a street kid, a runaway, one of the eternal hopefuls who left their small towns and got on buses to Hollywood with big dreams of fame, fortune, love—and ended up turning tricks on the Boulevard instead.

Boulevard of Broken Dreams, they called it. *You got that right,* she thought, feeling a flare of anger and grief.

The Boulevard was part of her Keeper jurisdiction, so she spent a lot of time with the street kids. She was drawn to them, she ached for them, most of them running away from exploitation at home only to fall into the hands of the same kind of predator on the streets.

Tiger was a shape-shifter, and like so many others, he'd thought he could use that talent to make his fortune.

But it was a sad fact that despite their incredible talents, shifters were rarely productive members of society. Their sense of self was too amorphous. After all, they could and would subtly alter their physical form to match other people's fantasies. And because of that inconstancy and lack of center, they tended toward indulgence of all kinds, which too often turned to addiction.

Along with that ability to create fantasy, they were also some of the most manipulative creatures on the planet. And they far too often got caught in their own manipulative traps.

Tiger was smart, and he was manipulative. Just sixteen or seventeen years old—Barrie had never been able to pin him down about his age—but already he was an expert hustler. He had been using his shifter talents to attract an upscale clientele. She had been sure he was also stealing as well as conducting any number of other illicit activities.

It had taken some time for him to trust her, but Barrie blended in well with the street waifs; at her height and weight she could easily look like no more than a kid herself.

She'd worked on Tiger, bought him meals, flattered him, joked with him, chided him, and time after time had hammered him that he could be using his talents for anything he chose, no dream too big. And she'd thought she'd gotten through to him. She'd persuaded him to check in to a local shelter, Out of the Shadows, that specialized in getting young prostitutes off the street and out of the life.

Not out far enough, as it turned out.

"Damn it," she said softly.

Someone spoke behind her, startling her. "Gryffald?"

She whirled in her chair—and saw Mick Townsend

looking down at her with an odd expression. She suddenly realized she was crying.

Townsend was staring at the tears running down her cheeks. "What is it?" he asked gruffly.

She swiped at her face. "Nothing. I'm fine."

He was about to speak again when she pushed her chair back, stood abruptly and walked out past him, willing herself not to break into tears again.

She made it across the newsroom and out without crying, but broke down again in the elevator.

Damn Townsend, anyway; he seemed to have a radar for every vulnerability. She hit the side of the elevator with her fist, pounding in frustration, and the concrete pain of it brought her back to herself. Somewhat.

She wasn't being fair, she knew. Townsend couldn't help the way he looked. Maybe he *had* come to L.A. to be an actor, as so many people did. And most came to their senses and realized the competition was hopeless and the ruthlessness required to act soul-killing, and wisely chose other professions.

But some were not so wise or so lucky. Those were the ones who clung to the desperate delusion that they would "make it," that stardom was just around that next corner. Instead they ended up used-up in their twenties…

Or like Tiger. Dead.

And most likely with no one even to claim his body.

She could do that for him, at least. So she swiped away her tears and stood straighter, resolved.

Chapter 2

Barrie wasn't exactly dressed for the morgue, so she changed in the car in the parking lot. She never knew where the job would take her, so she always carried several changes of clothes in her trunk. She chose old jeans and a tank top and hoodie, washable and discardable in case she got into an autopsy room. You never could quite get out the smell of the morgue.

Then she drove east, toward the L.A. County Coroner's Office, just minutes from downtown in Boyle Heights.

Her purpose was layered. She had to make sure the right medical examiner got assigned Tiger's autopsy; it wouldn't do to have a mortal cutting into a shifter. Too many questions could come up that were better avoided. Then she needed to see if there was anything unusual about the death, and whether there might be some danger for other shifters: a bad batch of meth, for example. Also with the recent scare of a blood disease affecting one species, she had to make sure there was nothing just plain bizarre going on. But mostly, she wanted to make arrangements for Tiger's funeral.

The coroner's office was in a gorgeous Baroque building, red with cream trim, dramatic steep front steps lit by streetlamps that cast eerie shadows as Barrie climbed the stairs toward the House of Death.

She signed in with the attendant on duty, telling him she had an appointment with Dr. Antony Brandt, and proceeded down the chilly hallways, trying not to look in through the doors where dozens of bodies in various stages of investigation and storage were laid out.

She reached an office with a plate on the door reading Dr. Antony Brandt, Senior Pathologist. Almost as soon as she'd knocked, Brandt was opening it. Tony Brandt looked every bit the werewolf, even if you didn't know he actually was one. He had a head full of thick, bushy hair, a powerful barrel torso, shaggy eyebrows over watchful eyes and an ever-present five-o'clock shadow.

He acknowledged Barrie with an ambiguous smile. "I knew you'd be here. Everyone else is lining up for a look-see at the Prince of Darkness."

Exactly what Mick Townsend had called him, Barrie thought. And, of course, it made sense that the coroner's office would be expediting Mayo's autopsy. In death, as in life, celebrities got the spotlight in Hollywood.

"Just as well," Brandt continued. "No one will bother with this kid."

So, already a main part of her mission was taken care

of. Brandt was taking Tiger's autopsy, and he was not about to reveal that Tiger had been a shifter. Any Others who worked in criminal justice were experts at hiding the existence of their fellows.

"Can I see him?" she asked.

Brandt led the way down the hall to one of the autopsy suites. In the observation room he handed her a white gown, mask and gloves, which she slipped on before they entered the cutting room.

It was a large space; several procedures could take place at one time. Now, however, the room was quiet and dim, and a single body lay on a single gurney on the far left.

Barrie was startled to see that Tiger was already laid out, not to mention that he had the room to himself. L.A.'s crime rate being what it was, it was about as hard to get a table at the morgue as it was to get one at the town's latest, hippest restaurant. But Brandt had his own priorities, and they were much like hers, namely to keep the existence of the Otherworld community a secret from the mortal one.

Brandt spoke, as if in answer to her silent thoughts. "Moved him to the head of the list. No one's going to notice while Mayo is lying in state."

Barrie thought that a revealingly cynical remark. Even for a studio head, Mayo had a lot of ill will swirling around him.

She approached the table and looked down at the young shifter, so pale on the slab. They always looked so much smaller in death. She felt tears prickling her eyes again. Such a smart, cheeky kid. Such a waste. Such a *crime*.

"I'm so sorry," she whispered to him, and touched his hand. It was cold, and she shivered. If she'd only tried harder, followed up sooner…

Brandt was watching her. "You knew him, then."

She set her jaw, trying to compose herself. She wasn't going to do Tiger any good by falling apart now.

"Who caught the call?" she asked Brandt.

He named a couple of homicide detectives in the Hollywood Division. "They didn't think it was important enough to involve Robbery Homicide," he added.

Robbery Homicide was a special division in the LAPD, the most coveted assignment. It handled the highest-profile murders. Certainly Mayo would have been moved there instantly. The haves and have-nots again.

"Is there any chance it was suicide?" Barrie didn't think so, but she had to ask.

"Oh, this was no suicide."

She tensed up in every muscle. "Why?"

"He didn't die in that alley. The body was moved. That's clear from the patterns of livor mortis."

Barrie knew that livor mortis meant the settling of the blood after death due to gravity. It appeared as bluish, blotchy discoloration of the skin where the blood had pooled. She listened closely as Brandt continued, indicating regions of Tiger's body with a short metal pointer as he spoke.

"Lividity does not appear anywhere that the body has been in direct contact with the ground. He was found sitting up, slumped against a wall, but if you look at the pattern here, you'll see there is no lividity in the relevant parts of his legs. He died lying down on his back. He was positioned sitting up at some later time."

Brandt loved to expound, and she was grateful for it; she picked up all kinds of useful information from his mini-lectures.

"Now ask me what else is interesting about this," he said.

Barrie tensed up. "What else is interesting about this?" she asked softly.

He held her eyes with his piercing ones. "I'm not entirely sure, but it looks to me like the unfortunate young man may have had some help."

"Some help *dying?*" Barrie stammered. "So, he was murdered?"

"You're getting ahead of yourself, fair Rosalind." There weren't many people Barrie allowed to call her by her real name, but Brandt was one. It was his Shakespearean quality; everything he said sounded vaguely Elizabethan. "But these bother me." He aimed the pointer at some faint purple circles at the top of Tiger's arm. They looked almost like—

"Fingerprints?" she asked, feeling a prickling at the back of her neck. "You think he was held? Forced?"

"Could be. On the other hand, it's common for addicts to help each other shoot up. And an addict bruises easily, so it may mean nothing. I am merely pointing it out as an anomaly, and in fact...I never said it. But it's something to keep in mind."

"Now, moving a body is a crime, but it's not necessarily murder. If he was shooting up in a gallery and someone didn't want the cops around, they may just have dumped him. But I don't think so. I think someone wanted this kid dead. He definitely didn't stick that needle in his own arm."

"Murder..." Barrie said, her thoughts far away. And she knew exactly where to go to find out what she needed to know. "I have to go," she mumbled.

Brandt raised his impressive eyebrows. "I'm cutting him in a half hour. You don't want to stay?"

Barrie shuddered. True, she regularly worked with the undead, but the actual dead were a different story. And she had no desire at all to see Brandt slice into Tiger.

"I need to get out to Hollywood to see someone. Can I check back with you about the tox screen and whatever else you find?"

"Of course. And I'll make sure your soon-to-be-cousin knows."

Barrie had to blink to understand that Brandt was referring to Brodie McKay.

"Thanks. And, Tony..." She had to swallow to get the words out. "I'll claim the body if no one else does. I'll make sure the Council gives him a proper burial."

He smiled at her sadly. "You're a good kid, kid."

Barrie was both buzzed and depressed as she left the coroner's building. She could feel the adrenaline rush of a mystery, the thrill of the hunt; at the same time she was grieving Tiger's death and the possibility of evil intent behind it, which kicked her protective Keeper instincts into high gear.

If a shifter had been murdered on her turf, there was going to be hell to pay.

Chapter 3

There were two main east-west boulevards that ran through the district called Hollywood: Sunset Boulevard and iconic Hollywood Boulevard itself. Despite the tourist trappings of the day, at night the Boulevards had a shadowy, sleazy side. Between those thoroughfares every conceivable taste could be serviced: girls, boys, top, bottom, pain, pleasure…and some tastes inconceivable to most human beings.

This no-man's-land was where Tiger's body had been found, and where Barrie was headed next. She knew Tiger ran with another young prostitute who called himself Phoenix, and he would be her best bet for information. The street kids often banded together for protection and community; Tiger and Phoenix had cribbed together, sometimes in one of the appalling motels that lined the side streets of Hollywood, sometimes on the stoops of shops or warehouses late at night. Whether the boys' intimacy translated to actual sex was an open question; Barrie suspected the two had been lovers as well, in some ambiguous way, but drugs often killed any real sex drive. Phoenix was a shifter, too, but nowhere near as skilled as Tiger was. She reflected that it was a talent a bit like acting, in a way. Some had a little; only a very few were stars. Tiger had been a star. Not that it had helped him, apparently.

She found Phoenix in a foul but atmospherically lit alley where she knew a lot of the street kids congregated in between tricks to recover, dose and socialize. He was sitting on a dirty stoop, smoke from a cigarette curling around his head. A perfectly cinematic shot, if not for his obvious agony. He was ravaged with weeping, and broke down again when he saw Barrie. All he managed was "You heard," before his words dissolved in tears.

She had delivered Phoenix to the Out of the Shadows shelter at the same time as she'd taken Tiger there; the two youths were joined at the hip, so to speak. She'd suspected at the time that Phoenix, by far the weaker of the two, would be back on the street in no time. She'd had higher hopes for Tiger.

She sat beside him and rubbed his back lightly as he cried, careful not to touch too hard, too much.

"He was working again?"

"Not the street!" Phoenix said defiantly. "He was moving up. Building a real list."

Barrie bit her lip to suppress an outburst, considering that a "list" was basically a collection of sexual predators. What there was about prostitution that could

be considered "moving up" in any way was so far beyond her that she couldn't even begin to process it, but
she didn't want to insult or alienate Phoenix. She wasn't
about to denigrate any bit of pride the boy could take in
his profession. And pride was what Phoenix was express-
ing, as his words spilled out about his friend.

"Tiger was *good*. He could do anyone. Jimmy, Kurt,
Jim, Heath, Johnny. He was goin' places."

Phoenix meant that Tiger could change his appearance to look like the dead stars Phoenix named. Barrie realized with a shiver that they were all stars who'd
died tragically young, either from addiction or their own
reckless behavior, shooting stars who burned out too fast
on their talent and lifestyles: James Dean in a car wreck
at twenty-four, Kurt Cobain a suicide at twenty-seven,
Jim Morrison of a heroin overdose (hotly disputed) at
twenty-seven, and the youngest of all of them, Johnny
Love, a sixteen-year-old movie idol who in the 1990s
had burned up the screen in cult classics like *Race the
Night* and *Youngbloods* and then died shooting up a lethal speedball at sixteen, just after the huge success of
his last movie, *Otherworld*.

Barrie thought uncomfortably, and not for the first
time, how chillingly easy it was to become what you
pretended to be. Now Tiger had joined the list of his
dead idols.

She shook her head and tried to focus on the boy beside her. "Was he working for someone?" She avoided
the word "pimp."

Phoenix straightened his shoulders, clearly proud of
his dead friend. "He was doin' it himself. He hooked

up with someone big. Real big. He had a regular date with someone in the movies, really connected, who was into shifters big-time. And he was paying big money for Tiger to shift."

Barrie's heart started beating faster. "Someone in the movies? Do you know who?"

Phoenix shook his head. "Someone who was going to do things for him. Get him parts. Tiger was really high about it."

Could it be? A connection between Tiger and Saul Mayo? Barrie had the strongest feeling, an almost psychic hit, that she was on to something. Maybe something huge.

"A producer? Director? Actor?" she asked, trying to be casual.

"Tiger didn't say much."

"Did you ever actually see this guy?"

Phoenix shook his head. "I saw his car once. A limo."

Not helpful. Every third car in this town was a limo.

"If that person—or anyone—comes around looking for Tiger, can you let me know?" She gave Phoenix a card; he looked down at it listlessly and shrugged. Her heart tore. "Phoenix, I can drop you at Out of the Shadows. You know Lara would be glad to have you."

His eyes grew hooded. "Maybe I'll cruise over later."

She sighed. It was so hard to get the kids out of the life. It was abuse, but for them it was abuse on their own terms. She touched his arm.

"You call me if you need anything, Phoenix. I'm so very sorry about Tiger."

* * *

Mayo's body had been discovered at the Chateau Marmont. The hotel was a Hollywood institution, built in the 1920s and modeled after a French castle, with one elegant old main building towering over a spread of luxury bungalows that fairly dripped old film studio elegance. It was known for its beautiful views, ornate turrets and tiny wooden elevators, the junglelike pool area, and the young celebrity clientele populating the hopping cocktail bar.

Barrie pulled into the side alley where the front entrance was tucked away and looked up at the Gothic palace on the hill. Its aura had been paid for in blood, the hotel being the site of several legendary tragedies: John Belushi's death from a drug overdose, and the near death of Jim Morrison, who used to joke that he used up the eighth of his nine lives when he fell headfirst onto a garden shed while trying to swing from a drainpipe to his window at the Chateau.

And tragically, sixteen-year-old Johnny Love.

Barrie recalled uneasily that Phoenix had said Johnny was one of Tiger's favorite shifts.

And Johnny Love had died of an apparent overdose in his teens.

Just like Tiger, Barrie thought. *So much like Tiger.*

It was not much more than the cruel chance of Hollywood that one had ascended to iconic superstardom and the other had died anonymously in an alley.

She frowned as something prickled at the edges of her consciousness, some fact that she knew was important but that she couldn't quite get to.

As she was grasping for the thought, she was distracted by the sight of a hearse pulling up, a Hollywood Ghost Bus loaded with tourists out to see "the darker side of Tinseltown." Barrie grimaced; it was all oh-so-edgy and cool from the outside, but tonight she couldn't see anything even resembling humor.

And now, she realized, the movie mogul Saul Mayo would be part of the tour, maybe even more of a celebrity in death than he had been in life. It was outrageous, enraging. And so very, very Hollywood.

Barrie breathed in to calm herself. Then she gave up her Peugeot to a valet and walked into the hotel through the side alley entrance.

As she entered the dim, elegant, edgy lobby, her mind was going a mile a minute. She knew she was going to have to play this carefully. She was bound to run into other journalists digging up dirt on Mayo's death, and she didn't want anyone else, not *any*one, picking up on a possible connection between Mayo and Tiger.

Least of all Mick Townsend. But here he was, larger than life, strolling around the sunken, tiled lobby, looking irritatingly suave and baronial in the lush surroundings that came complete with grand piano, heavy velvet drapes and candelabra. He seemed not just at home but as if he owned the place.

"Gryffald," he said, apparently unsurprised to see her. "Selling out and going for the Mayo story after all?"

"Just like you, I guess," she retorted, but she was secretly glad he'd jumped to that conclusion. It would save her the trouble of making up a story to keep him from guessing the real trail she was on.

"So, how'd he die?" she asked. If Townsend was going to be so damned chummy she could at least get some information out of him.

"OD," Townsend said shortly. "Some exotic drug cocktail. Coke, heroin and belladonna."

Belladonna? Barrie thought, startled. Coke and heroin was a common combination, called a speedball, among hard-core drug users. Adding a hallucinogen, particularly one with such an occult history as belladonna, was more Other territory than human, although in Hollywood Others often started edgy trends that humans then adopted without knowing the Otherworldly source.

Mick continued, "Of course, we're not allowed to report that. Total blackout until it's confirmed beyond a shadow of a doubt—or lawsuit."

He circled the piano, stopped to run his fingers lightly and expertly over the keys. She recognized the opening of an old jazz standard, one of her dance favorites.

Damn, he could play the piano, too. Perfection was so annoying. Barrie felt a warmth spreading through her and was alarmed to find herself wondering what it would feel like to have him run those skilled fingers over her body.

All right, that has to stop now.

Townsend pushed back abruptly from the piano, grimacing. "The story's already jumped the shark. It's not enough that Mayo died of an OD at the Chateau Marmont. There's some genius of a bellhop insisting that he checked into a bungalow with a young guy who was the spitting image of Johnny Love. Ghosts, for God's sake," he said, disgusted.

Now it was adrenaline Barrie felt racing through her, accelerating her thoughts.

A bellhop saw Johnny Love?

Phoenix said Johnny Love was one of Tiger's favorite shifts.

Tiger had a powerful Hollywood client who paid big money for shifting.

Tiger's body was moved from somewhere else into that alley.

She'd been right. There was a connection between Mayo and Tiger.

She was very still, letting none of her thoughts show on her face. In fact, she used a little glamour—a temporary illusion, a very unstable form of shifting that her father had taught her when she was just a little girl—to keep her expression neutral, a trick a shifter or shifter Keeper could do to make sure she wasn't giving anything away.

It was a huge lead. What if Tiger had died *here,* with Mayo? What if—

Her breath momentarily stopped at the next thought.

What if they both *had been killed here? Together?*

She had to contact Brandt right away.

She swallowed to be sure her voice was steady and said, "That's ridiculous. The ghost of Johnny Love? The hotel must be getting a kickback from the ghost tours."

Townsend laughed, a rich, genuine sound that made Barrie's face suddenly flush warm. "I bet they are." Then he looked at her, a long look that made her even warmer. "I think we should have dinner and talk about it."

She was caught totally off guard. "It's almost two in the morning," she pointed out.

"Breakfast, then," he said. "Brunch. Cocktails. Whatever your body clock has in mind."

She was itching to get to Brandt, which was why she responded without thinking. *Really* without thinking. "All I have in mind is bed."

Townsend half smiled, but even his half smile sizzled through her whole body. "Even better."

"I meant sleep," she mumbled.

"Sleep is always good," he said seriously. "Eventually."

Feeling completely out of control, Barrie said, "'Eventually' won't work for me. Have a good night." She turned and walked out of the lobby with whatever was left of her dignity, and immediately ducked into the ladies' to avoid running into Mick again. She sat in front of one of the makeup mirrors and was extremely annoyed to see the red in her cheeks.

"You look like you're in heat," she muttered. But looking in the mirror gave her an idea. She put her hands flat on the top of the vanity, and as she stared into her reflection in the mirror, she slowed her breathing and concentrated on her auric body, the energetic field that a shifter manipulates in order to shift. As her eyes bored into the mirror, she began to see the faint outline of light around her own reflection. She pushed with her mind… and slipped on a different kind of glamour, what she thought of as a beauty spell, that would at least temporarily make her devastatingly attractive to anyone who looked at her. She closed her eyes, and felt the glamour float over her head and settle delicately over her entire body, like a gauzy dream of a dress, a sexy and intoxicating softness....

She opened her eyes....

The woman who looked back at her from the mirror had her features and coloring, but magically enhanced: a classic Hollywood goddess, too beautiful to be real. In this moment she could have given Lauren Bacall or Myrna Loy or Rita Hayworth a run for her money.

Barrie breathed in, feeling the pure power of that beauty. Then she stood and went out in search of the bellhop.

With the glamour on all she had to do was smile at the young male desk clerk and say she would just *love* to talk to the man who'd seen the ghost. The clerk pointed her toward the bell stand with a felled-by-lightning sort of look on his face.

The bellhop was in his late twenties but still had the gangly awkwardness of adolescence, and looked equally starstruck to see Barrie coming toward him.

"M-may I help you?" he stammered.

She gave him a dazzling smile. "I hope so. Did you really see the ghost of Johnny Love?"

"I'm not supposed to talk to any more reporters," he said without much conviction.

"Good thing I'm not a reporter, then," she said, and watched him waver, captivated by her false loveliness.

He glanced around to see if anyone could overhear them and then leaned toward her. "It wasn't a ghost, it was a real person. He just looked exactly like Johnny."

Not a ghost, then. A shifter, Barrie thought, and felt her pulse spike. *Was it Tiger?*

"And he checked in with Mayo?" she asked.

"I'm not supposed to say that," the bellhop said, still enraptured.

"Good thing you didn't, then." She twinkled at him. "It will be our little secret."

As she was turning away from him, she heard footsteps and an already achingly familiar voice speaking behind her. "Ah, there you are…darling."

Darling? And what's with the British accent?

As she turned, Mick Townsend was at her side, taking her hand, lifting it to kiss her fingers.

Whoa!

Even as desire rushed through her bloodstream at the feel of his lips on her skin, Barrie was reeling with confusion. *What* is *this?*

Mick gave her a look that sizzled through her to her toes as he spoke. The British accent was perfect, one of her perpetual downfalls, as intoxicating as catnip to a kitten. "I've just been telling this gentleman about our dilemma, and he's been kind enough to find us a suite for the night."

Barrie realized that the desk clerk was hovering behind him, and from the look he gave her it was clear the glamour she'd put on was still working.

She tried to focus and sort out what was going on. *Our dilemma? A suite?* Even as she wanted to rip into Townsend for whatever game he was playing, her intuition was telling her to go along with him, at least until she knew what was going on.

"It's a bungalow, darling," Mick said pointedly, and stroked her cheek, making her pulse skyrocket. "Poolside."

Bungalow. Mayo died in one of the bungalows. Her eyes widened, and although she kept her thoughts to herself, she saw Mick give her the barest nod. *Can he really have talked his way into Mayo's suite?*

"That's so very lovely of you," she told the desk clerk, smiling as sweetly as she could. "We were—"

"—not looking forward to spending our wedding night at the airport," Mick finished for her smoothly, his fingers now tracing an erotic pattern on her forearms.

Wedding night? Now, that's just too much. She shot Mick a blistering look, and he smiled at her with mock adoration. "I explained all about the flight delay, our bags being held hostage. But none of that matters tonight. We have this beautiful place, we have each other...."

He bent suddenly and kissed her. A lingering, promising, maddening touch of that full, firm mouth. Barrie felt the ground cartwheel beneath her.

Mick drew slowly back, his eyes on hers...then slid his fingers down her arm to take her hand and turned her so they both faced the desk clerk. "May we see it?"

Mick steered her after the desk clerk, and Barrie followed along in shock, down an abbeylike hall toward a set of heavy wooden doors. "He's really putting us in Mayo's room?" she whispered to Mick. It was a crime scene, or at least under investigation. She couldn't imagine how he'd managed it.

"Not exactly," he said, barely moving his lips.

She opened her mouth again, and when he put a fin-

ger on her lips to silence her, she could feel the tingle
start from somewhere in her core. He nodded toward the
desk clerk, and she went along in silence.

The clerk held the door open for them and they
stepped outside into the junglelike plaza. The landscaping of the Chateau was lush and tropical—with tiny
lights sprinkled in the trees for a fairy-tale glow—and
designed for maximum privacy; as they followed the
clerk, Barrie could barely see the outlines of the bungalows down the paths that curved off into the foliage.
She was hyperconscious of Mick's hand closed warmly
around hers, his thumb stroking her fingers with a light,
sensual touch…and hyperconscious that he was one of
the most beautiful men she had ever seen. He carried
himself like a rock star. She might have put on an artificial glamour, but there was a natural glamour about
him that was almost hypnotic. She felt like the mistress
of some exotic celebrity, suddenly transported into a
Hollywood fantasy.

Ahead, the shimmering water of the pool glowed blue
and inviting in the center of the buildings. The lights,
the softly rippling water, the light breeze on her skin,
the heat coming off the gorgeous man beside her… Barrie was having all kinds of ideas she didn't want at all.
Mick glanced at the pool and then at her face, and she
suddenly had the uncomfortable feeling he knew exactly
what she was thinking.

They had turned down one of the pale curving paths,
and the desk clerk stopped in front of a bungalow that
seemed to have appeared out of nowhere. There was an
arched door with windows on either side completing

the curve, white roses and lilies in the planters beside it wafting an intoxicating scent. "Here we are," the clerk said, and glanced at Barrie. Mick nudged her, and she gave the clerk a big smile.

"Gorgeous," she said. "We're so very grateful."

The clerk opened the door, and she and Mick stepped into an elegantly retro cottage, low lights revealing clean lines and lots of windows with gauzy curtains, and everything impeccably decorated in old Hollywood style: Art Deco mirrors and tile, low curved couches, a small kitchen. Through a half-open door, Barrie caught a glimpse of a bedroom with a four-poster bed.

To her mortification, Mick caught her look and held her eyes before he turned to the desk clerk.

"It's perfect, my man. We're going to name our first child after you," he declared, whipping out what Barrie was sure was a hundred-dollar bill, even as she was blushing as crimson as the desk clerk at the idea of a first child.

"There are robes in the closet, and…well…" The clerk cast around for something safe to say. "Enjoy."

He backed out with one last furtive look at Barrie as he closed the door behind him.

"Beautiful," Mick said, looking straight at her with a heart-stopping intensity, and for a moment she wondered if he meant the success of their ruse—or her. She was suddenly regretting changing into jeans and a hoodie. And then she realized where her thoughts were going and ordered herself to focus.

"Was this Mayo's suite?" she demanded, moving far-

ther inside, partly to get some distance from Mick, who
was radiating way too much…everything. In every way.

"No. Two bungalows down," he said, and she was in-
furiated to see he was holding back a smile that seemed
all-too-knowing in the circumstances. "I saw the crime
scene tape," he added.

"What are you planning to do, break in?"

He turned his hand over and displayed a key in his
palm. "Grabbed it from behind the desk while he was
ogling you."

Damn the man, he thought of everything.

"You can drop the accent now, you know," she told
him. It was making her want to sink into that four-poster
bed and do unspeakable things to him. Or let him do
unspeakable things to her. Or…

Stop that.

She had to keep her head.

"Oh, of course," he said in his normal voice. "If you
insist. Let's see what we've got."

He stepped to the front door and opened it a wedge
to look out onto the dimly lit walkway, then nodded to
Barrie. She moved past him through the door, a little
too close for comfort. It seemed anytime she got within
three feet of him her whole body started to melt down.

Mick came after her. "This way," he said, and reached
for her hand; she pulled away and stopped on the shadowed path. "Why bring me along?" she demanded. Journalists weren't big on sharing scoops; the whole setup
was highly suspicious.

He half smiled in the dark. "Because I needed to get
out to the cottages and that clerk was so obviously smit-

ten with you, I knew he'd bend over backward to help if you were involved."

Barrie had to admit the glamour had done its work. In fact it even seemed to be affecting Mick a little; he kept looking at her in a way that was making it hard to concentrate on rooting out a story or even breathing.

"Are you coming or not?" he asked, and started down the path again.

She stood for a moment, then followed. "And what do you think you're going to find in Mayo's bungalow?" she said too crossly as she caught up with him.

The smile disappeared from his face; he looked serious, even grim. "I have no idea, but don't you want to see?"

She had to admit she did.

She felt a thrill of the illicit as she followed him under the crime scene ribbon, stretched discreetly back from the main walkway. He gallantly held it up for her to slip under, and then they both moved down the path toward the door of the dark bungalow. It was bigger than the one the desk clerk had given them. Two bedrooms, Barrie thought, and higher ceilings.

Mick inserted the key in the lock, and she found herself holding her breath as the door swung open.

They stood for a moment letting their eyes adjust to the dimness.

The bungalow was even more luxurious than the clean-lined and pretty one they had just left. Here there was dark wood, velvet couches and stained glass in the arched windows, with thick Persian rugs on the hardwood floors. The lights from outside were an eerie glow through the colors of the stained glass.

Barrie looked around her in the dark, and even though she knew it was mostly her imagination, she felt a chill, a dark heaviness to the air. *Did Tiger die here? Tiger and Mayo both? What intruder was here with them?*

Mick moved forward slowly, stepping silently on the luxurious rugs. "Feel anything?" he asked her, his voice low and tense. She was unnerved, wondering what he could possibly mean.

"Creepy," she said softly, surprising herself.

"Yeah," he answered, and moved into the bedroom. She stood for a moment in the pools of red and blue and amber light, and then followed him.

The bed, like the one in the other suite, was four-poster, but this one was massive, with heavy and intricately carved posts, and the window screens were covered with iron filigree. There were standing candelabra lined up beside the bed; the whole setup had a medieval look that gave Barrie another shiver. *Tiger, what did you get yourself into?* she thought, her heart wrenching with sorrow. And then she felt a surge of blistering anger at the middle-aged mogul who had deliberately, maliciously brought a teenage boy into this kind of gilded prison to use for his narcissistic pleasures.

"The Prince of Darkness," Mick said, his voice taut, almost as if he'd heard her thoughts, and Barrie heard the same strange bitterness in his voice that she'd noticed when he spoke of Mayo in the newsroom.

Why is *that?* she wondered. *And what does he think*

he's going to find here that the cops wouldn't have already taken away?

Even as she thought it, Mick pulled something dark and metallic from his jacket pocket. Barrie's heart constricted in fear.

Oh, my God...a gun....

And then she went limp as she realized it was a small flashlight.

He turned it on and shielded the beam with his hand to keep the light away from the windows, then stepped to the bed where he ran the flashlight beam up the post closest to him.

Barrie watched, mystified. Mick stopped the light on the wooden post about a foot above the mattress and leaned in to examine the wood. She could see by the tightening of his body that he'd found whatever it was he was looking for.

"What is it?" she said, and heard her voice quaver.

He moved abruptly back and strode around to her side of the bed. She backed away to let him pass. He trained the light on the other post, at the same level as he had before, and once again she saw the change in his body language.

He looked at her and nodded toward the post, holding the flashlight steady, and she stepped warily in beside him to look.

She saw scratches in the post, light marks where the wood had been scraped.

"What...?" she started, and then she had a sinking feeling she understood.

"Handcuffs," Mick said tightly.

"What does that...?"

"It means he *did* have a kid here with him. The scratches are fresh, and the evidence fits with Mayo's... proclivities."

Barrie was opening her mouth to demand how he knew, when suddenly they both froze at the sound of the door opening in the outer room.

A male voice called from the living room, "Who's in here?"

Mick killed the flashlight and grabbed her hand, pulling her toward the closet. He silently hustled her inside, edging the door closed behind them. The closet was large, empty except for two plush terry-cloth spa robes hanging from the bar, an ironing board clipped to a rack and a shelf of spare pillows and blankets. He pulled her back against the wall and up against his side, behind the robes. Not enough cover by any means; if whoever was outside opened the closet door they would be discovered.

Barrie's heart was pounding, and she could feel Mick's heart beating the same fast tattoo beside her. He still had hold of her hand and even through her fear she was wildly aware of his body against hers, long, hard muscles and a faint musky cologne that only enhanced his purely intoxicating male scent. Barrie was faint with terror, adrenaline and a sudden, unwanted desire.

Footsteps approached on the hardwood floor. Whoever had been outside was in the bedroom now. A crack of light suddenly appeared under the closet door.

Barrie's eyes widened, and Mick put his fingers over her mouth, locking his eyes on hers, willing her to be still.

Whoever was outside was silent, but she could feel his presence, hovering…and at the same time she was roiling inside from the touch of Mick's fingers…her insides seemed molten.

Then the steps retreated and the crack of light under the closet door went dark.

Barrie breathed shallowly and silently, straining to hear. *Someone just checking the room? Were they gone?* Mick's eyes were fixed on hers, and she felt a surge of relief…and attraction so strong her legs buckled underneath her.

Suddenly his arm was around her waist and he was leaning down to kiss her. Not a light brush of the lips this time, but a full-on, hungry, demanding kiss. Barrie gasped, shocked and terrified, but unable to push him away or protest. And then as his mouth opened hers and his hands moved on her waist, she didn't want to protest; she was kissing him back, silently, greedily devouring him, biting his lips, her own hands slipping under his jacket, pulling up his shirt, to find hot, smooth skin. His hard stomach jumped as she stroked his skin, her hand moving lower…. His fingers were on her throat, and his tongue surged against hers, thrusting deeper.

She felt her body melting into his, opening herself to the hardness of his sex and thighs as he pressed her against the closet wall and kissed her neck, licking the hollow of her throat. Her breasts were full in his hands, her nipples taut against his palms, and she wrapped her leg around his, and he lifted her hips so she could feel him hard and wanting, moving against her…seeking, straining through the fabric of their clothing….

Barrie was breathing shallowly, aching to have him inside her. He pulled down the zip of her hoodie and bent to tongue her nipples through the thin cloth of her tank top, and she breathed into his ear, "Please…please…" and she didn't know if she was saying *please yes* or *please no*…

And then terror overcame lust and she managed to push him away and they stood panting in the darkness.

In silence.

"He's gone," she said in a small voice.

Mick stepped forward, his face taut with desire. "Come here," he said roughly, and reached for her again. She gasped and ducked and fled through the dark bungalow and into the night.

Driving was a challenge; her whole body was vibrating from Mick's kisses, his maddening touches, the feel of his body hard on hers…. She was so weak with thwarted desire she could barely concentrate on the road.

But even in her confused—and aroused—state, she couldn't rest until she swung back by the morgue to see Brandt.

From the time she was young, Barrie had been instructed never to speak of Keeper business on the phone or in email or a text; you never knew what conversation might be picked up in these zero-privacy days. She and her cousins had developed their own language to use if they needed to use the phone, and they had a code word they changed every week that clued the others in to a Keeper-related message. There was a whole set of codes used by Keepers and Others. But she needed to see Brandt to ask him a question she didn't dare ask on the phone, even in code.

Five minutes in and out, and she had her answer.

Tiger's tox screen had showed the same lethal combination of heroin, cocaine and belladonna as Saul Mayo's.

Chapter 4

Barrie finally made it back to the canyon about dawn. The hills were bathed with rose-gold light, and the traffic…well, okay, the traffic had started hours ago, in the predawn dark, but she turned up the road toward the House of the Rising Sun, the compound she shared with her cousins, before the real gridlock kicked in.

She'd managed to curb the obsessive random images of sex with Mick in every conceivable position…by getting angry.

I don't even know him. He doesn't know me. And, okay, that was probably just the desk clerk outside the closet door, checking up on the room because he saw the light. But what if it wasn't? Of all the stupid, dangerous, inappropriate things to do…

Her inner rant was momentarily silenced by another full-body flashback of Mick kissing her while he slowly ground his hard and oh-so-enticing length between her thighs....

Stop it.

She clenched her fingers on the steering wheel and stared hard out the windshield to focus...and realized she was home.

The House of the Rising Sun—really a set of three houses—was protected by a tall stone wall that encircled it on multiple levels. She buzzed open the massive electric gate with a remote, and it swung wide to allow entry to the haunting drive, revealing the beautiful stone facades of the houses. Each of the cousins had her own, all part of the estate that had been left to their grandfather by his friend Merlin the Great: magician extraordinaire, aka Ivan Schwartz. The senior Gryffalds had passed the houses on to their three Keeper sons; Barrie had grown up in the house called Gwydion's Cave, after a mythological Welsh magician. And now that their fathers had been called to council, the international gathering of Keepers, the three houses belonged to the three cousins.

Barrie parked her car in the circle and walked through the pool area with its gazebo and jasmine-covered trellises toward the Cave, as she thought of it.

The pool brought on another very unwelcome flashback of the dark sensuality of the Chateau and the feeling of Mick's hands on her skin, her breasts....

Stop it.

Barrie ran the last steps to her door and flung it open. Inside, she slammed the door behind her and had at least a moment of peace as she let herself relax in the familiar luxury of home.

Gwydion's Cave was decorated with old peacock fans, marble pieces, antique mirrors and rich remnants of decadence from the days of the speakeasies. There was even a Victrola with a collection of recordings of the bawdiest songs from the 1920s.

It was a period Barrie especially vibrated to, a time when women threw off their corsets, claimed the vote and danced their way into independence in society. But she also loved the twenties for their sheer style, one of the few traits she shared with her complicated mother, so being able to live in the Cave, in such old Hollywood splendor, was icing on the cake of her Keeper existence.

She started down the hall lined with antique mirrors and felt a wave of exhaustion that had her swaying on her feet. A double murder, an Otherworldly mystery, and a powerful unexpected attraction…and it was up to her to sort it all.…

Sleep. I need to sleep. This all won't seem so…overwhelming…in the morning.

She barely had the energy to engage the elaborate security system behind her, then she stumbled off to bed.

But of course she couldn't sleep. She lay in her bed, a carved canopied thing with satin sheets and pillows, and could think only of Mick Townsend.

God, she *wanted* him. Her whole body was on fire… the slightest move of her clothing or the sheets on her skin was making her crazy with desire.

She closed her eyes and stretched her arms out to

her sides, imagining Mick holding her down, the whole delicious weight of him on top of her, his mouth on her breasts, his knee parting her thighs so his hot hard length could slide into her core....

The fantasy was so strong, the memory of his touch so vivid, she could almost feel him on top of her, his hands on her wrists, the tip of him teasing her open... and then the thrust of him, the massive pleasure of his sex inside her, filling her, inflaming her....

She moaned and writhed underneath him, and his thrusts deepened...quickened...driving her to the brink... it was so good...so real....

Her eyes flew open and above her she saw—

Golden skin, blond hair, blue eyes...

She gasped aloud and sat straight up in shock and terror.

Daylight streamed through the cracks in the drapes. She was alone.

Well, not completely alone. Her cat, Princess Sophie, was curled up on a pillow beside her. Sophie lifted her head to blink at her sleepily.

Barrie caught her breath and lay slowly back. "Johnny Love," she said softly. "Oh, my God."

That was the dream image she'd had before she'd woken up. Not Mick, but the young dead actor.

She shivered, disturbed.

But she knew where the image had come from.

As she'd hit the bed last night—this morning—she'd kept her eyes open long enough to reach for her iPad and search "Saul Mayo and Johnny Love" on Google. She had learned one very interesting thing. Mayo had been the producer of Johnny Love's last movie, the cult classic *Otherworld*. So, the two had known each other, worked together.

And she'd incorporated the photos of Johnny Love she'd been looking at into her dream.

She shivered to shake off a strange chill and grabbed for her phone to check the time.

11:00 a.m., which meant Sailor was probably back from her run, the little freak. If Barrie was lucky, both her cousins were still at home. She definitely needed to talk.

And there would be no more obsessing over Mick Townsend. It was daylight; it was over. "It never happened," she said aloud.

She even felt a touch of guilt. After all, in the rush of hormones she'd completely forgotten, but the fact was she *had* glamoured herself. "It was an *attraction* spell, for heaven's sake," she murmured. Which meant that everything would undoubtedly be completely normal when she saw him again. Which made her feel relieved...and a little sad.

She sat up in bed and was confronted with myriad images of herself. There were mirrors all over the bedroom. But despite her appalling behavior with Mick Townsend last night, it wasn't like she was some sex-crazed exhibitionist. She'd grown up with a wall-size mirror as a constant companion in the dance classes she'd taken as a child, and she had always been especially fond of mirrors set across from each other to create infinite images. As shape-shifter Keeper, she dealt with beings whose specialty was multiple and deceiving images, so the metaphor fit. It was her bedroom, after all, so why shouldn't she have it the way she wanted it? Secretly she was thrilled that Merlin had decorated Gwydion's Cave like a Roaring Twenties cathouse; it meant she could live surrounded by that decadence and pretend that it wasn't her own taste.

She stretched her way out of bed, then pulled on her favorite tangerine silk Chinese-dragon-patterned robe and stepped out onto her patio adjacent to the pool. It was a perfect time of day and perfectly lovely; the hills were bright with sunshine, and the estate was deep enough in the canyon to always feel far removed from the city hustle.

She could see both her cousins' cars parked in the drive, so she hurried through the pool area over to the main house, enjoying the feel of the warm dry breeze on her skin.

As they'd settled into their Keeper duties, the cousins had established a morning ritual, the Morning Report, a meeting of the three of them over coffee while they discussed any Keeper or house-related issues. Since Barrie was almost always on the night shift, and both Rhiannon and Sailor often kept odd hours themselves, it was often more like a prenoon meeting.

Barrie punched the code into the keypad by the front door and entered Sailor's Mediterranean Gothic mansion, with its several bedrooms upstairs, a grand living room and staircase, and a family room that led out to the pool. All three of the cousins' houses might have been curio museums; they were filled with Merlin's collections from a lifetime of loving magic—and the eccentric.

Rhiannon's house featured superb carnival attractions: glass booths housing an animatronic gypsy fortune-teller and a magician who seemed to have a mind of his own. In the main Castle House, now Sailor's place, there were Tiffany lamps and Edwardian furniture, and busts and statues and all manner of art.

Barrie found Sailor and Rhiannon in the kitchen at the breakfast table enjoying extra-large cups of coffee. There was a whole pot steaming fragrantly in the coffeemaker and pastries arranged on a plate, the heavenly muffins and scones Rhiannon was always scoring from the Mystic Café where she played guitar and sang several nights a week.

Both her cousins looked up at Barrie as she stepped into the kitchen: Rhiannon, a fiery beauty with flaming red hair, and Sailor, with her movie-star profile, softer auburn hair and gorgeous eyes.

They looked so expectant that Barrie asked automatically, "What happened?"

"That's what we're waiting for you to tell us," Rhiannon said.

Sailor overlapped her. "You were out all night, we were hoping there was a man involved."

"Only if he's good enough for you," Rhiannon qualified.

Oh, no, Barrie thought to herself grimly. *There is no man. No man at all.*

Aloud she said lightly, "Not *a* man. Two of them. Only they're dead."

"Oh, it was business," Sailor said, and sounded disappointed, which gave Barrie a surge of irritation. Now that her cousins were happily paired off she was constantly feeling the pressure of their hopeful expectations for her. *Well, it's not that easy to find someone in L.A.,* she thought at them resentfully…and instantly had a sudden, unwelcome memory of Mick Townsend crushing her against him. She felt her stomach flip with desire. She had to force herself away from the thought to focus on Rhiannon.

"I said, 'Who's dead?'" Rhiannon repeated.

"I'm sure you've heard about the first one. Saul Mayo," Barrie answered, and watched their faces.

"Oh, my God, of course I heard, it's all over town!" Sailor exclaimed. And then she frowned. "But he's not one of ours."

"I know. There was another, a shifter," Barrie said, and suddenly felt the prickle of tears. "He died on the Boulevard…"

"Oh, no, Barrie, not Tiger," Rhiannon guessed, and reached across the table to take her hand. Her cousins knew all about Barrie's crusade to help the young street shifters.

Barrie nodded and swallowed back the tears. "It looked like an OD, but I think they're connected."

"Tiger and Mayo?" Sailor gasped. "That's *huge.*"

"I know," Barrie said, feeling a flush of anger. "And I'm not going to let whoever did it get away with it."

"What do you need?" Rhiannon asked.

Barrie felt another rush of warmth, this time affection. The cousins were new to Keeperdom. But in a matter of just months, Rhiannon, as Canyon Vampire Keeper, had captured a murderous vampire, and Sailor,

Elven Keeper, had tracked down the source of a rare blood disease fatal to Elven, and their successes were largely because of the cousins' pledge of loyalty to each other before any other Keeper alliances.

"Well, here's the thing," Barrie told them. "I think you *can* help."

She filled Sailor and Rhiannon in on everything she had learned last night, leaving out all encounters with Mick Townsend, because, of course, none of that ever happened.

She was gratified by the gasps from her cousins when she told them about Tiger's special ability to portray dead Hollywood stars and the bellhop's statement that Mayo had checked into the Chateau with a young man who looked like Johnny Love. She left out the whole sneaking-into-the-bungalow-where-Mayo-died incident, and especially the almost-sex-in-the-closet-with-Mick-Townsend incident, and ended with, "I searched Johnny Love and Mayo on Google, and Mayo produced *Otherworld,* Johnny's last movie."

"Otherworld!" both cousins exclaimed in unison.

Of course they knew the movie. They *all* knew the movie. It had come out just as the cousins were going boy crazy, and the movie had been cast with the most gorgeous of all up-and-coming stars. The three leads in particular were a collection of teenage heartthrobs who positively burned up the screen.

And it had been scandalous in the community, because all three were actual Others playing Others. It walked a very dangerous line, which added to the controversy.

"We were thirteen," Sailor remembered.

"And we had to beg our parents for weeks to let us see it," Rhiannon added wryly.

"Too gory!" Sailor exclaimed in mock parental shock.

"Too sexy!" Barrie gasped, and put her hand to her head as if she were about to faint.

"You're too young!" Rhiannon scolded. The three of them giggled like thirteen-year-olds.

"But we wore them down," Sailor said with satisfaction.

"We were nothing short of insufferable," Rhiannon agreed.

"And then we went back...how many times?" Barrie wondered.

"Dozens, I'm sure," Rhiannon said.

The film had exceeded all teenage expectations and parental fears: bloody, gory, sexy and *so* controversial. At the time the filmmakers, a collection of Others with a few key humans like Mayo who were in the know, were pushing the envelope, portraying Others so authentically. It was always dangerous to flirt with that boundary between the worlds, and danger was seductive.

"Never has such a bounty of male lusciousness been assembled all in one place," Sailor said.

"I remember that every week you had a different favorite," Barrie teased her. "Oh, Johnny. Oh, Robbie. Oh, DJ..." She pretended to swoon over each young actor in turn.

"*I* remember you didn't eat for weeks, you were so gone on Robbie Anderson," Sailor retorted.

Despite herself, Barrie felt a blush rising in her chest

and cheeks. It was true. She'd had a painful crush on the
young shifter. She had written him dozens of letters that
she'd never sent, pouring her heart out, telling him why
they were meant for each other. She was destined to be
a shifter Keeper, after all....

"He was the first shifter you wanted to Keep—for
yourself," Sailor crowed, voicing Barrie's own thoughts.

"Oh, Lord, the pain of it," Rhiannon sighed. "I
wouldn't be a tween again for all the money in the
world."

Truthfully Barrie was shocked at how strongly the
memories of that crush were hitting her; it was as if she'd
never grown out of it.

*Or maybe you just have sex on the brain. Damn Mick
Townsend.*

Rhiannon was looking at her probingly. "What's the
matter?"

Barrie shook off the feeling and focused on the present.

"I keep going back to the fact that Mayo checked
into the Chateau last night with a young man who was a
dead ringer for Johnny Love. And that Tiger's specialty
was shifting as dead movie stars. And that Johnny Love
died at the Chateau. *And* I found out from Tony Brandt
that they both died of overdoses of a drug cocktail that
sounds really Other: heavy on the belladonna."

"But what does all this have to do with *Otherworld?*"
Rhiannon asked practically.

"I don't know yet, but I'm thinking the movie *has* to
have something to do with my cases."

"But only Tiger is your case," Sailor worried. "Mayo wasn't an Other."

Barrie felt her defenses going up. "No, he wasn't, but his death is related. I can't investigate Tiger's death without investigating Mayo's."

Now both her cousins looked concerned. "You need to be really careful about this, hon," Rhiannon said. "There's going to be a lot of heat on the Mayo investigation."

"But no one else knows the two are related, and I'm going to keep it that way," Barrie answered stubbornly. "And don't worry," she said before Rhiannon could object. "I'll talk to Brodie first thing."

Rhiannon's fiancé wasn't only a homicide detective with the elite LAPD Robbery Homicide division, he was an Elven.

Like Brandt and the other Others who worked in law enforcement and criminal justice, Brodie subtly used his position to get assigned to Other-related cases, to ensure that the existence of the Others was kept secret. And now Barrie had a feeling her soon-to-be familial connection to Brodie was going to come in very handy.

Rhiannon looked somewhat mollified. "Well…as long as you're careful."

"What's up next?" Sailor asked.

"I'm going to find out everything I can about Johnny Love and Mayo and the movie."

And she knew exactly who she needed to see to get the inside scoop.

Chapter 5

Barrie showered and dressed and fed the cat, then headed down the canyon to the flatlands, the Fairfax District where NBS, one of the major television networks, had its soundstages.

On the way she listened to the news on the radio to see how Mayo's death was being reported. The mainstream media was being incredibly tactful, as they always were with celebrity deaths, not speculating on the manner of death; the official word was that he had "collapsed" in his bungalow at the Chateau. She would have to check the Net for the more fringe theories.

As usual the NBS parking lot was jammed with busloads of tourists there to see the tapings of various television shows. Barrie had never seen the appeal of tapings, she found them incredibly boring herself, but she knew NBS's most popular reality show, *That's Dancing!* was filming today, and that would be where she could find Harvey Hodge.

Harvey was NBS's self-proclaimed "Entertainment Connection," the on-camera entertainment reporter for NBS News. H.H., as he was known, was a shifter who always had all the best Hollywood gossip because he could literally be a fly on the wall and pick up any dirt that was to be had on anyone.

And Barrie knew that Harvey never missed a taping of *That's Dancing!*

Harvey was a handful, but Barrie had taken great pains to cultivate him as a source. Luckily being a Keeper was its own modest form of fame, and she was able to use that to her advantage. She'd sussed out Harvey's great weakness: he wanted to be as much of a celebrity as the stars he reported on, and she knew how to play the starstruck kid. It was a lot of work, but she could usually wheedle and flatter Harvey into talking to her, and he really *did* know everything about every Other in show business.

The tough part would be making it onto the set of *That's Dancing!* The show was down to the last few episodes, with just four couples left, and it seemed from the lines that every dance fan in the world was trying to crash the gate.

The guard was militantly checking soundstage passes, so Barrie called up what she could vaguely remember about one of the contestants and glamoured her way by him in a swish of tulle and sequins. The effort left her gasping for breath on the other side, but at least she was in.

She found Harvey in the press pit, a corner of the soundstage draped with curtains for reporters to conduct their interviews and film their stand-ups.

He was in a foul mood. "Weres are *beastly* dancers," he complained without even bothering to say hello as Barrie approached him. "I don't know why they ever let them on to begin with."

"So, who's going to win it?" she asked, feigning interest.

"How would I know?" he said coyly.

"Oh, come on, H.H.," she coaxed. "If not you, who?"

"I'll never tell."

"Not even a hint?"

But she'd gone too far. Harvey looked her over shrewdly. "I'm short on time and temper, and you are *so* not here as a *Dancing!* fan, *Keeper*. So, what are you after?"

Barrie felt caught out, and then realized it was better just to lay it on the table.

"I need the scoop on Mayo," she told him.

He rolled his eyes. "You and half the town."

"I need to know about Mayo and Johnny Love."

Harvey stopped and really looked at her for the first time, his gaze narrowing. "That's original of you, doll. What about them?"

"Exactly. What about them?" She lowered her voice. "You know what I'm saying, H.H. Did Mayo have a thing for Johnny Love? Was there anything between them? Like, during the filming of *Otherworld?*"

"Funny. That yummy Mick Townsend asked me the same thing."

She stared at Harvey in disbelief. Was there any way to escape Mick? "You were talking to someone outside the community about Other business?"

"*No,* I was talking to a fellow *journalist* about a *story.* He asked me if Mayo had a thing for Johnny Love, just like you just did, and I told him that Mayo had a thing for all kinds of things."

"But what do *you* think?" Barrie asked the question with a kind of ingenue breathlessness that made it sound like Harvey's opinion was the only one that mattered. Sailor wasn't the only actress in the family.

Apparently it worked, because Harvey glanced around them, as if checking for prying eyes and ears. "It's an interesting thing. There were rumors." Then he looked straight at her. "But I'll tell you—the great Mayo always had a thing for shifters. The younger, the better. *I* don't think he ever got over Johnny dying. But you know, things were such a nightmare for everyone after *Otherworld* came out. It was one of the great cursed films of Hollywood. So much tragedy associated with it. First Johnny, of course, that nasty OD."

"It was some special speedball, wasn't it?" she asked. "Something exotic?"

"Heroin, cocaine and atropine," Harvey said, and Barrie felt a rush. Atropine was the hallucinogen found in belladonna. The same combination that had killed Mayo and Tiger. "And DJ, well, you *could* say fame and fortune is no kind of bad luck, but…"

DJ, no last name required, was a vampire who had played a teen vampire in the film. Currently one of the highest-paid actors in Hollywood, he was a total recluse and rumored to be nearly impossible to work with. Blood wasn't his only addiction, and when you added an actor's temperament to a vampire's, then threw in his dark past…it all spelled constant trouble. In fact, DJ was famous for being so unreliable that 90 percent of his salary on any film was withheld until the end of shooting, just to make sure the film was completed.

"Right, DJ…" Barrie murmured.

Harvey shrugged. "Let's just say I'm not the only one who updates his obituary every few months just to have it ready. It's a miracle he's lasted this long. No one in town would give him the time of day if he weren't, well, brilliant."

Harvey was starting to warm to the topic, a great thing for Barrie, who now only had to prompt him with wide-eyed attention and the occasional little exclamation. "Then, of course, Robbie Anderson disappeared without a trace. A lot of people think he died not long after Johnny, but no one could ever prove anything. It's just that…someone *that* gorgeous and talented? He couldn't have stayed away from acting."

"No," Barrie murmured. "Probably not." But privately she thought that anyone who had suffered the death of one of his best friends and been witness to the crippling addictions of the other might not be all that hot on the profession. She herself would have fled for her life. She thought of Robbie with a pang, that surreally beautiful teenager, and silently hoped that he'd gotten out and started a new life far from the corruption of Hollywood that he'd been thrust into far too young. Robbie had been British, had never known his mother and was estranged from his father; he'd filed for emancipation when he was just fourteen. He could have disappeared back home, but the media had tracked him relentlessly; it seemed that someone would have found him—if he'd still been alive. The thought gave Barrie a chill. *"So much tragedy associated with"* this film is right.

"Mayo was opening quite the can of worms when he decided to remake it," Harvey was saying.

Barrie jolted back to the present. "Mayo was going to remake *Otherworld?* I hadn't heard anything like that." Not that she followed production news religiously, but certainly news like that would have registered with her or one of her cousins at least.

"Oh, it hadn't been announced yet, but he was gearing up for it. And you can bet your buttons the community wasn't too thrilled about it."

Barrie knew that Harvey wasn't talking about the film community now, but *their* community, the underground.

"The interspecies politics are such a mess on these paranormal films," he sighed. "Everyone's got an agenda."

"So, a lot of people didn't want this remake to go through," she said, and thought to herself, *That's a lot of potential suspects.*

"It's not even just political. Think about it. Three white-hot rising superstars: one kills himself, one disappears, one's a total train wreck… The town is superstitious, darling, and that's looking a lot like a curse to me."

Despite herself, Barrie felt a chill.

The "Dancing!" stars—well, minor celebrities— swirled onto the soundstage with their pro dancer partners, and Harvey went on journalistic alert. Her interview was done.

"Thanks, H.H.," she said quickly. "I owe you."

"Yes, you do-o," he trilled back at her, and gave her a backward wave as he rushed to meet the stars.

As Barrie was walking off the soundstage, musing over the idea of a cursed film, she saw a tall, familiar figure strolling toward her. *Oh, great,* she thought, even as her heart started racing a mile a minute. *Be calm. Just be calm. It was just the glamour, remember?*

She struggled to keep her expression disinterested as she stopped in front of Mick Townsend in the center of what was ironically an absurdly romantic set: white roses trailing over a gazebo, a bridge over a mirrored stream. Probably the backdrop to a waltz competition.

"Don't tell me you're a 'Dancing!' fan," she said dryly, and was proud of her nonchalance.

"I never miss it," he deadpanned back.

He sounded so almost-serious that for a moment Barrie had a fantasy of what it would be like to dance with him. Of course she was dreaming—men just didn't dance anymore—but if he could...oh, if he could lead even half as well as he kissed...

Focus, she ordered herself.

"You're following me," she accused aloud.

"Or maybe great minds think alike," he suggested. "You were just here to see H.H., right?"

She was silent, unable to deny it.

He gave her a killer smile. "That's why we need to

team up. This is a big enough story for two people, and we're obviously on the same track...."

She raised an eyebrow. "If we're thinking alike, what is it we're thinking?"

His luminous green eyes met hers and held them. "I'm thinking about last night."

Immediately her heart was racing again, and she was finding it hard to breathe. She struggled for distance and control. "Last night was—inappropriate. Adrenaline rush, the circumstances...it happens, but it doesn't mean anything. If you want to team up on this, then we have to focus on the case and the story."

For a moment she thought she saw a flash of amusement on his face, but he nodded seriously and said, "Perfectly understood. Strictly business." He held out a hand for her to shake.

She hesitated, then put her hand in his. "Strictly business," she echoed, even as a betraying rush of lust raced through her veins at his touch. She pulled her hand away quickly. "So, what are we thinking? About the *case?*"

"That the same person killed Mayo and that poor kid," he said softly, and she felt a jolt, realizing that he *did* know about Tiger, and more than that: he seemed to care. He continued, still holding her gaze. "That someone didn't want the remake of *Otherworld* to go forward, so that someone hired Tiger to lure Mayo to his death, dose him with a fatal exotic cocktail, and then the killer fed Tiger the same stuff."

She had to hand it to him: it was exactly what she was thinking. But she wasn't about to let him know that. Not yet.

"Is anyone saying there was a third person in that bungalow at the Chateau?" she demanded. If he wanted to work with her, he had to prove he had something to offer besides lethal charm.

"Not that I've been able to find out. Most of the rest of the town is so focused on Mayo they're not looking anywhere else."

"*And* someone went to a great deal of trouble to make Mayo and Tiger look like unrelated cases," she pointed out.

"Someone who knows how the LAPD is structured," Mick agreed. "Mayo's case went straight to Robbery Homicide, while the Hollywood division detectives who caught Tiger's case just accepted the obvious."

Damn, he was good. Barrie could feel herself weakening, even though she knew it was madness. But how *much* did he know? That was the question.

"So, why do you think this someone used Tiger to get to Mayo?" she hedged, probing.

Mick looked grim. "Mayo wouldn't be the first power player to have a taste for underage prostitutes. Word is this Tiger had some kind of resemblance to Johnny Love," he said distastefully. "Which explains the bellhop saying he saw Johnny with Mayo. Add a touch of pseudo necrophilia to Mayo's list of perversions."

So, he's assuming Tiger looked *like Johnny Love.* She was relieved, but also suddenly deeply conflicted.

What am I doing? I can't work with a mortal.

It was against all the rules. One of her primary duties as a Keeper was to guard the existence of the Others. She couldn't very well team up with Mick without revealing far too much unless she flat-out lied to him. And that was just too risky. As discreet as she knew how to be, it would be too hard to keep up the front if they were actually working together. She felt a kind of pang, too, a surprising realization that she didn't *want* to lie to him.

Yes, the real puzzlement here was this pull she had to work with him, even knowing that it would be nothing but trouble, that it would violate every aspect of her job.

Mick was watching her. "What's wrong?" he asked directly, and she realized she hadn't said anything for several moments.

"I just… I'm sorry, I have another appointment," she said lamely. "Not related to the case," she added quickly, in case he decided to follow her, although so far there didn't seem to be any way to stop him. "But I have to go."

"Are you sure you don't want to sit somewhere and talk?" he asked, and those green eyes were on hers again. "I think I can spring for coffee at the Farmers' Market."

"Can I get a rain check?" she hedged, and immediately regretted it. Now she would just have to fend him off again. And the problem was, she didn't *want* to fend him off.

It was all too confusing. She had to think.

"I have to go," she repeated gracelessly, and left him, hurrying over the bridge, past the luxuriant fake white roses.

She was upset enough over the encounter that she decided to drive straight home. She needed to remember who she was. It was absolutely crazy to bring a mortal into Keeper business; there was something wrong with her head that she had even been contemplating it. But she was sure her cousins could set her straight.

She made one stop, though, on her way up toward the canyon: the great Amoeba Records on Sunset, where she bought a collector's edition DVD of *Otherworld*.

She had homework to do.

Chapter 6

Barrie staggered into the main house, her arms loaded down with bags of microwave popcorn, M&M's, ice cream bon bons—all her favorite movie foods—plus a bottle of good red wine and the *Otherworld* DVD. She'd made another spur-of-the-moment stop on the way back to the house for munchies—might as well make work fun—and also called her cousins, requesting an emergency meeting. Luckily both of Rhiannon's employers were Keepers themselves, though of different districts, and were accommodating of her sometimes unusual schedule. And Sailor didn't have to be at the House of Illusion, her night job, this week because she'd landed a voice-over gig.

"I've got treats, too," Sailor told Barrie, standing by the butcher-block table in the kitchen and waving a knife. Barrie dumped her bags on a counter and peered over her cousin's shoulder suspiciously. As usual, Sailor's idea of treats was not Barrie's—everything looked morbidly healthy and low-fat and sugar-free: cut-up fruit and vegetables and fat-free dips.

Barrie sighed pointedly, and Sailor leveled the knife at her. "Just because you have the metabolism of a hummingbird…"

Not true, of course, it was just that Barrie often forgot to eat. "I do some of my best thinking on sugar," she justified, ripping into the M&M's.

Rhiannon floated in through the back door, her face lit up like a Roman candle, a sure sign she'd just been on the phone with Brodie. Sure enough, the first words out of her mouth were "Brodie can't make it till later. But he's looking into everything he can on his end."

Barrie murmured, "Bless him." She liked her cousin-in-law-to-be very much, but it was especially useful to have a homicide detective in the family.

How's that for connected? she said silently in her head, and then realized, unnerved, that she was talking to Mick.

"This is going to be flashback city," Rhiannon said, reaching for a freshly made bowl of popcorn as Barrie opened the wine.

They trooped into the great room, where Sailor already had a fire blazing atmospherically in the fireplace, and turned off the lights and fired up the *Otherworld* DVD, then settled in on the couch, like the thirteen-year-olds they had been, for a gory, sexy flashback of a night. Made fifteen years earlier, the film still held up, from the vertiginous, exhilarating swoop of the opening shot to the hazy, erotic, psychedelic underground party scenes, to the thrilling climax on Catalina Island. The story had been written and directed by the werewolf Travis Branson, and it followed the exploits of a young vampire, shape-shifter and Elven, decadent young princes of the Otherworld who topped each other in hedonism and rivalry until they were forced to come of age and join forces to defeat a threat to the underworld kingdom in a supernatural Three Musketeers–like final battle.

All Barrie's thoughts of Mick Townsend vanished as she gave herself over to the thrills of the film. There were times when the cousins gasped aloud at how close the movie came to revealing secrets that, as Keepers, they were sworn to protect. And they all sighed over the breathtaking beauty of the three stars, each magnetic in his own right but soul-meltingly charismatic together. The cousins shrieked and clutched each other during iconic scenes, like the one in which Johnny Love crawled across the floor toward the screen with deliciously predatory intent, and screamed at the gruesome death by crucifixion of a werewolf who had been captured by the bad guys, sparking off a war.

Barrie could be really cynical about Hollywood in general and actors in particular. After living in L.A. all her life, and being raised by a wannabe-actress mother on top of that, she felt she was entitled to her skepticism. But sometimes movies were just magic, and now she sat in awe over the raw talent of the three young actors.

As she watched Robbie Anderson on-screen, Barrie felt herself transported back to the heartbreaking longing of her teen years. Just the way he moved, with the lithe power of an animal, the way his golden eyes gazed soulfully out of the screen, sent shivers through her body.

But as much as she ached for Robbie, a part of her had to admit Johnny Love was especially incandescent. A phenomenal actor, he seemed to be a completely different person in the final battle when he finally realized and declared where his loyalties lay. As much as Barrie was attracted to the shifter Robbie Anderson, she was left with a powerful draw to the dead young Elven.

The climactic set piece in an abandoned ballroom on Catalina Island was as psychedelically Gothic as anyone could want, ending with the mirrored palace going up in a spectacular inferno.

As the closing credits ran, with haunting music underneath, the cousins sat, stunned and moved.

"Such talent," Sailor whispered, mesmerized.

"Such a waste," Barrie said so heatedly the other two jumped in the dark.

"You know, the movie really walked the line on the Other question," Rhiannon said thoughtfully.

"It crossed the line, if you ask me," Sailor declared. "The filmmakers thought they were being oh-so-hip but they were playing with hundreds of thousands of lives."

Barrie and Rhiannon murmured agreement.

"'Non-disclosure is the first rule of the Otherworld,'" Barrie quoted. "They were all thumbing their noses at the Code."

"Now I understand why our dads were so upset about the film," Rhiannon reflected.

"It's true. It had nothing to do with the sex at all," Sailor chimed in. Barrie and Rhiannon looked at her.

"Okay, it had *something* to do with the sex. But the politics—yike."

"I wonder who was the instigator?" Barrie mused. Her cousins both looked at her. "I mean, obviously they got away with what they did in the film. No one stopped the production or the release. So, someone on the film must have been powerful enough that the councils let them do it."

"The studio itself wouldn't necessarily know that it was all true, though," Sailor said.

"Factual," Rhiannon corrected her absently.

"Based in fact," Barrie agreed. "But the councils must have known. And the thing is, the writer/director, Travis Branson, and producer, Mayo, were at the beginning of their careers. It's not like they had all the power they have—had—today. So, why didn't the councils stop them, or at least pressure Branson to tone it down?"

"Maybe they were flying under the radar," Sailor suggested. "Sometimes these cult films come out of nowhere and no one expects them to be any kind of success, and then suddenly they take off." She looked wistful. "It's what everyone always hopes for. Kind of like winning the lottery."

"Why do you care who was behind it?" Rhiannon probed.

Barrie frowned. "Harvey Hodge said that Mayo was planning to remake *Otherworld*."

"You're kidding!" Sailor gasped. "I never heard that."

Barrie pointed at her. "Now, see—*you* hadn't heard, either. And the way you pore over the gossip rags—"

"Hey!" her cousin huffed.

"I mean, with your *vast* insider knowledge of the entertainment industry..." Barrie amended. Sailor looked slightly mollified. "Even *you* hadn't heard. So, only really connected people—I mean, the most connected people—knew about the remake. And whoever those people are, some of them weren't happy about it. At least according to Harvey."

"Harvey's dirt is usually gold," Sailor admitted.

The cousins all nodded agreement.

"So, what are you thinking, Barrie?" Rhiannon prodded.

Barrie looked at her cousins and gathered her thoughts. "I'm thinking there's a lot of death and destruction associated with this movie. And then, before a remake is even officially in the works, we've got two deaths potentially associated with it. So, I'm thinking I'm looking for someone who was associated with the first movie and, for whatever reason, doesn't want a remake made. Who didn't want it enough to kill over it."

Her cousins nodded thoughtfully, then more excitedly.

"I think you're on to something, Rosalind Barrymore," Rhiannon said, and for a moment Barrie heard her father in her cousin's voice.

"So, now what?" Sailor asked.

"So, now I have to find out what really happened during that movie," Barrie said, resolved.

"Wow," Sailor said in a hushed voice. "Maybe you can figure out what really happened to Johnny Love."

"And Robbie Anderson," Barrie said, and suddenly realized she was about to investigate one of the great mysteries of her childhood.

"And DJ," Rhiannon added, and both cousins looked at her. "He didn't come out of all that unscathed," she pointed out. "Yeah, he's a star, but did he ever really have a *life* after the film?"

The other cousins nodded solemnly.

"Maybe it *is* a cursed film," Barrie said uneasily.

A silence fell over the candlelit room, suddenly broken by the *pop* of a log bursting in the fire. All three cousins jumped...and then burst into laughter.

Barrie turned serious again. "The problem is going to be getting close to anyone connected with the film."

"You know the Pack had their own band..." Rhiannon said reflectively.

"Who could forget?" Sailor started to sing. "'I'll follow you to death's door...meet you on that final shore...'"

As if superstardom in the film arena hadn't been enough, the three young actors had been packaged into a boy band. They'd recorded a couple of numbers for the film and then, as had been popular for movie stars to do in the nineties, they'd even done some gigs in L.A. and on the road.

Sailor pointed at Rhiannon. "You had a poster up in your room."

"Guilty as charged," Rhiannon admitted. "Hey, they were the best eye candy any of us had ever seen. But they did a few gigs in L.A., remember? We couldn't get in because the shows were all in bars, no one under eighteen admitted, but..."

Sailor and Barrie both caught Rhiannon's drift in the same instant. "Declan would know them," Sailor said.

Her fiancé owned the underground club known as the Snake Pit and was highly connected in the music scene.

"I don't know if even Declan could get me in to see DJ," Barrie said morosely.

"You never know," Sailor said.

"Do you still have that poster?" Barrie asked Rhiannon with a quickening interest.

Rhiannon shrugged. "It's probably up in the attic, along with the whole rest of our childhoods. You know how Merlin is about holding on to things."

Fueled by wine and their own nostalgia, the cousins trooped up the staircase, then up a narrower, rarely used set of stairs to the attic.

Barrie fumbled against the wall for a switch and flicked on the lights. Typical Merlin, the fixtures were designed to look like candelabra, flickering and all, which gave the attic an otherworldly glow. It had a high, sloped roof and dusty floorboards and an amazing collection of junk—or treasure, depending on your point of view.

The cousins turned, looking over the remnants of their often-shared past. Then there were Merlin's magic equipment, top hats, racks of glittering dresses in thick plastic wardrobe bags. There was also a collection of old-fashioned leather-fastened trunks. As Barrie stepped forward to examine them she saw she was in luck; most were labeled with names. She spotted her father's, Rhiannon's father's, her mother's....

"Oh, my God, my stuffed animals!" Sailor cried, flinging herself down in front of a trunk.

"Let's stay focused here," Rhiannon suggested.

Barrie moved forward in the dim light and saw a pale figure step toward her from a corner. She gasped, pulled back...and then realized she was staring into her own reflection in a cloudy gilt mirror. She laughed shakily.

"Guys, look."

Barrie turned away from the mirror to see Rhiannon pulling a long paper tube from a trunk. Sailor helped her unroll it...and the Pack of three young actors looked out at them with heated stares. They were in a classic band pose, brandishing instruments as if they were weapons, perfect flesh exposed under artfully ripped clothing.

"It's probably worth a fortune at a collectibles shop," Sailor said. "Maybe we can sell it and pay the utilities this month."

Barrie slugged her in the arm.

"Ow. Kidding."

"I'm claiming it until I solve the case. For inspiration," Barrie said.

"Sweetie, if you solve the case you can *have* it," Rhiannon told her, and handed it over.

"Yeah, I can't see Brodie going for hanging *that* up in the house," Sailor teased her.

Rhiannon answered automatically, "I don't see why he'd have any objection to..." She looked more closely at the mouthwatering trio. "Maybe you're right," she admitted.

They all looked at the image of the three actors and were silent.

"It would be freaky-weird if DJ turned out to be a killer," Sailor said. Rhiannon arched an eyebrow, and the cousins all thought about it. Certainly the star was volatile and unpredictable.

"Or Robbie Anderson," Barrie said slowly.

The other two looked at her.

"Think about it. Is he dead? Does he know what happened to Johnny? Is he maybe...back?"

The electric candelabra flickered exactly as if there had been a breeze, and Barrie shivered.

"Oh, great," Sailor said gloomily. "Good luck sleeping tonight."

Suddenly not so keen on staying up in the spooky attic, the cousins moved quickly for the door.

They descended the stairs in troubled silence. As they reached the balcony, a huge shadow loomed up in front of them and all three screamed.

"Easy, easy," a resonant and familiar voice soothed, as Brodie McKay, six feet five inches of golden-haired, alpha Elven cop, stepped out of the shadows and smiled at them. "It's only me."

"Brodie!" Rhiannon rushed for his arms, and then stopped in her tracks and pushed at his chest, indignant. "You just about scared us to death."

"I gathered that," he said, enclosing her in a reassuring embrace. Barrie felt a tug of...not jealousy, she was thrilled for Rhiannon's happiness and certainly had no designs on Brodie. It was more like a longing, for someone comforting of her own....

And suddenly her thoughts of Mick Townsend were back in full force.

"What have you been up to that's got you so spooked?" Brodie frowned as he looked from one cousin to another.

Barrie shook her head to banish Mick and unfurled the Pack poster to show Brodie.

"Ah," he said, and looked troubled. "'Live fast, die young' in a nutshell."

"I've been wondering about the LAPD investigation of Johnny Love's death," Barrie told him. "Like who was the Elven Keeper of the district and who were the detectives assigned to the case?"

"Before my time," Brodie said. "I was just starting college. But cases like that one are always a nightmare. You've got the Keeper of the deceased's Kind, the regular cops to massage into seeing things a certain way, and hopefully you have an Other detective embedded deep enough into the appropriate department that all Other-related details are 'handled'—and all of them working under intense media scrutiny, not to mention intense civilian interest. Deflecting the press alone takes some skilled sleight of hand not to let anything we don't want out, out."

Barrie winced just thinking about it. She saw similar looks on her cousins' faces. "So, who managed it?" she asked. "And what really happened?"

"I'll ask Alessande who the Elven Keeper was that handled the death," Sailor offered. It wasn't information you could get by just searching Google, and though Sailor's Elven friend looked no older than any of the cousins, Alessande was an Ancient; she would remember the case.

Barrie shot her a grateful look. "That would be fantastic."

"And I'll see how it was handled in the LAPD," Brodie said.

"Do you think you could get the original case files?" Barrie asked.

"I'll see what I can do," he promised her.

"Has the coroner come up with a ruling on Mayo's death yet?" Barrie had checked her phone. No messages from Brandt, coded or otherwise.

"The ruling is 'Pending,'" Brodie told her. "Which means the case requires additional investigation. Robbery Homicide has it." Barrie knew that already. Brodie continued. "I didn't ask for Mayo's case—I didn't know it was going to turn out to be Other-related. But I've told Captain Riley that it has to be handled with kid gloves." Brodie's captain, Edwin Riley, was one of the few humans trusted by L.A.'s Other community, being the son of a practicing Wiccan high priestess. The community depended on him to steer investigations away from sensitive issues as long as secrecy would not compromise a case.

"It's a *good* thing no one has seen the connection," Barrie said. "Can you imagine the heat the community would be taking if Mayo hadn't kept his predilection for Others under wraps?"

They all knew a sudden drawing back of the curtain on the Others' existence would create havoc in both the mortal and Other worlds; Barrie often had nightmarish visions of a mass psychotic break. There was even a word for it in the Otherworld community: the Shattering.

"It's bad enough that Mayo was so powerful that some

Others broke the Code and let him in. And fraternized with him," Rhiannon said.

"'Fraternize' is putting it mildly," Barrie muttered.

"And it's a textbook example of why we shouldn't," Sailor said vehemently.

Barrie could have talked shop all night, but she could see Brodie and Rhiannon eyeing each other in That Way, so she thanked her cousins for keeping her company, waved good-night to everyone with the rolled-up poster and headed across the patio for her own house.

In her room, just before she got into bed, she tacked the poster up above her bureau and stood looking at the trio of stars.

"Well, boys…talk to me," she said, and turned out the light.

Chapter 7

She is in the movie, in Otherworld, *wearing some sparkling gold fantasy of a dress, walking through the arches of the balcony of the round oceanfront ballroom, with the shimmering waves crashing below.*

Someone is following her, stepping in and out of the arches just behind her, staying tantalizingly out of sight, but she can feel his presence as an aching longing in her entire body....

She wakes suddenly, with flickering candlelight all around her, to find herself in a huge canopy bed. She gasps as someone steps from the shadows...a gorgeous, haunted figure...

Robbie Anderson, as preternaturally stunning as he appeared in the film. He moves to her and bends to kiss her, running his fingers down her arms with a touch like fire, then suddenly lifting her hands to pin her wrists above her head, and stares down into her eyes. He is no longer a teenager, but older, more demanding, though every bit as beautiful. He moves on top of her, opening her mouth under his, opening her legs with his hips to rock against her, rubbing the ramrod bulge of him against her, slow and teasing, as his right hand caresses her breasts until moans are coming out of her throat as the feel of him excites her into madness, and she arches her back, urging him inside her…. "Please…"

She opens her eyes to look up into his golden gaze…

And then suddenly the face above hers is not Robbie's but the Elven face of Johnny Love.

Barrie gasped awake, for real this time. Her heart was pounding, and she felt…well, disturbed. Her phone was vibrating on her night table.

She had every intention of ignoring it, but then she remembered Brodie had promised to check into the case files on Johnny Love's death.

She grabbed for the phone.

"Brodie?" she mumbled.

There was a slight pause. "Brodie?" a man asked roughly on the other end.

A familiar voice. She couldn't place it at first yet, oddly, found herself blushing. And then she realized who it was.

"Townsend?" she said, and sat up, pulling the covers around her as if he could see her. "What are you… What do you want?"

There was nothing but silence on the other end. Mick—or whoever the caller was—had hung up.

She set her phone down and leaned back on her pillows, looking across the room at the poster of the three *Otherworld* actors on her wall. And she shivered, hugging herself, remembering her dream.

It was already late afternoon when Barrie hit the freeway, crawling with the rest of the traffic toward downtown.

There was no sign of Mick Townsend at the newspaper office. A blessing; she wouldn't have to avoid him. She still felt off balance after her dream, and she didn't want to face his keen scrutiny. And if he *had* been the one to call and wake her? What did that mean? How had he even gotten her number?

She checked in with her editor, and then dashed out of the newsroom and headed straight for the coroner's office. Brandt had not been picking up his phone, and she was impatient to get the coroner's report on Johnny Love; she was sure that Tony would pull it for her.

But in his office, Brandt just shook his head at her request. "I can't get you the L.A. coroner's report on Johnny Love because there isn't one."

She stared at him. "It was stolen?"

"There never was one. There's no evidence whatsoever that Johnny Love died in Los Angeles. I just got finished telling Brodie the same thing—he said he was checking into it for you."

"But…Johnny died at the— I mean, everyone says he died at the Chateau Marmont," she said.

"That'll teach you not to believe what you read on

the Net," he said, sounding annoyingly like her father for a moment.

"Where did he die, then?" she demanded.

"I don't know." After a long beat, he added, "I'd be happy to look into it, but it's a big country. That is, if he even died in this country. It would help if I had some idea where to start."

"I'm on it," Barrie told him. "Thanks, Tony."

She left him, feeling in a state of shock.

Back in her car, Barrie reached for her phone to call Alessande, but she knew that at Alessande's age—over a hundred years now—she wasn't big on phones, and when the call went straight to voice mail Barrie decided to drive up into the canyon to see her in person.

Alessande Salisbury was Elven and almost a neighbor, the way such things were measured in L.A. She lived in Laurel Canyon, maybe two miles from the House of the Rising Sun, in a rustic dwelling that looked like a cabin from the outside but was actually a rather luxurious and sophisticated setup inside, with arching bay windows, solar panels and a state-of-the-art kitchen. Alessande was a bit of a recluse but had become a good friend of all three of the Keeper cousins, since she'd saved Sailor's life, or helped to, when Sailor had recently come under attack by a shape-shifter who had been infecting Elven actresses with an ancient disease.

Barrie parked in the drive outside the cabin, and when no one responded to her knock at the front door, she circled the house toward the garden in the back. A witch's dream, it was stocked with spiky, feathery, fragrant

herbs that could cure or curse any mortal or Other with
whatever remedy or malady you would care to name.
The sun was setting over the hills, and a whispery wind
rustled through the old-growth trees, wind chimes tin-
kled from somewhere in the garden, and it was all so
private it could have been unsettling, if Barrie weren't
so well acquainted with the house and its owner by now.

As she wound her way through the lush growth, she
spotted Alessande on her knees and digging, attacking
what looked like a stubborn and unnervingly human-
looking bit of root. As occupied as she seemed to be, she
threw the trowel down, brushed off her hands and stood
to face Barrie before Barrie could say a word in greet-
ing. Being Elven, Alessande was typically stunning, and
she towered over Barrie: six feet tall with white-blond
hair and green eyes, and a knockout figure, both voluptuous and athletic. And she didn't look a day over thirty,
much less the hundred and six Sailor claimed she was.
Barrie wondered sometimes how anyone could possibly
mistake her for human, even with beauty being as com-
monplace as it was in L.A.

She gave Barrie a warm hug—awkward as that was
given their height difference: nearly a foot between them.
As she pulled back, she looked serenely unsurprised to
see Barrie, had probably sensed her as soon as Barrie
had the thought to drive up to see her. The Ancients were
in possession of a psychic sensitivity more characteristic of witches than Others.

And even as Barrie thought it, Alessande gave her
a probing look. "You're looking rather radiant today. Is
there something new in your life?"

Barrie was about to answer an automatic "no" when Alessande added, "Or some*one,* maybe?"

Barrie felt herself blushing to the roots of her hair. "No," she lied. "I don't know wh-what you mean."

Alessande raised her eyebrows, but to Barrie's relief, she dropped the subject. "You're late," she said instead, lifting her hair from her neck. "I've been wrestling with that mandrake for an hour. Let's sit and have some tea."

Barrie followed her onto the semi-enclosed patio with a sweeping view of the sinking sun. A frosty glass pitcher of iced tea was already waiting on a mosaic-topped table with two glasses and a plate of decadent-looking cakes. Barrie reached for one and sniffed it suspiciously; she was sure there were all kinds of herbs in them.

Alessande smiled her cat smile. "Oh, go ahead, you'll like them."

Barrie bit into an explosion of chocolate and berry deliciousness. Whatever its healing properties, the cake was also loaded with sugar, more proof that Alessande had seen her coming.

Alessande sat and poured them both tall glasses of rosily glowing tea. She pushed one glass toward Barrie and got straight down to business. "Sailor told me you're looking for information on the death of Johnny Love, and I've been looking into it."

"You're an angel," Barrie said, meaning it. "Thank you."

Alessande nodded distractedly. "You're very welcome, but there's actually a troubling dearth of knowledge about this incident, given that it's one of the most

notorious celebrity deaths of the end of the century."
She had a way of talking that made history sound long
and vibrant—not surprising, considering her age and
relationship to time. She continued, serenely and seriously.

"No Elven I spoke with seems to know anything
about what happened to him. There was no Elven Keeper
I can track who had anything to do with the investigation into the death or the autopsy." Pale as she was, her
lovely face was shadowed. "It is extremely troubling.
It's almost as if...wherever Johnny died, there were no
other Elven in the vicinity at all."

"That *is* strange," Barrie murmured, and reached for
another cake. There was nothing about the case that
wasn't strange.

"I can only think that very powerful Others were involved in this cover-up. They would have to be, to cir-
cumvent the Elven Council so completely."

Barrie frowned, frustrated. That was no help in narrowing suspects down. In Hollywood, power was the
coin of the realm.

"What do I do, Alessande?" she asked.

"I think any paperwork you'll be able to find on the
case will be completely false," the beautiful Elven said
soberly. "You must find direct witnesses. People who
knew Johnny. People or Others who were actually there
at the time, who can tell you their story."

Barrie nodded, feeling a rush of excitement. She knew
exactly where to start.

"I'm thinking Declan Wainwright," she said aloud.

Alessande smiled. "I'm thinking you're right."

* * *

Sailor's fiancé owned two clubs on Sunset, which in that zip code pretty much constituted a dynasty. One club was completely "out" and legit, a popular hangout for the mainstream mortal population of Los Angeles and a popular destination for tourists wanting a taste of the "real" L.A. The other club was grungy and edgy, showcasing up-and-coming underground bands and sometimes popular bands who wanted to get back to their down and dirty roots. And *after* after hours…that club opened by invitation only, to Others only.

At least technically speaking.

The truth was, though, that there was a certain segment of the human population of L.A. that just *knew* about the Others.

Artists are a different breed from ordinary mortals. They push the boundaries of society and civilization. It was not an accident that for centuries actors had not been allowed to be buried in hallowed ground.

Just as in the segregated past white patrons had sought out the jazz clubs of Harlem, just as people from all walks of life had risked arrest to have the speakeasy experience in the Roaring Twenties, there was today a small slice of humanity that sensed the presence of Others and sought to learn more about them.

The denizens of L.A. were especially apt to seek out the edgy, the bizarre, the occult, the outré, and artists had a long history of possessing a heightened sense of non-rational forces. And there was no earthly secret more outré and non-rational and exciting than the Otherworld. So, for as long as there had been artists and Others, they had been commingling. And those humans who knew of the Others, while not bound by any official Code of Silence, were surprisingly good at keeping the Others' existence secret, much as members of the film and music communities were surprisingly discreet about keeping the non-mainstream sexual preferences of film stars and other celebrities private. There were lots of open secrets in Hollywood, secrets that by mutual understanding *stayed* in Hollywood.

The existence of the Others was a more closely guarded secret even than sexuality, and through the years humans who had tried to break the silence had been silenced themselves, through blackmail, threats and sometimes even death.

So, the edgy and hidden nature of the Others-only clubs was a powerful draw for humans who were aware of the Others. Declan's underground club made a fortune in admissions from humans in the know who were willing to pay top dollar for the Other experience.

It occurred to Barrie that Mayo would have been one of them, and she made a mental note to ask Declan about him as she stormed the club after a stop at home to change into a VLBD (very little black dress) and her tallest heels, the outfit accented by a complicated necklace, an industrial-looking metal chain assemblage of copper and steel and glass, for edge.

The doorman, one of L.A.'s supertall leprechauns, knew her and lifted the velvet rope, waving her past the line. Inside the black box of a club she braced herself against the assault of sound and started to wend her way across the crowded, atmospherically misty floor in the direction of the bar. The manager's office was behind a spiral stairway, which led upstairs to a green room.

Barrie was an avid dancer and loved dance clubs in any form, but it always did her heart good to see Others mixing so happily and in such numbers. Now, as she looked out over the floor she saw vampires dancing with Elven, weres dancing with shifters, everyone having a great time, just as it should be. *Beats the hell out of interspecies war, that's for sure,* she thought.

As she moved to the pulse of the music and assessed the crowd, she got her share of appreciative looks from the males of every species, which she casually ignored. But then she caught sight of a tall Elven—well, okay, "tall Elven" was redundant—watching her from the sidelines with an intense enough look that she paused midstride before she looked away. She knew never to lock eyes with an Elven. They could read minds if they held your gaze. In a solid eye lock, you could read theirs as well, a disturbingly intimate thing. Barrie kept moving, but it was surprisingly hard not to look back at him. She didn't generally go for Elven; they were too uniformly gorgeous and…blond for her liking. But there was something about the quiet intensity of the one who had been watching her that made her think for a moment of Johnny Love and her disturbing—and disturbingly erotic—dream last night.

She shook her head almost violently to rid herself of the thought and was thankful to spot Declan casually leaning across the bar to speak to one of the bartenders.

He turned as she approached, as if sensing her presence. He was a striking Englishman of forty, with gorgeous cheekbones and raven-black hair, a taut swimmer's body and an impatient energy that often read as arrogance. Barrie would never have called him that, but he didn't suffer fools gladly.

"Cousin," Declan greeted her, and kissed her English-style, on both cheeks. "Sailor said you might be storming the gates tonight."

"I need to know about the Pack," she told him, without any further pleasantries. Declan was a shifter Keeper; she didn't need to pussyfoot around. He nodded and put his hand to her elbow to steer her into the office behind the bar, shutting the door behind them. The music still throbbed through the walls, but now they didn't have to shout—or risk being overheard. Barrie got right to it. "Did you know them?"

Declan looked conflicted. "I knew them about as much as anyone was allowed to get to know them at the time, which, truly, was not much. I've been in the business a long time, and I'll tell you, love, I've never seen anyone quite like those three. One by one they were charismatic, to be sure, but together? It was a whole other level of star power. And they knew it. And they *used* it."

Barrie picked up on his ambiguous tone. "Used it… and pissed people off, you mean?"

"That's putting it mildly."

Barrie felt cold. "Enough to kill them? Or one of them, anyway?"

Declan smiled wryly. "Ah, we're back to that, are we? 'Who Killed Johnny Love?'" he asked with ironic emphasis. "Who killed Kurt, who killed Jim, who killed Janis, Jimi... There's always a conspiracy when stars die young."

"You don't believe it, then."

Declan spread his hands. "I believe that Johnny had enough destruction in him to finish himself off all on his own."

She looked at him thoughtfully. She trusted him, and his steady skepticism gave her pause. Best not to go off half-cocked, after all.

"He didn't die in L.A., you know," she said, and she saw a brief jolt of surprise—or something—in his eyes.

"That I did not," he said. "Where, then?"

"I was hoping you could tell me."

His face was neutral. "I heard the same thing everyone did, I imagine. It was an overdose at the Chateau. If that's not the case, it's news to me."

Then he twitched and reached for his pocket to pull out a phone. He checked a message, and his face tightened. He glanced to Barrie.

"Could I just sit you down for about ten minutes? I have a drummer passed out up there and..."

"Oh, no," Barrie said in outraged sympathy. Artists. Universal flakes. "Don't worry about me. Go. Good luck."

He escorted her out of the office and back into the main room where he found her a barstool. He nodded to the bartender, who had the shaggy-around-the-edges look of a were, and indicated Barrie's drinks were on him.

He started off, then turned back to her and stepped

close to her so she would hear him but no one else could. "Barrie...be careful on this one. It's dangerous territory you're treading into. A whole studio lot full of skeletons that a lot of people won't want unburied."

Even with the raucous, jostling crowd around her, Barrie felt a shiver. "I'll be careful," she promised him. But as a Keeper he knew as well as anyone what the job was—which was whatever it had to be.

As the bartender turned toward her, she shouted over the music for a vodka tonic, then sat on the stool watching the dancers and brooding over what Declan had said.

The band finished its set to cheers, and recorded music came up over the speakers for the break. It was a classic funk tune Barrie loved, and she found herself looking around the room for potential partners.

And even as she thought it, she saw the Elven who'd noticed her as she came in heading purposefully toward her.

He stopped in front of her, towering and blond, and smiled. "Want to?" he asked, not quite shouting over the din.

Normally she would have been up on her feet in a second, especially for such a danceable song, but something about the Elven, his intensity, made her hesitate. Then she put her hand in his, and he led her out onto the floor.

He was a surprisingly fabulous dancer. Not many Elven really were; it was hard to compress all that height into the economy of movement that's such a pillar of good partner dancing. Barrie had always considered herself lucky that shifters were in general the best dancers of the Others; their natural talent at mimicry extended to physical movement. But this Elven was doing fine, more than fine, and she found herself relaxing into his expert lead. He was comfortable enough with himself to play around with the song, and she found herself laughing as she alternately followed and challenged him.

And then their eyes locked.

They were looking deep into each other's eyes, and try as she might Barrie couldn't look away. She felt fire through her whole body, and an almost paralyzing desire—not just desire but a longing so powerful she couldn't breathe....

Then she realized something was wrong.

The Elven was looking straight into her eyes and *she wasn't reading his thoughts*.

And then she understood. The being in front of her wasn't Elven at all.

She stopped still on the dance floor, jostled from all sides by the crowd, and forced the words out. "What are you playing at, shifter?"

She saw the jolt in his eyes, and before he could flee, she grabbed his wrist and held on.

She was unnerved by the strength of the shift; she had to focus her whole being on keeping hold of him until he began to shimmer....

And then Barrie jolted back in shock as the Elven resolved himself...

...into Mick Townsend.

For a moment she was more stunned than angry. First that Mick was a shifter at all, and second—she'd never seen a shifter duplicate an Elven, or any other Other, so well. But the anger came soon enough—anger at herself for not having seen it, anger at him for being so *good* at it. Not only had she not picked up that the Elven was a shifter, much less Mick, she'd never picked up that Mick was a shifter at all. It was an appalling failure on her part. She felt shame, humiliation and white-hot rage.

She turned and pushed her way off the dance floor. He followed her. "Gryffald, wait!"

Barrie darted through the dancers, but he was fast. He caught up with her at the door to the back hall and grabbed her arm, and she spun to face him in a fury. "Wait for what? So you can shift into a were or a leprechaun and trick me all over again?"

"I wasn't trying to trick you."

"What *were* you trying to do, then?"

"At the moment I was trying to dance with you."

That silenced her, at least momentarily. The dance had been really good, she had to admit. Which she didn't want to think about. She wanted to stay mad and storm off.

But there was one thing she needed to know, and that kept her there out of pure professional curiosity.

"How do you do it?" she asked grudgingly.

He seemed startled at the question, but he knew what she meant because he grinned. "Years and years of practice."

She felt another flare of resentment. "Well, now you have proof of how good you are. You fooled a shifter Keeper."

"I fool everyone," he said. "Is that why you're mad?" He suddenly grabbed her hand and pulled her into the back hall and out the exit door.

The quiet of the alley was deafening after the din of the club; Barrie was disoriented. Mick held her wrist, a maddeningly erotic touch, and forced her to face him. "Barrie, almost no one *ever* knows I'm a shifter."

It was probably the first time he'd ever said her first name, and she had to admit that it gave her a little thrill. But that disappeared as she registered what he'd said after her name.

"You're *passing?*" she asked in sheer disbelief. Of course, all Others were passing as far as humans were concerned, but she rarely came across an Other who was trying to pass as human to other Others. It was startling, it was unnerving, it seemed... Shifty was what it was.

"Most of the time," he admitted. "I don't usually reveal myself to anyone at all," he added.

That struck her as odd, in a strangely thrilling way. "Then...why me?" she managed.

"I wanted you to know," he told her, and a thick silence fell between them.

Barrie found it unnerving and had to move away from him to look out at the cars cruising by on Sunset at the end of the alley. He moved up behind her, but thankfully not as close as he had been.

"I thought it would make it easier for you to agree to team up with me if you knew I was an Other."

She glanced at him. She didn't want to admit it, but of course he was right on the money; she had virtually decided against doing any kind of work with him at all because it would be so hard not to break the Code.

"I do feel like an idiot for not seeing it," she said.

He suddenly grinned at her. "Hey, I've been doing it for so long even *I* forget I can shift sometimes."

In spite of herself, she laughed. She was still mad at him, but too curious to walk away. She looked at him quizzically. "But I don't understand. Why? Why would you want to hide it?"

It was his turn to step away, his face darkening even in the shadows of the alley. "You're a shifter Keeper. I don't have to tell you about the excesses of my kind. Being a shifter makes it easy to fool people. It makes you think you're powerful when really you're just conning people, taking advantage of their trust."

Barrie knew too well what he meant. Shifters were very much like actors: born chameleons and tricksters. It was their very nature to be inconstant.

Mick continued, and his voice had an edge; he sounded haunted.

"There have been things I've done that I'm not proud of. When I quit—some of the other stuff, I realized if I were really going to start over, I had to...not shift. I wanted to experience my life as just one person. So, I set out learning how to do that, to just be myself." He smiled ruefully. "Hardest thing I've ever done."

Barrie was moved by that; it took a lot of guts and commitment not to abuse the power that shifting offered. It was a brave thing to do...and a lonely one, too. She felt herself melting, and that was the last thing she wanted to do.

"Well, you haven't lost the talent. That was a pretty damn good imitation of an Elven," she said grudgingly.

He smiled slightly. "What gave me away?"

"Looking at me the way you did," she answered automatically, and then blushed, suddenly remembering their moment on the dance floor, remembering how very thoroughly he had looked at her, how his look had stopped her dead with a feeling of desire so strong it had taken her breath away. It did it again now.

"I couldn't read your thoughts," she managed to say. "That's how I knew."

"You couldn't read my thoughts?"

Barrie couldn't speak. The truth was, she *had* been able to read his thoughts at that moment—all too well. Just not in an Elven way.

Mick looked down at her as if he knew exactly what she was thinking, Elven or not, and his voice was suddenly husky. "I'm glad that much came through, anyway."

She moved away from him, trying to keep her head. "You *have* been following me, haven't you?"

"Well, maybe a little."

"A *little?* How do you follow someone a *little?*"

"Barrie," he said, and again she felt that thrill at the sound of his voice speaking her name. "I've been up front with you, haven't I? I've said that I want to work together, that I think we should team up."

"Why are you so keen to work together?"

He looked at her steadily. "Because no one cares as much as you do about that kid who died. And no one will work harder to do right by him."

She felt a little shaky, as if somehow he'd looked directly into her heart, and she had to turn away. "How do you know that?"

"I'm a shifter, aren't I? Even if I'm not living as one, I keep my hand in. You're the newest shifter Keeper. I watch these things."

She nodded distractedly; it made sense.

"And knowing you a little now..." He touched her face briefly, but the touch shivered through her. "I'd have to be blind or an idiot not to see that you care."

All kinds of unwanted feelings were welling up inside her, and she found herself dangerously close to tears. She stepped back from him abruptly to break the connection.

"So, if we *were* going to work together," she said, making sure not to indicate any kind of commitment or anything, "where were you thinking of starting?"

"Johnny Love," he said instantly.

"What about him?" she asked, maybe a little too quickly herself.

"He's the center of all of this." He paced in the alley, as if unable to contain his urgency. "There's a fifteen-year-old mystery about his death.... A talented young shifter is killed while playing Johnny for the sexual pleasure of the producer of the original movie who is planning to remake that movie. And both the shifter and the producer are killed with the same exotic drug cocktail that killed Johnny.... It's the obvious center of the investigation." He stopped his manic circling and turned to face her. "If we want to know what's happening now, we have to start with the past. So, we have to find out what really happened to Johnny Love."

Barrie felt a different kind of thrill now, because of course it was exactly what she had been thinking.

"And how would you want to proceed on that?" she asked coolly.

"Johnny didn't die in L.A."

Barrie felt dazed with shock. *He knows. How does he know?* Aloud she blustered, "And I suppose you know where he *did* die."

"Catalina," Mick said with absolute certainty, and Barrie stared at him, stupefied. He'd already tracked down the real place of death. Catalina was an island just off the coast, a resort oasis and the setting of the final scenes of *Otherworld.* Even as he said it, it had the ring of truth. She tried to focus through her excitement and gather the facts.

"How…how do you know that?"

"Sources," Mick said. "And I think we should go out there and find out what really happened to him. Now. Tonight."

Barrie knew she had no choice but to go with him if she wanted to be in on this case.

"All right," she said, forgetting all about waiting to talk to Declan. "Let's go."

The car the valet brought was a stunning silver Bentley, so polished and shining Barrie could see her own reflection in the hood, an unbelievably classy classic car. *And* way *too nice for a reporter's car.*

As the valet ran to open the passenger door for her, she was roiling with envy and suspicion and desire.

Who is *this guy?*

As she dropped into the passenger seat, she had a

momentary flash that she was doing exactly what she'd just promised Declan she wouldn't do.

Oh, come on, he's a coworker, she told herself. Even so, as Mick stood outside the car and tipped the valet, she took out her phone and texted both her cousins using code to let them know where she would be.

Mick went back to the trunk before getting into the car, and when he dropped behind the wheel he was carrying a coat, which he handed to her. "Not that I want you to cover those legs for any reason, but you'll need this out on the water," he said, and she blushed, pleased with the compliment and surprised at his thoughtfulness.

The coast road was gorgeous under an almost full moon as they drove down PCH, the Pacific Coast Highway, toward Marina del Rey where the ferry to Catalina docked.

Catalina was a small island off the coast, home of the town of Avalon, created as a resort in the 1920s. Barrie thought back to the last scene of *Otherworld;* Catalina had stood in for the fictional island depicted as the heart of the Otherworld kingdom. That part of the story was totally make-believe. There were certainly Others on Catalina, but not a large population, and they tended to be reclusive, mostly weres who wanted the wide-open spaces the island offered or who had a taste for bison, which roamed there in herds. Elven hated Catalina because of the water. Elven had a pathological dread of water; it was often lethal to them—a fact the movie never went into.

Barrie felt a stir of significance at that last thought,

but before she could pursue it, Mick spoke, looking out the windshield at the almost-full moon.

"Weres will be out on the prowl any minute," he joked, and she laughed and realized how comfortable it was to be with someone who just *knew,* who she didn't have to hide things from or struggle to keep the Code.

Her romantic history wasn't exactly a disaster, but she'd never been in love, real love, either, and it had started to feel like she was missing out on a rather large and essential part of life.

She wasn't like some Keepers who thought intermarriage between mortals and Keepers, or marriage between species, should be banned. That attitude smacked of miscegenation, and there were always couples—not many, but some—who could make it work. It just seemed to her a sensible policy to keep a professional distance from the species she was entrusted to protect.

But it was hard living between two worlds. It was hard to date Others because she knew their foibles too well, and they were, after all, a whole different species. And it was hard to date mortals because she couldn't talk about her life's work without breaking the Code. If she were ever to find that…One, then she would of course tell him everything about who she was and what she did, without reservation. The trouble was, she hadn't found him yet. Or he hadn't found her. And she was getting a little tired of waiting.

She envied her cousins, who seemed to have found their soul mates so easily. Rhiannon and Sailor hadn't even been back in town for six months before they'd run straight into the loves of their lives: Rhiannon wasn't having any trouble at all making it work with an Elven, and Sailor's fiancé, Declan, was a Keeper himself, as well as entrenched in the entertainment business, a perfect match.

"Penny for your thoughts," Mick said beside her, and Barrie jumped...then reddened. She couldn't very well tell him.

"Oh, I was just...wondering why Johnny was out on Catalina after the movie was wrapped." And then she realized what had been bothering her about it. "He was Elven. They hate water. Of course he'd tolerate it for the movie, actors do whatever it takes. But why would he ever voluntarily be on the island after they'd wrapped?"

Mick's face tightened, but he didn't answer; they'd arrived at the ferry dock, and the dark water of the Pacific spread out before them like a velvety carpet. "We'll have to hustle to make that last boat." He veered into a parking space and parked.

The boat to the island was a high-speed catamaran, and the trip was about an hour over the water. And of course in the grand old resort tradition, the party got started on the boat.

Barrie hadn't been out to Avalon in a long time, and she'd forgotten how luxe the night ferry was. The music was classic forties jazz, and the bar was cozy, with big wide couches and club chairs to sink into, and a sweeping Art Deco bar. Mick ordered perfect icy martinis and they found a booth against the wide windows looking out on the moonlit sea, a stunning view of dark ocean and receding city lights.

It was so romantic, in fact, that she had a sudden suspicion that he was just getting her out on the boat—and out to the island—to seduce her. She was immediately mortified for thinking it…and more…for wanting it.

She refocused herself on business. "Why do you think Johnny was out on the island?" she asked again.

Mick was lounging very enticingly against the booth and looking at her in a most distracting way.

"Maybe he liked the area. Or maybe he'd gotten to know someone out there."

"A lover, you mean. Was he gay?" she asked abruptly. There had been all kinds of stories of Johnny and various starlets, but in Hollywood being seen in female company was hardly proof of sexual preference. "I mean, I always wondered. The three of them, the Pack, were so close."

Now Mick glanced away. "I'm not sure who'd be able to answer that. I'm not sure Johnny knew himself. He was sixteen. That age, you're still finding yourself, and it's not easy when you can have whatever and whoever you want, anytime you want it. And of course when drugs are involved, the boundaries are even less clear." He stared out the window at the ocean sparkling under the moon. "He may never have had a chance to really know."

Barrie was truly impressed, even moved, by his insight. "You know a lot about him." She felt like a total slacker herself; she couldn't believe how much information he'd come up with. But it wasn't information, really, it was a *sense* Mick seemed to have about Johnny, an empathy, as if he understood him.

Mick shrugged. "I've been interviewing everyone I

could find who would talk. It's not easy. A lot of people claimed to know him and really had no clue. But that's all part of the legend, too, letting everyone think what they want to think of you—or sometimes, with actors, actually *being* what people want."

She said what she had been thinking earlier. "Acting is a lot like shifting, I guess."

"Exactly," he said bleakly.

Barrie pushed her martini away and got out her notepad. In a homicide investigation, reconstructing the victim's last day was key. But that was exactly what was maddening about the whole case. "We've got two big problems. One, this all happened fifteen years ago. Two, all the witnesses are celebrities. Hard to get to. I mean, listen, this is the witness—and suspect—list." She read from her notes. "Travis Branson, DJ, Robbie Anderson—if anyone could ever find him. The director of photography is dead, heart attack five years ago...." She went on through her list, naming several other big-name actors who had played roles in the film.

"Darius Simonides," Mick added.

"Darius?" Barrie looked at him in surprise. Darius was a senior agent for the huge Global Artists Agency, one of the most powerful men in Hollywood.

"He repped all three of the Pack," he said. "He still reps DJ."

"Darius I can get to," she said with a rush of excitement. "He's my cousin Sailor's godfather." It was exactly what Alessande had counseled her to do: find people who were actually there, who could tell the real story.

Mick was silent for a moment. "You know, it's like

you just said—all those guys on that list are hard to get to. Maybe we should start with someone who would know everything but would be more willing to talk to us."

Barrie felt a stirring of significance. "Like who?"

"The opposite end of the totem pole. Below the line. An assistant, a gaffer, or best boy or production assistant. Someone who would really be in the know, but not obvious."

Barrie stared at him, realizing. "You already found someone, didn't you."

"Well…"

She gritted her teeth. "Just tell me," she said.

He gave her an apologetic smile. "I was lucky on my source. I figured—like you said—none of the above-the-line people would want to talk to a lowly journalist, so I started at the bottom."

She stared at him. "That's a great idea," she said reluctantly, kicking herself that she hadn't thought of it herself.

He shrugged, as if it was no big deal. "Production assistants, especially—they're treated so badly, most of the time. They like to be asked."

She frowned at him. "How do you know so much about the business?"

He hesitated. "Don't tell anyone, but I worked my way up on the entertainment beat."

She burst out laughing. "Oh, no, you were a Harvey?"

He mock-grimaced. "If you tell anyone, you're dead."

She put a hand to her mouth to stop giggling. "Your secret's safe with me—if you behave yourself," she teased, but instantly got serious again. "So, who are we going out there to talk to?"

Barrie wasn't sure he even realized he was doing it, but he leaned forward and kept his voice low, so he couldn't be overheard. "This PA told me about an actor who lives on the island. Not a pro, but a local fisherman who showed up for a casting call for islanders as extras, and he ended up with a role because he had such a great look."

Barrie remembered the fisherman from the movie; he'd played the small but pivotal role of a ship's captain who helped the Pack by hiding them from their human pursuers.

"He *was* good," she said. "And what about him?"

"I'm not sure, but he was in some of the last scenes of the movie with Johnny. The PA said we should talk to him."

The boat was nearing the dock, and the two of them went up on deck with quite a few of the rest of the passengers to watch the approach into the crescent-shaped harbor. The lights of the town sparkled in uneven rows leading up the hill, and the boats in the harbor were lit up as well, with brilliant strings of lights, a fairy-tale picture. Barrie was glad to have Mick's coat, a soft, dark cashmere thing that swallowed her up and smelled deliciously of some faint cologne—and even more deliciously of Mick.

She gazed out over the water at the circular white facade of the Avalon Ballroom, a former casino, now ballroom and movie palace. It looked like a giant wedding cake towering over the water, and she was acutely aware of how fabulously elegant it was inside; she'd actually been there for ballroom dance events, but never with someone who would make the romance complete....

And those *are thoughts that are only going to get you in trouble,* she warned herself. *This is work. That's all.*

She forced herself toward thoughts of the case, the film, the mystery of Johnny Love.

As she and Mick debarked along the long diagonal slant of the ramp with the other passengers, it did feel exactly as if they were descending into the film. Catalina was an Otherworld of its own, a setting out of time.

The feeling continued as she walked beside Mick along the main street of town, with its old-fashioned streetlamps and upscale boutiques and open-air bars and restaurants, where couples sat at candlelit tables, sipping wine and gazing into each other's eyes.

She had just seen the movie, and it was an odd thing, traveling along the same streets that the young actors had strolled in the film. It was a feeling you often got, living in L.A.—so often there was a sense of déjà vu from coming across a location that was familiar from a favorite movie. It added to the fantasy world aspect of Hollywood; much more than merely romantic, it was hallucinatory, intoxicating.

And to be walking along these romantic streets with someone who was gorgeous enough to be in a movie himself...it was all very unsettling.

Mick glanced at her as if he knew what she was thinking and said, "It would be nice to come here *not* for work."

She cleared her throat. "Where does this captain live?"

He gave her a smile that was not quite a smile and gestured to a path leading down to a smaller harbor.

The fisherman lived on his own trawler, exactly as he had for the movie, although she was pretty sure the boat in the movie had been a newer, cleaned-up version. The captain was waiting for them on the well-worn deck, smoking a pipe and looking out over the shimmering water. Just as it was startling to walk onto a street you knew from a movie, it was always startling to meet someone who you knew from on-screen. The fisherman looked not that much older than he had in *Otherworld,* really, and he had the same authentic salt-of-the-earth energy that he'd brought to the role; she understood perfectly why he'd been cast.

Mick introduced the fisherman as Captain Livingston, and said Barrie was a colleague.

"It's such a pleasure to meet you," she told him honestly. "My cousins and I loved you in the movie."

Captain Livingston nodded thanks without speaking, and glanced at Mick.

"We appreciate you seeing us on such short notice," Mick said.

"Come downstairs and we'll talk," the captain said curtly, and turned to go through a door. Mick and Barrie followed him downstairs into the main cabin, a comfortable, masculine room with carefully stored nautical equipment and carved built-in furniture pieces, and a small galley separated from the rest of the room by a storage counter. Outside the wide windows other boats bobbed gently in the rippling current, and the moon stippled the dark water with blue light.

"I can offer you tea, or there's whiskey," the captain said in his brusque way.

"Tea would be wonderful, but I can get it for all of us," she offered. The captain looked her over, and nodded shortly.

She stepped into the galley. There were already mugs set out on the counter, and a kettle was on the burner. She poured tea as out in the main room Mick told the captain, "Steve Price said you might talk to us about the last few days on *Otherworld*."

The old fisherman puffed on his pipe. "Depends on what you want to know."

"We think that a false story was put out about Johnny Love's death," Mick said, getting right to the point. "You were on set those last few days before Johnny died. Your scenes with him were some of the last shots of the movie. So, we thought you might know, or have some idea, anyway."

The old man took his time answering. She brought out the mugs of tea and a plastic bear filled with honey, and handed them around, and it was still some time before the captain actually spoke.

"Most of what they all said about that Johnny Love was false," he finally said.

Barrie was about to jump in and ask him why, but Mick touched her leg and shook his head very slightly, and she kept silent. The old man sat in his chair, and she felt her body subtly swaying in the softly creaking boat, until finally he spoke again.

"Everyone called those three boys spoiled and arrogant, but it wasn't so. Not Johnny, anyway. I didn't know beans about acting, but he was always willing to help me out, explain what the bigger fish were saying. He went over all my scenes with me, practiced with me, talked over what everything meant. And as an actor he was up there with the greats. It's a crime what happened to him."

The way he said it, Barrie had to ask, "What *did* happen to him?"

The old man looked at her with eyes as dark as the water outside them. "I don't rightly know, but it's not what they say. Johnny Love died before they ever finished that movie," the old fisherman said flatly.

Barrie gasped. She looked to Mick, who looked grim—but not exactly surprised, she noted.

He knew, she thought.

She forced herself to focus on the old man. "Please. Please tell us."

The captain gazed into space, and the very air seemed to change around them as he remembered. "We were down to the last few days of filming. Then one morning Johnny never showed up for a call. It was our last scene together. No one knew what the problem was, but all the bigwigs were in an uproar. Everyone was scrambling. And finally toward the end of the day they had me shoot my scenes with someone else standing in. When you look at that last scene, you can see we were never shot together. Well, it's because Johnny wasn't there at all."

Barrie was feeling distinctly disoriented. She'd just seen the movie. "But Johnny is *in* those scenes…" she said weakly.

"They did it with computers," the fisherman said flatly. "And then they filmed the last scenes on a closed set, with only the director, cameraman and the actors."

Barrie was aware it could be done; it *had* been done in other movies where a lead actor had died before the end of principal photography. Editing techniques and digital animation and special effects being what they were, there was very little that couldn't be fixed in film. But the very thought of it, of what it meant...

She stammered, "You never said anything, all these years...."

"Didn't want anything more to do with it—ever." The captain's face was dark. "Those movie people are always playing a big game on everyone else. Thinking they're putting something over on us by mocking something that's real. But I'm not blind. I know what's out there in the night. I know some people aren't what they seem."

Barrie felt a chill. She also understood why the old man had been cast: he had a power that just resonated, in person and on-screen. Mick was being very silent beside her, and she glanced over to him—and was unnerved by the look she saw on his face. Either angry or disturbed or both, she couldn't tell, but something had come over him.

He didn't seem inclined to speak, either, so she swallowed and turned back to the captain. She spoke carefully. "Do you think someone...hurt Johnny?"

"Hurt him?" The old man looked at her directly.

"Killed him," she whispered.

The captain's eyes turned bleak. "I couldn't say. But someone was up to no good, and they ruined that kid."

He looked defensive and defiant, and his voice trembled as he spoke. "He was just a kid, and he was a good kid, no matter what anyone says."

Barrie leaned forward and put her hands on his. "I believe you."

Barrie and Mick left the boat in silence, with Barrie tendering their thanks and appreciation to the captain. Mick was still in that strange silence, brooding, sunk into himself.

"You knew." She confronted him once they reached the boardwalk, out of earshot of the boat. He looked for a moment caught.

"I didn't *know*," he countered. "I'd heard something—"

"From one of your *sources*," she said in total disbelief. *Does he ever tell the truth? Ever?* She felt faint, even sick.

"I'd heard about the closed set. There could have been any number of reasons why Mayo and Branson closed off the set for the last scenes. The captain isn't an Other, so of course he didn't know everything that was going on. There was a whole other level of reality that was being kept from him."

"They didn't keep it from him very well." She recalled the old man's eyes as he'd stated, *I know some people aren't what they seem.* She was fairly certain that he knew there were more things in heaven and earth than most people dreamed of.

Mick was silent, maybe knowing there was nothing he could say to her right then that would calm her. The water rippled behind them, a lulling and yet somehow ominous sound.

"Is there anything else you're not telling me?" she demanded.

Mick looked at her but didn't speak.

He knows too much, she thought. *He wants too much. I don't know why he cares about this...the way he does.*

She was suddenly acutely aware that they were completely alone on the pier. There might have been any number of people out on the boats tied up in their slips all around them, but no one was visible. She was out on an island in the middle of the night with a shifter, one of the least reliable beings on the planet, and suddenly she doubted every single thing he'd ever said to her. More than that, she was afraid. And she didn't like that feeling at all.

"All right," she said, and managed to keep her voice from shaking. "I'm going home now."

As she turned on her heel he caught her wrist, and she gasped. She swiveled around to face him, her heart in her throat, and he looked at her. "I wish you wouldn't," he said, barely audible.

And then he was pulling her forward and his mouth was on hers, and she felt herself turn to liquid at the touch of his lips, melting and burning and freezing all at once as she kissed him back, and felt the warmth of him and the smell of him enfold her....

She pulled back with a gasp, staring at him.

"Barrie," he said, his voice thick, and she knew in the core of her that whether she trusted him or not, whether he was telling the truth or not, if she let him pull her forward, she would be lost for all time. Then she jerked her arms away from him and fled, running all the way back to the ferry dock, not turning around until the boat back to the mainland was in sight. She paused, panting, staring back into the dark....

He hadn't followed her.

And despite everything, she wished he had.

Chapter 8

From the ferry landing in Marina del Rey she took a cab back to the Snake Pit for her car. Once again, it was well after 3:00 a.m. when she finally arrived back at home.

Her cousins' houses were both dark as she drove through the main gate and up to Gwydion's Cave.

I'm bringing new meaning to the idea of the night shift, she thought.

Her own kitchen light was the only one burning besides the outside lights of the estate; with her odd hours, she'd learned to leave a light on for herself. She was relieved and grateful that no one was waiting up for her; she couldn't possibly have explained where she had been or what she had been doing, or especially what she *felt,* since she didn't know that herself. But the feeling of Mick's kiss, of his arms pulling her against him, of the urgent fire of her own response, was making her dazed and light-headed.

She opened the front door and threw her keys in the bowl on the side table. Oddly, Sophie didn't come padding out to greet her as she almost always did. Barrie moved down toward the bedroom, frowning.

And then she heard a scuffling noise in the kitchen and froze.

Someone's here.

She took two noiseless steps forward to the panic button the Keepers had installed in every room in the house and hit the silent alarm to wake her cousins. Then she grabbed an umbrella from the coat stand to arm herself.

She crept toward the front door, holding her breath as she approached the archway into the living room. Two shadows loomed up in the darkness…and she came face-to-face with her cousins. All three of them screamed.

Barrie dropped the umbrella, going limp with relief. "You guys! You scared me half to death!"

"You're the one coming home at three in the morning!" Rhiannon accused.

"We were worried!" Sailor said on top of her. "You send us some text about going off to Catalina in the middle of the night."

"With some guy."

"In the middle of a murder investigation."

"What were we supposed to think?" Rhiannon finished.

Barrie looked at both of them, a little overwhelmed. Then again, maybe she hadn't been clear enough. "Well, he's not just some guy, he's on the *Courier*."

Sailor and Rhiannon looked at each other. "All right, you're starting from the beginning," Rhiannon said, and herded them all into the kitchen to make tea.

Barrie filled them in over steaming cups of her favorite, black currant. Truthfully, in her own kitchen, with her cat purring in her lap, it was hard to be as spooked as she had been out there on the island, in the dark, with the feeling of the movie all around her. "Mick Townsend is a new hire on the paper," she started.

"Mick Townsend," Sailor repeated. "He sounds hot."

"That is so not the point," Barrie said murderously, and Rhiannon gave Sailor a warning look. Barrie continued warily. "He's been following the connection between Tiger and Saul Mayo, too. And tonight we went out to Catalina to talk to this old fisherman from *Otherworld*—"

"The one in the boat scenes?" Rhiannon interrupted. "He was great."

"He's for real," Barrie said. "As real as it gets."

She quickly filled her cousins in on their interview with Captain Livingston, and his startling insistence that Johnny Love had died during production.

"Oh, my *God!*" they exclaimed at once.

"I know," Barrie agreed.

"So, that's why I haven't been able to find out anything about the Elven Keeper who handled Johnny's death," Sailor said.

"Exactly. He didn't die in L.A.," Barrie said. "And I think the reason no Elven knows the real scoop about his death is the *water*. It happened out on the island. There are no Elven out there. It must have been excruciating for Johnny to be out there filming."

"I can't believe he did it," Rhiannon said.

"He was an actor," Sailor argued. "A role like that? Anyone would have done it, excruciating or not."

"I agree," Barrie said. "But for sure there wouldn't have been any other Elven out there with him. So, if he did die out there—on set or off—there was no one of his Kind out there to help him or attest to what happened."

The cousins fell silent, contemplating this. Finally Barrie spoke.

"The thing is, I think Mick already knew. Not just that Johnny died on Catalina, but that he died during filming." She looked at her cousins. "Look at the way you two just reacted. It's *huge*. It changes everything we think about Johnny's death. But Mick—when Captain Livingston told us about Johnny, Mick acted a little surprised, but not anywhere near what you would expect." Talking it out, she realized at least part of what was bothering her so much about the situation. "So, why would he take me all the way out to Catalina in the middle of the night to find this guy and interview him when it was something he already *knew?*"

"Maybe he was trying to seduce you," Sailor said, the exact same thing that Barrie had been thinking earlier in the evening.

"Sailor, this is serious," Rhiannon reprimanded her. "If Barrie thinks there's something off about it, she has to be very careful about this guy. What do you know about him, anyway?" she asked Barrie.

"Besides that you like him," Sailor said.

"I don't *like* him," Barrie started, but the words sounded like a lie even to her. "Okay, maybe he's smart, and perceptive, and an ace journalist...."

"And hot?" Sailor suggested.

"*Yes,* and hot. And a great dancer," Barrie said, a little wistfully.

Sailor raised an eyebrow. "He sounds like a dream. So, what's bothering you about the guy?"

Barrie could never get anything past her cousins; they all knew each other too well.

"Well, for starters he's a shifter," she said. "But it's hard to explain. I think he's lying to me about something." In fact she *knew* he was lying; she just didn't have any proof.

"The thing is, he's not just a shifter, he was *concealing* being a shifter, completely passing as human...and he did it so freaking *well*. I had no idea. Really, none. It's kind of scary."

"I'm going to have Brodie check him out," Rhiannon declared, and Barrie was about to protest when she realized that Rhiannon was right; it would be useful to have Brodie get some real background on Townsend.

"That would be great," Barrie thanked her. "And, Sailor, I need a huge favor from you, too."

"Anything, honey," her cousin offered instantly.

"I need to talk to Darius Simonides."

"Why? I mean, of course, I'll call him first thing in the morning, but why do you need to talk to him?"

"He repped all three of the Pack, and Travis Branson, too."

"Of course, that makes sense," Sailor murmured. She sounded troubled.

"But really, I need to talk to DJ," Barrie said.

"Talk to DJ!" Sailor exclaimed.

Rhiannon looked equally startled, and Barrie knew why. The actor was so famous it was sort of like saying she wanted an audience with Kate and William, and somehow crazily expecting to get one.

"I know," she told them. "But he's the one who's really going to know what happened on set. Well, him, and Travis Branson, the director. Captain Livingston said they were shooting the last scenes on a closed set, and only the principal actors were there. And realistically, DJ and Branson are prime suspects. God knows I'd love to talk to Robbie Anderson, too, but—"

She stopped, with a sudden thrill of realization.

"Maybe I *can*. If Robbie is dead, then there's a chance I *can* talk to him. And Johnny Love, too."

She stood, then hurried out the back kitchen door toward the main house.

Inside Sailor's house, Barrie moved into the back wing where Merlin kept his own room.

Merlin was the most polite ghost imaginable, an impeccable gentleman, and very firm about keeping civilized human boundaries. He would never think of just appearing in a room; he used doors just like anyone else, and when any of the cousins wanted to get in touch with him, she knocked on his door just the same as she would for anyone.

Barrie knocked, and waited, and after a moment the

door opened, as if by itself. It took Merlin a moment to fully appear; he must have been out of the house—somewhere *else*—when she'd knocked. He'd been a man of medium height and weight, with a charmingly lined face, bright blue eyes and a cap of snow-white hair, and that was how he appeared as a ghost, as well. At the moment, though, he looked anxious.

"Barrie, my dear. Is something wrong?"

His concern made her remember the hour. "No, nothing like that," she reassured him. "I'm sorry to disturb you so late."

"Oh, the hour doesn't matter in the slightest, as long as you and your cousins are all right."

"We're all fine, truly. But we're discussing a case, and you may be able to help."

"How lovely. I'd be delighted."

The door closed behind him on its own, and he followed her out into the great room where Sailor and Rhiannon were already waiting. There were air kisses all around; not that any of the Gryffalds were into air kisses as opposed to the real thing, but with a ghost, air kisses were what you got.

When all the women were seated, and not a second before, Merlin took a seat on the sofa and put his delicate hands on his knees expectantly.

"Now, what can I do for you girls?"

"I'm looking for a ghost," Barrie told him. "That is, the case I'm investigating revolves around a dead actor, and possibly two. One of them—I don't know if he's really dead, and if he's not, it would be really useful to know, so that I can start looking for him. The other one is definitely dead…." She stopped, wondering if she could even assume that much. "Probably definitely. But, since we have this most excellent connection to the spirit world, I thought…if there was any way of getting in touch with him—or them…"

"Who are these fine ex-personages?" Merlin asked her.

"Johnny Love and Robbie Anderson."

"Ah, yes," Merlin said. "I remember what a stir that caused, those two young men. So much talent, snuffed out so quickly."

Barrie quickly did the math in her head and realized that Merlin had still been alive when Johnny died.

Merlin nodded as if he knew what she was thinking. "Of course, I was still on this earth plane when Johnny Love made his transition, so I have no idea what kind of stir there may have been in the afterlife. I've never run into him over there, but you know, there are so many levels—continents, really—and it's not as if I've been looking. I'll certainly nose around and see what I can find out."

"Thanks, Merlin," Barrie said in real gratitude, and Sailor and Rhiannon echoed her. "And if you *could* see what you can find out about Robbie Anderson, too… The thing is, I just don't know. He disappeared at about the same time, and there's definitely something wrong with the whole situation, and it seems to be the key to a couple of recent deaths as well, a shifter and a mortal."

"My, my," Merlin tutted. "Very complicated. I assure you, I shall do my best."

It was really useful, sometimes, having a house ghost.

Chapter 9

She was in a huge round domed room with three ornate thrones set in a triangle in the center of a parquet floor, and candles blazing in wrought-iron candelabra. The three young actors slouched in the chairs like indolent crowned princes: Johnny Love, as blond as the sun; DJ, black-haired and black-eyed; and Robbie Anderson, hair the color of an antique gold piece and flecks of gold in his eyes. They were drunk, passing a flagon of wine and drinking from silver goblets.

And none of them could see the flames all around them, creeping higher and higher, across the floor toward the thrones....

Barrie woke with her heart pounding and a strangled scream in her throat. Sophie meowed her concern from

the pillow beside her, and Barrie picked up the little cat
and held her to her chest to calm down.

Of course you were dreaming the movie, she chided
herself. *Being over there on Catalina was like walking
into the film. This is all getting under your skin. Just follow the clues, do your interviews—and try not to lose it.*

She sleepwalked to the kitchen for coffee, and while
she fed the cat and the caffeine started to spike through
her veins, she discovered she had a text from Sailor con-
firming a two-thirty appointment with Darius Simonides. Barrie was impressed; she hadn't at all expected
to be able to get in to see the agent so soon. Thx, S. IOU,
she texted back.

It was already well past noon, so she showered quickly
and found something expensive and marginally conser-
vative in her closet, a tight-fitted, tailored skirt and suit
coat that looked like something Rosalind Russell would
have worn, with forties heels to match. Then she ran out
to her car and got herself down to Beverly Hills.

The Global Artists Agency offices were built to in-
timidate, and they did. The three-story building was an
imposing pink rectangle, grim as a prison. Barrie gave
her name to the guard on the first floor, who asked her to
wait in the atrium. Instead of seating herself, she drifted.
Inside, the building was gorgeous, airy, clearly designed
with impeccable attention to feng shui and the flow of
energy. The atrium was lined with modern art. Despite
the airiness, the place was terrifying, and not just for
the blatant display of money; the entire feeling of it was
heartless and cold. She understood why people in town
called the agency "The Forbidden Planet."

She sensed movement above her and looked up as a young, bright-eyed and hard-edged assistant came down the stairs to meet her. Barrie recognized him instantly as a shifter, and the way he eyed her made her think that he recognized her as a Keeper, too, though he didn't say anything of the sort. Instead they made small talk about the traffic as he led her up the broad spiraling staircase to the second floor, where he ushered her into the inner sanctum.

It was an exquisite office: huge, with a wraparound wall of windows that looked out over the city. Designer chairs were set in front of the chrome-and-glass desk; a spacious conversation area boasted a full stereo, wide-screen system and a wet bar; and another door led to a private bathroom.

Darius turned from one of the glass walls as she walked in. He was a little over six feet, a striking man with sharp hazel eyes and dark, slightly graying hair, who radiated the dangerous sensuality of his kind. Barrie had no idea how old he was; with vampires, any guess would almost surely be wrong. The overwhelming aura was *power,* a feral and dangerous charisma. Combine a superagent with a vampire and multiply by ten, and that was Darius.

He stopped a few feet in front of her and looked her over. It was not a sexual look; Barrie felt more that her every physical characteristic was being assessed and assigned a monetary value. She half expected him to ask her to open her mouth and show him her teeth. She was willing herself not to redden when finally he spoke.

"You Gryffald girls did well in the gene pool. If you

ever decided to give up this Keeper business, I could have you all up on-screen in no time, not just Sailor."

She had to suppress a shudder at the thought. Her mother had wanted the acting life, and because of that Barrie knew too much about it ever to be tempted. Besides, she knew full well that Darius hadn't exactly supercharged Sailor's career to date, and he could have if he'd chosen to.

"I'll stick to being a Keeper," she said with a forced smile. "Acting's riskier."

"Perhaps," he said cryptically.

He raised an elegant, long-fingered hand, motioning her to the conversation area of low couches and designer chairs, and remained standing until she sat, a chivalry that always threw her. When she was settled on a sofa, he seated himself in the largest chair. Earlier the assistant had placed drinks on the table in front of them: sparkling water for her and a tall glass of red liquid for Darius. She knew better than to ask.

"Thank you for seeing me," she began. "I—"

"Sailor tells me you have questions about *Otherworld*," he said bluntly, before she could finish the sentence.

Time is money, I guess, she thought.

"Is this something to do with Saul Mayo's death?" he demanded. Well, not exactly demanded, but his tone was challenging, to say the least.

"It's possible," she said, and was proud of herself for her cool tone.

His eyes narrowed. "My dear, you're a shifter Keeper. Mayo was not Other. I'm aware that you're new to your calling, but may I remind you that it's not part of your job description to investigate mortal passings?"

"I'm not investigating Mayo," she said, and could see that her brevity was getting under Darius's skin. She didn't want to alienate him, but she wasn't about to tell him about Tiger, either. "But since we're on the subject… you knew him well, didn't you?"

"Professionally," he said. "We've done quite a bit of business together."

"Do you think he was murdered?" she asked point-blank.

He smiled slowly, and for a moment, only because she knew to look, she caught the gleam of fangs.

"Almost certainly," he said. "Half the town wanted him dead. The trouble would be finding someone with the actual balls to do it."

She had to suppress a shiver.

Darius looked at her. "But we're not talking about Mayo, are we?"

Barrie recovered herself. "No. This is a possibly re-lated incident. A suspicious death that seems to be tied to *Otherworld*."

He flicked a hand dismissively. "I've heard that rumor. That someone had Mayo killed because of the remake. The denizens of our little community are the worst gossips in Hollywood. Why should anyone kill anyone over a remake?"

She answered carefully. "Didn't the original movie cause a lot of controversy in the community because it came so close to revealing the existence of the Oth-erworld? Maybe someone felt there was a danger that

Mayo—or someone—would go further and actually break the Code with this new film."

"Utter nonsense," Darius said. "Mayo didn't break the Code with *Otherworld,* and he hasn't since. He liked to think he was flirting with the edge, but the truth is, he always stayed safely behind the line. He enjoyed the power and prestige of knowing something very few mortals are ever privy to, and he wasn't about to make that secret common knowledge. The clear proof is he's had fifteen years since *Otherworld* with multiple opportunities to expose the Otherworld, and he never has."

Barrie had to admit Darius had a point.

The agent smiled as if he'd heard her thought, and continued, "My dear, mortals see what they're comfortable seeing. In the end, it's nothing but a movie, all sets and makeup and special effects, and we Others go on as we always have—unseen, unsung."

He sat back and sipped his drink, which left his mouth just a little too red.

"Now, I strongly suggest you leave Mayo's death to the police. There are ten thousand mortals who would have liked to see Mayo dead. The chances that the killer is one of ours is very slim, and there's no sense in your getting involved."

Then you don't know about Tiger. Or you're pretending you don't, Barrie thought.

"I really don't have any intention of investigating Mayo," she said.

He raised an eyebrow. "Then, what exactly are we talking about?"

"I'm trying to find Robbie Anderson," she said. Up

until the moment the words left her mouth, she'd had no idea that she was going to say them. But from the startled look on Darius's face, she realized it had been the right thing to say. It wasn't easy to catch him off-guard, and yet she'd managed it.

"Well, well," he said softly, and for a moment his eyes were far away. "Don't think I haven't tried. Losing Johnny and Robbie at the same time, and the way we did—that was half my client base at the time, and more talent than I've seen before or since." His business mask had slipped, and the look on his face was something like regret.

"You really have no idea what happened to him?" she asked.

"I think he's dead."

He sounded so certain. Barrie felt a chill…and a strange sense of grief. Why? Robbie Anderson was just a childhood fantasy, an abstraction on the screen.

"Why do you say that?" she managed.

"Shifters have a tendency to die badly," he said. "Something I hardly need to tell you, Keeper."

He looked straight into her eyes, a compelling, almost hypnotic gaze. "Believe me, my dear, if he were alive on this planet I would have found him and had him back in the business long ago. He could have named his price."

Barrie found she had to make an effort to pull her eyes from his. *Damn mesmerizing vampires.* She felt a little weak from the intensity of his stare and reached for her glass of water to give her a moment to recover her balance. Her overwhelming feeling was that Darius was telling the truth, but that was what was so tricky about vampires and Others generally. Under the right circumstances, they could make you believe…anything.

She put her glass down and smiled at him while being sure, this time, not to look directly at him. "Maybe I'll find him for you," she said nonchalantly. "I'll be sure to keep you posted."

She was shocked at her own audacity, but exhilarated, too.

"You do that," Darius said, with an edge of wariness, and for a moment she was sure he was going to dismiss her. But then he asked, "Is there anything else?"

"As a matter of fact, there is. I've come across the most interesting rumor." She glanced at him without making eye contact. "Is it true that Johnny Love died on set, before *Otherworld* even finished shooting?"

Darius looked as shocked as if she'd staked him. "Certainly not. I was on set for the last few days of shooting, and Johnny was most assuredly there. Do you think I wouldn't have noticed if my own client had dropped dead?"

He sounded truly incredulous.

Instinctively she nodded, as if she completely agreed with him. "That's what I thought. It was just so outrageous…. I mean, we've all seen the film. No one could possibly have kept a secret like that."

Darius shook his head, as if still trying to recover from the idea. "Where on earth would you have heard something like that?"

"It was an anonymous source. Really left-field…but of course I have to check out every lead."

He was watching her in a way that made her feel a

little like a mouse with the huge shadow of a hawk circling her. He rose and moved around the couch, rendering her even more profoundly uncomfortable. She hated to have her back to a vampire.

"I must say, I'm concerned that your father and uncles are so far away. I do hope you're not meeting any of these 'sources' in dark alleys."

She was fairly certain his words were a coincidence, but she couldn't help but think of the alley where Tiger had been dumped.

"Well, there's one source who might be able to clear everything up for me right away. But I need your help to get to him."

"And who might that be?"

Barrie took a breath. "I need to see DJ."

The vampire actually laughed out loud in disbelief as he sat back down. "See DJ?"

For a moment she expected him to say, *No one sees DJ.*

"If anyone knows what was happening on that movie, it would be him," she pointed out.

Darius chuckled and leaned forward to pat her hand indulgently. "You're overestimating your reach and mine," he told her. "DJ doesn't inhabit the same planet as any of the rest of us. You might as well ask to see Johnny Love."

Don't worry, I'm already on it, she thought silently. But what she said aloud was "I don't need a private appointment. The premiere of his new movie is tonight. If you can just get me in, I'll take it from there."

He frowned. "There's been a wait list for tonight for months, but I'll do what I can."

Liar, she thought. *As if you can't get tickets to anything, anywhere, anytime you want.* "That would be great, Darius, thank you so much."

He rose, signaling the end of the interview.

"Even if you can talk to him, I wouldn't count on the clarity of his memories. DJ's—" he paused delicately "—habits...started long ago."

Drugs again. There are drugs all through this case.

"Do keep me apprised," he told her at the door. Not a request.

"Of course," she told him, lying.

Darius's shifter assistant walked her to the staircase, and she was aware of him still standing above her, watching as she walked down the slow spiral of the staircase.

She pushed out the doors with a feeling of release and relief. But as she walked down the curving path toward the adjoining garage, the feeling of being watched, *tracked,* continued.

It was one of those huge Century City garages, with confusing levels and half levels. As she headed toward her car, heels clicking, she became aware that she was essentially alone in the labyrinth of concrete pillars and rows of cars. And yet, she didn't *feel* alone....

She didn't change her pace but focused her attention on her astral body, the aura of energy perception that surrounds every living being, human and animal. It was the astral body that shifters learned to manipulate. As a shifter Keeper, she also had a certain natural facility with manipulating the astral body. It was what allowed her to put on a glamour, and she could also tune in to the heightened perceptions of her astral body to sense people and beings around her.

Her heart began to beat faster as she realized there was indeed someone following her, someone who was intently focused on her. Then she was unnerved to feel a rush of heat through her body, an undeniably erotic charge.

She stopped in her tracks in shock.

And then she realized what was happening.

She turned around and faced the dimness of the garage.

"Shifter, I feel you. Show yourself!"

There was a shimmer in the darkness, and then Mick Townsend was standing there looking at her.

"Following me?" she accused, furious.

"I can't seem to stay away from you, Gryffald," he said with a half smile.

"Maybe a restraining order would help."

She moved to brush by him and reach her car, but he caught her forearms, and she felt an electric shock of attraction.

"Barrie," he said, and she had to look at him, then found she couldn't breathe. "Things got a little intense last night."

That was the understatement of the year. She couldn't even work up the strength for a retort.

"I just wanted to make sure you're all right," he continued, and damn him, he would not stop looking at her with those eyes, those green, green eyes....

"Well, I'm fine, obviously, so you can stop now."

He shook his head. "You never quit, do you? Walking right in to see Darius."

"This is my *job*," she flung back at him.

"You don't have to do it all by yourself every second, do you? This isn't something you should be nosing around in alone."

Safer than doing it with you, she wanted to say, but didn't.

"Barrie, there's more to it than you think there is— *and* more to whoever is behind it."

"That's really not something you have to be concerned about," she began coolly, but he tightened his grip on her arms.

"But I *am* concerned," he said roughly. "That should be obvious by now."

"I just don't understand why—"

"Yes, you do," he said, and pulled her to him to kiss her. Her mouth opened under his, and she felt arousal coil through her like a snake. His hands moved on her waist, his legs were hard against hers, and her whole body flashed back to him kissing her the night before, a sense memory of his hands on her. And her skin, her limbs, her blood, responded in the same way, right there in the garage.

I am in such trouble, she thought. *I am gone....* And then there were no thoughts at all, just an aching, delicious desire.

When he finally lifted his head from hers, she felt as if the whole garage was spinning. They stood in the concrete dimness, both breathing hard.

"Tonight," he said, his voice a low and intoxicating murmur, his hands caressing her waist. "Not business, a date. Just us. I'll pick you up after work. Seven o'clock."

"Okay," she said with absolutely no control over her responses. He bent and kissed her again, this time backing her against the side of the car, and she could feel his legs and his throbbing sex and the garage spiraled as her legs shook underneath her.

Then he stepped back, took her key and opened the car door for her. "Seven," he reminded her.

"Uh-huh," she said.

He shut the door on her, closing her inside, and she sat in a limp daze…watching as he turned and slowly walked down the aisle of parked cars, and she suddenly remembered that she was supposed to be trying to get into DJ's premiere that night but all she could think was *Seven? How am I going to last the whole day?*

And then she felt a twinge.

After work? Did he just say "after work"?

Mick had the same schedule she did, the night shift. So, what work was he talking about?

She sat up, suddenly alert again, and stared out the windshield.

Halfway down the aisle, Mick was stopped beside the Bentley. He zapped the door open and lowered himself into the elegant car.

Not even valet parked, she thought, which made her even more sure he had been following her. *And that's way too much car for a journalist,* she told herself grimly, and started her engine.

Then she followed him out of the garage.

The Bentley rolled out onto the street, smooth as glass, and she turned after it, trailing it crosstown, west on Wilshire, always hanging back, concealing her little Peugeot behind larger vehicles.

Mick drove the car like an L.A. native, switching lanes often and gliding around slower cars to time the lights perfectly. Barrie prided herself on her driving but had to admit a grudging respect; he wasn't just driving well, he *understood* the traffic. And having to admit it just pissed her off.

In Westwood he turned abruptly into the parking garage of a tall office building. She made the turn into the garage herself, and as her eyes adjusted to the dark, she saw the Bentley stopped at the valet station. Mick was just handing over his keys to an attendant. As she watched, Mick said something to the valet, who laughed and nodded. Mick tapped the man's arm in a familiar gesture, and the valet gave him a little half salute. Her eyes narrowed. *That valet knows him.*

She watched as Mick pushed through the inner glass doors toward the elevators, then sped up to the valet station and let the next valet take her keys. As he handed over her ticket, she asked him, "Who was that man with the Bentley?"

The valet didn't have to ask who she meant. "Mr. Stuart."

Barrie felt a surge of cold shock, but outwardly she did no more than raise her eyebrows. "Mr. Stuart, of course. What floor is he on?"

"Sixteen, miss."

"Thank you so much," she said sweetly, and headed for the glass doors.

The elevator took her up to a three-storied modernistic lobby, and she strode up to the building directory, a gleaming marble slab with names and numbers carved into the surface.

Her eyes scanned for the sixteenth floor and then stopped, staring, at the name of the company that occupied it: *The Circle Foundation.*

And the name of the CEO: Michael Stuart.

Chapter 10

The elevator doors opened on the sixteenth floor, and Barrie stepped out into a waiting room worthy of a museum. She took great pleasure in L.A.'s architecture: the surreal silver curves of the Disney Concert Hall; the Streamline Moderne of LACMA, the County Museum of Art; the oh-so-noir geometric patterned staircases of the Bradbury Building.

But the lobby of the Circle Foundation was one of the best examples of modern design she'd ever seen.

Money, she thought, dazed. *So much money here.* It didn't just rival GAA's offices, it surpassed them—in artistry, anyway.

Across the vast space of the lobby, a sleek receptionist with a haircut as modern as the decor sat at an island of a—*desk? counter?*—speaking into her Bluetooth.

Barry moved slowly forward into the space.

There were two huge, clear glass panels standing in the light of a domed skylight, etched with names and looking vaguely like the tablets of the Ten Commandments. One side held the names of donors to the Circle Foundation, the other a list of endowed charities and causes. She recognized the names of quite a few of the organizations: homeless shelters, scholarship foundations, intervention centers for at-risk youth. And they all had something in common: they quietly catered to the needs of Others.

Her eyes stopped on one familiar name, and she froze.

Out of the Shadows.

The shelter where Tiger had been living briefly before he went back on the street.

"May I help you?" the receptionist asked from her island. The acoustics of the room were so good it sounded as if she were standing right beside Barrie.

Barrie turned to her, startled, and walked forward, improvising. "Oh, hello. I'm affiliated with Out of the Shadows," she said smoothly. "I was in the building, and I've heard so much about the Circle's offices. I just thought I'd pop in and take a look." She faked an appreciative glance around the lobby. "Just as beautiful as everyone says."

The receptionist gave her a practiced smile. "Yes, it's a wonderful place to work."

"I'm sure," Barrie smiled back. "And I had no *idea* how many other organizations Circle is funding! Mr. Stuart is so modest about it all. Is he fairly new as CEO?"

"Not at all, he founded the company," the receptionist answered, and then apologized as she reached to answer the phone.

Barrie glanced up at the glass monument in front of her, at the date etched in the clear surface.

Established 2005.

As the receptionist spoke into the phone, two men in suits came out through the glass doors leading into the inner offices.

As the doors began to close behind them, Barrie moved quickly toward them and darted through.

She heard the receptionist's voice calling behind her, but she strode grimly along the inner hall, straight down toward what was clearly the corner office.

Another sleekly gorgeous secretary rose from her desk as Barrie barreled forward.

"I'm sorry, did you have an appointment with Mr. Stuart?"

"Yes," Barrie said through clenched teeth, and pushed through the door.

Mick sat behind a massive desk, talking into his Bluetooth as he leaned back in an ergonomic chair, looking out on his sweeping view of Santa Monica and the ocean beyond.

He caught one glimpse of Barrie and his feet hit the floor. "Call you back," he snapped into his headpiece, and threw it on the desk as he stood, facing her.

"Mick Townsend? Michael Stuart? J. Paul Getty? Who the hell are you?" she demanded.

"Barrie, look, sit down, let's talk—"

"Not until I know who I'm talking to. And I mean

the truth. Except, oh, right, you're incapable of telling the truth." She was aware that she was ranting but she couldn't help herself. She was furious.

"Barrie—"

She sidestepped him, not letting him come near her. "*Everything* about you is a lie."

"Come on, now, be fair. Do you tell everyone you're a Keeper?"

The question stopped her dead.

"Our lives are secret, they have to be," he said reasonably.

But you were keeping it from me, she thought, and was immediately uncomfortable with her assumption that he should tell her everything, because...

Because of what's happening between us.

"I wanted to tell you," he said, as if hearing her unspoken thought. "I was going to tell you—"

"When?" she demanded.

"Tonight," he said immediately. "Why do you think I wanted to see you? Everything's been happening so fast...."

What is he talking about? she wondered, and then he continued, and she knew.

"I was suddenly so deep with you and I didn't know how to go back to the beginning."

She felt warm all over.

No. Don't get sucked into this. He has some major explaining to do.

She turned in a circle, spreading her arms to indicate the enormous office.

"What the hell are you doing pretending to be a journalist?"

He ran a hand through his hair, a gesture that made her want to twine her own hands into his hair again. *Stop it.*

"Pretty much the same as you," he answered. "Keeping an eye on Others. There's no better place than a newspaper to get a sense of what's going on out there, on the street level. The owner of the *Courier* is a friend, and I went in last month to establish an identity that I could use to get access to certain situations…criminal investigations. It was only supposed to be temporary, just long enough that I could throw the right names around in a pinch, but…"

"But what?" she demanded.

"But then I met you." He looked at her. "And the plan changed."

I don't believe you, she thought, but only because she wanted to believe him so badly.

Don't cave, she ordered herself. *Make him tell you what's really going on.*

She was a little breathless as she demanded, "So, essentially you've set yourself up to be some kind of—of undercover watchdog of the Otherworld."

"If you want to call it that," he said, not contradicting her.

"In case you hadn't noticed, that's the Keepers' job."

Some kind of understanding flickered on his face. "I know that. And I have the highest respect for what you Keepers do. I think you and your cousins have been doing a miraculous job since you stepped in. But, Barrie, you know the system in L.A. is broken. It's a mess. The infighting and secrecy are making any regulation all but impossible. It's not just frustrating, it's dangerous. You above anyone should know that unprecedented crimes are taking place in the Otherworld."

That brought her up short. It *was* disturbing, beyond the norm, that in the few short months that she and her cousins had been Keepers, Rhiannon and Sailor had been embroiled in solving vicious serial murders. It did seem like something larger was bubbling up from somewhere dark and unfathomable.…

Mick was watching her face. "Sooner or later—and I think sooner—something is going to blow up, and it could rip the lid off the Otherworld. You know what I'm talking about."

She did; he meant the Shattering. A full disclosure of the existence of the Otherworld.

She tried to slow her racing thoughts, groped for journalistic detachment. What she needed right now were answers, not emotions.

"So…just back up. What is all this?" She indicated the offices. "What is it you do here? Exactly?"

"We fund organizations and charities that have a specific focus on helping Others. Microloans for Others in poverty who are trying to start their own businesses. Shelters like Out of the Shadows that help get young Others off the streets."

As he continued the list, detailing the work of the various organizations, Barrie was struggling with herself. There was no way she could fault the work that he was doing. It was almost the opposite; he was practically a saint.

On the other hand, he was essentially going rogue, leaping over the long-established systems for keeping the peace and becoming his own fixer. As right as he was that the system was—well, that it needed fixing—she hated to hear it.

And he'd lied to her. Repeatedly. So, what guarantee did she have that the whole saint act wasn't some front for...something?

He must have sensed she was wavering, because he jumped in. "Barrie, why do you think I want to work with you? We want the same things. While the L.A. Keepers are fighting bureaucratic turf wars, Others like Tiger are slipping through the cracks. It doesn't have to be that way. I know how committed you are to protecting Others who need help finding their way. That's what I want, too."

He was so passionate and, all right, so *gorgeous,* that she found herself melting. And he must have sensed that, too, because he moved in closer, and the force between them was magnetic; she could barely stand. As he leaned in toward her, she summoned just enough strength to put a hand on his chest and push him away. She felt her blood rushing and realized she hadn't felt so giddy since she was a teenager. She didn't know if that was good or disastrous.

"I...need to think."

"Okay." He sounded breathless himself. He walked in a circle, as if trying to compose himself, and then said, "Okay. But I'm still picking you up at seven."

"Picking me up?" she repeated, feeling a fresh surge of outrage coming on. "Oh, no. Tonight is definitely off."

"Even if I said I have tickets for DJ's premiere?" he said with a gleam in his eye that almost made her lose her professionalism and grab him. "That was what you were hoping for, wasn't it?"

"You can get in?" She felt light-headed.

He shrugged. "Connections." He glanced at his on-line calendar. "Seven o'clock, and we can talk about everything then. It's black tie, by the way." And then he gave her a look that turned her insides molten. "I'll see you tonight."

Just business, she told herself.

Yeah, right.

Chapter 11

Barrie was having trouble keeping her feet on the ground as she got out of her car in the drive of the House of the Rising Sun and headed for her house.

Just business, she reminded herself sternly. But she was feeling distinctly unbusinesslike.

And then Mick's words came back to her.

Black tie.

She felt a flutter of panic. *Oh, yike. Black tie at a major Hollywood premiere. That's going to require a major dress.*

She sped up toward the house.

Two hours later Barrie sat in her bedroom in the middle of piles of discarded clothing, flushed, worn out and in complete despair. It wasn't that she didn't have some wonderful dresses. It was just that for a DJ premiere at which she actually expected—*needed*—to talk to DJ herself, it had to be not *a* dress but *the* dress.

And okay, yes, maybe she was thinking a little of what Mick would think when he saw her. A dress that would have the desired effect. Which would be to drive him wild. In a professional sense, that is.

Borrowing from Rhiannon or Sailor was no good; they were much taller than she was. And besides, as lovely as they both were, her style was just different.

She needed something amazing. Something old Hollywood.

What she needed was something like her mother used to wear.

"That's it!" she told Sophie, who was having great fun playing hide-and-seek with herself in the piles of dresses.

A minute later she was pounding on the door of Castle House.

Sailor pulled open the door. "Hey! How'd it go with Darius?"

"Darius?" Barrie repeated, puzzled. "Oh, right, Darius. Not so well, actually."

"Oh no, really? Tell." Sailor opened the door wider, pulling Barrie inside.

"Okay, but you have to come up to the attic with me. I need to go through some of my mom's trunks."

"Ooh, I sense a story."

As the cousins climbed the mahogany stairs toward the attic, Barrie recapped the meeting with Darius. "He flat-out laughed at the idea that Johnny died during production."

"Well, it *is* kind of crazy."

"No crazier than anything else about that movie."

"True."

"But the weirder thing was that he acted like he couldn't get me in to the premiere tonight. Now, since when can Darius Simonides not get anyone into anything he wants to? So, why doesn't he want me there?"

Sailor frowned. "It doesn't mean he doesn't *want* you there...."

They had reached the top landing, and Barrie was breathless from their rapid-fire conversation. "No, but I got the distinct impression he didn't want me talking to DJ."

"Darius has always been super-protective of his clients. By the way, why are we going up to the attic?"

"Because I need a dress for the premiere tonight."

"I thought you said—"

"The plot thickens."

By the time they'd made it up the narrower attic stairs and located the trunk Barrie was thinking of, she'd told Sailor all about Mick and the Circle Foundation. Well, not absolutely everything. She left out the kissing and the way her heart couldn't seem to stop racing whenever she was with him.

"My, my," Sailor marveled. "So, as well as being brilliant and gorgeous, he's loaded and a powerhouse philanthropist. That's wonderful! When can we meet him?"

"Sailor, you're missing the point," Barrie chided her. She didn't need her cousin going further off the deep end than Barrie herself was already.

"What's the point?"

"The point is I have no idea who this guy is anymore. Not that I ever did. He's created a shadow Keeper organization of his own, completely outside regular channels. He's got all of this money from who knows where. And everywhere I go, he's there."

And I'm falling for him so hard I can't see straight, she thought but didn't say.

"I wouldn't say he's got a shadow Keeper organization," Sailor said, pondering. "He raises money for charities that help Others. I think it's kind of great. In fact, I think you may be trying to create this sinister backstory because you're afraid to fall for him."

As usual, her cousin was right on the money.

Barrie hauled out the trunk to avoid having to respond to Sailor's observation. "Here it is."

"Oh, I get it," Sailor said when Barrie opened the lid. "These are your mom's things. She always did dress like a total star."

It was true. Rose Gryffald might not have become the star she'd come to Hollywood hoping to be, but she'd always managed to look like one. Barrie's memories of childhood included a constant feeling of inferiority, the sense that she could never possibly become half the woman her mother was.

As she and Sailor pulled out one plastic-sheathed confection after another, exclaiming over silks and sequins and chiffons, Barrie couldn't help feeling a pain in her heart. She remembered her father and mother, dressed to the hilt, going out to premieres like the one she would be attending tonight, a beautiful, magical couple. But her mother's insatiable desire for fame, for stardom, started to twist in her heart with every year that went by when she didn't "make it." And then the fighting started between her parents, her mother attacking her father's profession, unfairly, Barrie thought, attributing her failure in Hollywood to the secrecy of his life. It made no sense to Barrie, but the fighting escalated, ending inevitably in divorce. And Barrie, at fourteen, was still young enough to believe that she herself had somehow caused the split, or simply had not been *enough:* strong enough, interesting enough, loved enough to keep her parents together.

Her mother had remarried within the year, to a wealthy older businessman who had already raised two separate families from two previous marriages and had no desire to do so a third time. Barrie was more than happy, if that was the word for it, to stay with her father. Who was so brokenhearted by her mother's departure that he never, to her knowledge, had a relationship with a woman again.

Sailor turned to look at her and said, "Hey," in a voice so concerned that Barrie realized she was crying.

She quickly brushed at her eyes. "It's nothing. Nothing but memories, anyway."

Sailor put her hands on Barrie's shoulders and looked her square in the face. "Barrie Gryffald, you are *nothing* like your mother. You never have to worry about that."

Of course I'm not like my mother, Barrie thought. *My mother was beautiful and unforgettable. I'm just...me.*

"I know I'm not," she said aloud. She held a midnight-blue gown up to her chest, eyeing it. "But I sure wish I had her cleavage right about now."

Sailor squeaked and dove into the trunk to pull out another dress. "Hah! This is the one. This will look stunning on you."

It was a shimmering copper creation, embroidered in beads and sequins, exactly matching the lightest highlights of Barrie's hair. Sailor held it up against Barrie and turned her to face the oval standing mirror. And Barrie stood, arrested by the vision of herself and the dress.

Sailor and Barrie took the dress downstairs to Sailor's bedroom, which included an impressive mirrored dressing room. Sailor, a longtime expert at last-minute wardrobe alterations, went to work fitting the dress to Barrie's figure. Barrie was shorter and less voluptuous than her mother, but otherwise there wasn't much to be done.

"This could have been made for you!" Sailor enthused as she taped and pinned and stitched.

A voice came from the dressing room doorway. "What's all this?"

Sailor and Barrie and their reflections turned to see Rhiannon standing in the doorway.

"Barrie has a date to DJ's premiere with the hot shifter," Sailor answered cheerfully.

"It's business," Barrie insisted.

Rhiannon was already frowning. "Now wait a minute. I just heard back from Brodie, and he wasn't able to find anything at all on a 'Mick Townsend.'"

Barrie sighed. "That's because he doesn't exist," she admitted.

Rhiannon looked about to hit the roof. "If you

think I'm letting you go anywhere with a nonexistent shifter—"

"No, I mean he's someone else. It looks pretty legit." But even as she said it, Barrie felt a little flutter of anxiety. "Anyway, I'm not going to be alone with him. Much. And it's my chance to get into the premiere." She could see Rhiannon wasn't convinced, so she told her, "You can meet him and decide for yourself. He's picking me up. And it's not like he's going to...I don't know, abduct me or anything. Not when both of you see us leaving together."

Rhiannon finally relented. She even got into the spirit of things and ran across to Pandora's Box for a coppery gold wrap and an evening bag to contribute to the overall effect.

Of course Merlin showed up for the unveiling, and Sailor coaxed him into the dressing room to see Barrie reflected in all the mirrors.

"Oh, my," he said reverently. "You are a vision, my dear. Absolutely stunning."

Barrie looked at herself in the mirrors, glimmering in copper. The dress brought out the shining highlights of her hair, her eyes.

Merlin cleared his throat. "I don't want to interrupt your preparations, but I have been asking around the afterlife after your two young men."

Barrie whirled to face him and didn't bother to correct him that they weren't *her* young men. "Merlin, you're a doll. Is there anything you can tell me?"

"I have to say, it's perplexing," the elderly ghost admitted. "The one you call Robbie Anderson... I haven't been able to find a trace of him. Are you sure he's passed on?"

"I'm not sure of anything," Barrie admitted.

"My own guess would be that he has not," Merlin told her. "Johnny Love is a different story. But he is not fully present in the afterlife. There is no place I can reach him there."

The cousins looked around at each other, mystified. "Not fully present in the afterlife? What does that mean, Merlin?" Rhiannon asked.

"When someone dies tragically, a suicide or some other traumatic death, the soul often retains an attachment to the earth that makes it difficult for the soul to fully pass into the afterlife. It's different from visiting earth in the way that I do. Visiting earth is one thing. Clinging to it without fully accepting death is a half existence, very sad."

"Does that mean Johnny committed suicide?" Barrie asked intently.

"Not necessarily," the ghost explained. "It can happen with any traumatic death—suicide, murder, a fatal accident so sudden that the soul has no time to assimilate its situation. Even death that's accompanied by an emotional shock like betrayal. I'm sorry I can't be more specific."

Barrie bit her lip, thinking. "No, no, you've been incredibly helpful. Thank you, Merlin."

He excused himself so "you girls can get back to your primping," and Barrie sat on the edge of a divan and tried to process what he'd just told them. "I'm not sure I know anything more than I did before," she admitted. "I think we all knew Johnny didn't die peacefully."

"You don't have to think about it now," Sailor said, and turned to her, lifting her enormous makeup kit. "What you need to do is hold still."

Barrie rarely wore any makeup besides lipstick and mascara, but actress Sailor had mad skills with the stuff. "Just a little," Sailor coaxed. "Remember, you'll be under spotlights." And so Barrie held still as her cousin dusted and painted and powdered.

Somehow the whole afternoon had dissolved, and the cousins were interrupted from their oohing and aahing over Barrie when the security panel in the kitchen buzzed, indicating a car at the gate.

Barrie felt her heart drop. "He's here."

Rhiannon and Sailor looked at each other, and Sailor even rubbed her hands together. "Well, let's look him over."

It was senseless to plead with her cousins to be discreet. Barrie started to follow them downstairs, but Sailor turned around and stopped her. "No way. You're going to make an entrance. Go powder your nose and wait till we call you."

So, Barrie trailed back upstairs, so nervous she could barely make her feet move.

On the landing she crouched beside the stair railing and listened over the thudding of her heart as the door opened and her cousins' voices mixed with another, a low male rumbling that sent waves of desire through her.

Mick's voice.

I can't do this, I'm going to faint, she thought wildly.

And then Sailor called, "Barrie!"

Barrie gulped a breath and pulled herself up to her feet. She focused every ounce of will she could muster on walking steadily down the stairs.

Her cousins and Mick were standing in the entry hall. Mick was in a tux, and Barrie's breath was knocked out of her as he looked up toward her. He really did look like a movie star himself, too gorgeous to be real.

The look on his face was dazed.

"You look amazing," he murmured as she stopped on the stair in front of him. He had flowers in one hand, a spray of coral roses.

They couldn't stop looking at each other.

"I'll just put those in water for you," Rhiannon said, and took the flowers from him. Sailor snagged one and tucked it into Barrie's hair.

"There. Perfect."

"Well," said Rhiannon.

"Well," said Sailor.

"It was a pleasure to meet you, Mick," Rhiannon said, and Barrie had the distinct impression she was having trouble keeping a straight face.

"You two have a wonderful time," Sailor chimed in.

"Hope we see you again soon," Rhiannon added.

Sailor kissed and hugged Barrie goodbye, whispering, *"Dreamy!"* in her ear. On Barrie's other side, Rhiannon's whispered evaluation was *"Perfect!"*

Mick offered Barrie his arm, which she took gratefully; because even though she nearly melted at his touch, she also needed the support to walk.

Then they strolled past her cousins and out the door.

Chapter 12

Mick had not brought the Bentley but an actual limo, with an actual driver behind the partition, so they glided down the canyon and onto Hollywood Boulevard like actual movie stars. There was jazz on the stereo and champagne chilling in a bucket in the built-in bar, and Mick casually poured it into two beautifully carved flutes as the limo cruised the curving road.

Barrie took hers and drank too quickly, nervous as she was.

"Your cousins…" he said.

"I know, they're out of control," she said.

He smiled. "I was going to say they're charming. You must have a lot of fun."

"We do," she said, and laughed, which relaxed her. The champagne was probably helping, too.

"You three remind me of—" he said, and then stopped.

"We remind you of what?" she asked, curious.

"You remind me of stars," he said. "Real stars. Movie stars and star stars."

Barrie felt herself flush warm, and this time it wasn't just the champagne.

The premiere was at the Chinese, the famous theater where stars had been putting their shoe prints and handprints and signatures into slabs of cement since 1927. The theater itself was red and black, built in the style of a pagoda with Hollywood's idea of Asian flourishes in neon, and the courtyard was paved with the iconic handprinted slabs.

The limo glided past the Walk of Fame, the Hollywood sidewalks that bore the brass stars of famous film, TV, radio and music personalities, and came to a stop in front of the Chinese Theater. It was the full red-carpet scenario, with huge spotlight beams crisscrossing the sky, and a press line rushing the red carpet as limos pulled up beside the curb to disgorge celebrity after celebrity.

Barrie found herself suddenly frozen in terror, but then the limo door opened, and the driver stood at attention outside. Mick got out and reached down a hand to help her from the car. And with her hand in his, she found herself emerging with effortless grace, feeling every bit the star he had said she looked like.

Flashbulbs popped wildly; Barrie couldn't believe the flood of lights. It was as bright as high noon on the beach from all the kliegs—to provide the best backdrop for photos and filming, she knew, but she'd never been the one *in* the lights. It was dazzling and overwhelming.

But Mick guided her nonchalantly down the red carpet toward the theater entrance as paparazzi snapped and flashed.

At the guard pedestal, the doorman simply bowed to them and let them through.

"You don't need tickets?" Barrie asked him under her breath.

"Well, I didn't actually have them, so I used Plan B," he confessed, and turned his face to her.

She gasped.

George Clooney looked back at her, with that roguish George Clooney smile on his face. Mick had shifted; no wonder the doorman hadn't asked for tickets. That face was all the entrée anyone could ask for.

Clooney grinned and then dissolved back into Mick.

"I thought you didn't do that kind of shifting anymore," she accused, a little stunned.

"Only in emergencies."

"And this is what you call an emergency?"

"I have to keep in practice for real emergencies, don't I?" he asked innocently.

With premieres, the movie came first, the party after, so they had little time to talk as they moved with the crowd into the lush red-curtained theater and found seats. Barrie scanned the premiere-goers for DJ and Travis Branson, but there were too many people, and the lights dimmed shortly after they were seated.

At first Barrie was so distracted by Mick's warm,

live presence in the seat beside her, his thigh pressed up against hers, that she couldn't concentrate on the movie. But gradually the action on the screen captured her attention.

Rocket Man was not a film that she would ever have bothered to see if DJ hadn't been the star. But even without her case, she probably would have seen the movie simply because DJ was in it. Based on a wildly popular graphic novel series—*Meaning comic book,* she thought disdainfully—it was a megabudget "tentpole" film: one of those that the studios hope will spawn numerous sequels, spin-offs, video games, toy and clothing lines, even amusement park rides. It was full of car and helicopter chases, all manner of things blowing up, and macho dialogue. In fact, the only watchable thing about it, from Barrie's point of view, was DJ.

But his casting was what made the movie. Of course a vampire, or any Other, always brought a certain extra something to a performance, but the whole idea of having a quirky, volatile, unpredictable actor known for his excruciatingly intense character roles playing a comic superhero meant that clichéd fight scenes suddenly turned into laugh riots, and the absurd plot points seemed laced with satirical commentary, and there was an underlying mystery and darkness to the character that elevated the proceedings above their comic book roots. Despite his troubled life, or probably because of it, DJ remained as mesmerizingly watchable as he had been all those years ago in *Otherworld.*

Beside her, Mick seemed oddly riveted himself. At one point she leaned in to him and said, "He's so *good.*"

Mick said, "Yes, he is." His tone was ambiguous.

Even though the explosions took over for actual plot in the end, Barrie had to admit that the movie was much better than she had ever expected it to be, and she joined the applause as the credits rolled.

Instead of moving to a different venue for the premiere party, the studio had walled off Grauman's famous courtyard and dressed it with parts of the *Rocket Man* set and some pretty magnificent lighting. She had to admit there were some things that Hollywood just got right, and spectacle was way up there on the list. It was a fabulous party, everything designed to make people feel like the innest of the in-crowd just to be there at all.

Mick went off in search of drinks, and she stood beside a column, scanning the crowd.

All around her partygoers drifted and schmoozed and star-watched, holding their drinks and appetizers: a spread of Asian delicacies, since the main action of the film was a romp throughout Asia.

She caught sight of Darius in the throng, surrounded by men in high-powered suits. Her first instinct was to hide, but he had already spotted her. He excused himself to his entourage and moved toward her, sharklike in his ability to part the crowd.

As he approached her, he took a flute of champagne from a circulating waiter and presented it to her with a small bow.

"Delighted to see you here, my dear."

"Are you?" she asked, and immediately worried that she'd gone too far.

He smiled thinly. "But of course. You're proving as

resourceful as your father. Much better than my handing everything to you, isn't it?"

I see, this was all some kind of lesson from the kindly mentor, she thought cynically.

"Did you enjoy the film?"

"DJ is amazing," she said, glad to have something honest to say.

"Sensational. The film will break three hundred, easily."

Meaning three hundred million, domestic box office. She knew she shouldn't be surprised by the inevitable focus on the financial bottom line, but it repulsed her.

"I'm sure you're right," she said, forcing a pleasant tone.

Darius seemed to spot someone important in the crowd; he held up a finger as if asking the person to wait and turned a smooth smile on Barrie. "I do hope you find what you're looking for tonight."

"Oh, I have no doubt," she assured him.

He gave her a slight bow. "Happy hunting, then."

As Darius glided away, she looked over the crowd, searching for DJ. She knew it would be a trick getting to talk to him; every person—and Other—at the party would be lining up to fawn over him. Even so, she was determined to try, but as of yet, there was no sign of him. There was no sign of Mick, either.

Then she saw a familiar face, flitting from group to group.

Harvey Hodge was tuxed to the max and hobnobbing for all he was worth, but he seemed to sense Barrie's gaze on him. He turned and spotted her, and then, to her surprise, he made a beeline toward her through the crowd.

"Darling, you look *fabulous*," he gushed, and airkissed both her cheeks. She was a little stunned at his enthusiasm; while Harvey was often useful, he had never been much more than condescending to her. Even at his gossipy best, he had a very set hierarchy of who was important and who wasn't. Yet here he was, acting as if she were the only person at the party who counted.

He dropped his voice and leaned in to her. "I saw you came with Clooney," he confided.

So, that's it.

"Oh…well," she hedged. "Business, you know."

"And so tight with Simonides, too. I had no i*dea* you were so connected."

Barrie shrugged modestly. "Deep down they're just people. Or vampires."

She had no idea what she was doing in this conversation. She looked desperately around for Mick to save her.

Harvey's eyes narrowed. "That's a quaint way to put it," he said, dripping skepticism.

"That's me. Quaint. So, how did you like the film?" she asked, floundering.

"That's tomorrow's column, sweets," he said. "You can read it in mock-up."

And without another word, he was off again.

Talk about a hit-and-run, Barrie thought. But something was bothering her about the brief encounter, something that didn't fit, that even felt like it might be significant if only she could figure out what it was.

Left to herself in a sea of glamorous strangers, she

found herself searching the cement slabs of the courtyard for one she remembered from her childhood. She
drifted by the handprints of Myrna Loy and William
Powell, the wand prints of the *Harry Potter* kids, the
hoofprints of Roy Rogers's horse, Trigger…and stopped,
looking down at a slab that had three sets of handprints,
three sets of footprints: the Pack—DJ, Robbie Anderson
and Johnny Love.

She felt a chill, a heightened sense that almost seemed
psychic, as if she could feel the presence of the three
stars.

And then someone spoke right by her side, startling
her; she hadn't sensed anyone approaching.

"Is this a professional interest, Keeper?"

Barrie looked up—and was stunned to see DJ himself, in Armani, with glistening sequined Converse Hi-
Tops on his feet. He balanced a drink rather unsteadily
in his hand and was looking her over with predatory
intensity.

Meeting actors in real life was always a disorienting
experience. They were always smaller than on-screen,
naturally, when one was used to seeing their images
thirty feet high. But good actors always had a larger-
than-life aura, and Barrie almost felt rocked on her heels
in the presence of it. First, there was that feral charisma
of a vampire. Vampires were all about appetites—for
blood, for wine, for life force, for fame. And on top of
that there was the pure star power of the actor.

Of course most Others could spot a Keeper just as
most Keepers could spot an Other, but it was still slightly

surreal that he recognized her. She felt like Cinderella, singled out by the Prince.

"I heard you wanted to talk to me," he said in a way that made her think he knew exactly how off balance she felt. His voice had a slightly slurred, sexual quality, and his eyes were dilated to huge black circles, which might mean drugs or that he had just fed on blood. Considering this was DJ, quite probably both.

"Yes. I wanted to talk to you about what really happened on Catalina," she said quickly.

He smiled, but his eyes took on a wary quality. "You want to know what's real? In *this* place? Good luck with that."

Her heart sank. She'd lost him.

He turned his back to her, but oddly, didn't move. Then she heard his voice. "My house. Tomorrow."

She jolted. *What? Was that an invitation? What does he mean?*

And then he was strolling off, as if they had never talked.

"When?" she called after him.

He turned back with a mocking bow. "Dusk, of course."

As he moved into the crowd, he was instantly surrounded by people vying for his attention, and she wondered if he'd made himself invisible to others during their brief exchange.

Before she had time to process her thoughts, Mick was at her side again, with champagne flutes in hand.

"Oh! I was wondering where you were," she said. He had been away a long time.

Instead of looking at her, he stared after DJ; his face was taut, unhappy.

"I didn't want to interrupt. It seemed as if you were—" he paused slightly "—getting somewhere."

I was. I did, she thought with a little thrill. "He wants to see me tomorrow." She still couldn't believe her luck. "I guess Darius talked to him after all," she mused, and then looked down at the cement slab at their feet. "Unless…"

"Unless what?"

She laughed a little. "It's silly, but Merlin, our house ghost, says that often ghosts can most easily be called at significant places. I know DJ isn't a ghost, but…maybe it works for the living, too. Or the undead. I was standing here, thinking about the three of them, and DJ just appeared."

Mick looked down at the slab with a strange expression on his face. "It's not silly," he said.

"It *was* a little like being haunted," she confessed. "He's not just Other, he's so much bigger than life. They all were," she added, looking down at the signatures and handprints and footprints at their feet.

"For all the good it did them," he said tightly. "Immortal at sixteen—and dead. That's no life."

She was surprised at his depth of feeling. Then again, he had devoted his life to helping Others, pretty much the definition of passion.

She had a question forming in her mind, but then suddenly she spotted Travis Branson in the crowd. "Look." She touched Mick's arm and nodded toward the director. In his mid-forties, lean and handsome, he had that restless, intensely focused energy that she associated with film directors, along with a were's usual profusion of facial hair, trimmed neatly into a Van Dyke beard.

She murmured to Mick, "You know everything about everyone. Tell me something about Branson."

He glanced down at her, then over at Branson. "Werewolf, as you know. He wrote the script of *Otherworld* when he was only in his late twenties and held out to direct it. It was his debut, obviously a smash, and after that he didn't write his own movies anymore."

She watched the director expounding to a circle of young men, all of whom had the hungry, slightly desperate look of aspiring actors and filmmakers.

"It's unusual, isn't it? You don't usually see weres as directors."

Mick smiled slightly. "Very unusual. They don't tend to have the focus."

In the background, the swing band launched into one of Barrie's favorite jazz standards, "Ain't That a Kick in the Head?" She glanced out over the dance floor. As usual at a Hollywood party, there were very few couples out on the floor; there was too much schmoozing to be done for anyone to waste their time dancing. *And no one knows how to dance anymore,* she thought.

She refocused on the problem at hand. "What else do you know about him?" she prodded Mick.

"Apparently he had a huge cocaine problem while they were filming *Otherworld.* But he's cleaned himself up since then." Then he said abruptly, "Enough business. I love this tune." And suddenly she was in his arms and they were on the floor, dancing.

Her memory hadn't exaggerated one bit; he really could dance.

Barrie was such a control freak in her real life that no one would believe the secret pleasure she got out of just giving herself over to a partner who knew what he was doing. And Mick *did* know. He led her and figured out what she liked to do, then did more of it. They found a perfect rhythm, coming together and pushing apart in a sexy, sensual tandem. He was like an anchor, strong and lithe as he swirled her and spun her and lifted her, and every touch was like a promise of things to come.

He really was perfect, just perfect.

"You're perfect," he whispered.

He even did a mock Fred Astaire tap break as the music changed. And as the song finished he swept her off her feet and dipped her expertly over his muscular thigh, to delighted applause from the onlookers around them.

As he set Barrie slowly back on her feet, his hands lingering on her waist, she was flushed and speechless.

He laughed at her expression and took her hand. "Come on, let's walk."

It was a beautiful Hollywood night, warm, with a dry Santa Ana breeze that rustled through the fronds of the palm trees and made the neon of the street shimmer in the air, and they walked along the glittering sidewalk sprinkled with the bronze and terrazzo stars of radio, TV, film and music personalities.

Mick strolled along with his coat thrown casually over his shoulder, very *GQ,* and his hand firmly around hers.

"Where did you learn to dance like that?" she demanded.

"Where did *you?*" he countered. "Look, Barbara Stanwyck." He pointed down at a star as they passed.

"Are you sure you're not an actor?" she asked, suspiciously.

"I swear." He put his hand on his heart. "I just learned to dance to get girls."

"Huh," she said. "Most men aren't that smart."

"Most men aren't that *ambitious.* Rita Hayworth," he said, and pointed at a star. And then he added, "You're not all that fond of actors, are you?" It was more a statement than a question.

She looked away uncomfortably. "I've lived here all my life," she said defensively.

"That would do it," he agreed. He pointed down again. "Jimmy Durante." Then he looked back up at her. "Is there something else, though?" He paused. "An actor broke your heart, maybe?"

"Not an actor. An actress," she confessed impulsively.

Mick looked startled.

"My mother," she told him. "She had *the dream.* But it didn't happen for her. Just bit parts, a lot of—"

"'Sound and fury, signifying nothing,'" he finished for her.

She looked at him wryly. "Exactly."

"That's rough."

She shook her head. "*Rough* is not the word. I can't feel sorry for myself. I had absolutely everything growing up. My father loved me, and my mother—she loved me, too, in her way. I had a great education, a wonderful home. I have my cousins, I have Merlin, I have my job...."

"But you had a mother who was never there for you. Don't make light of it, sweetheart, it hurts." He stopped on the sidewalk and brushed a hand through her hair, looking into her eyes with that penetrating green gaze. "You don't have to play tough with me." His fingers were moving on her face, and it was all she could do not to melt into him and be lost.

She pulled away with effort. "You sound like you know something about actors."

He smiled faintly. "I've lived here all my life."

And then it suddenly hit her what was bothering her about her conversation with Harvey Hodge. He'd been so impressed that she'd walked in with "George Clooney." But Harvey was a shifter himself; he should have been able to see that the "Clooney" she'd been with was a fake.

But he hadn't.

Why?

She didn't for a moment think that Mick *was* George Clooney, nothing like that. And she knew he was a highly skilled shifter. It was just that another highly skilled shifter—and professional gossip—like Harvey should have been able to spot the deception.

Mick was watching her closely. "All right, what are you brooding about?"

"I'm not brooding," she began.

"Oh yes, you are. When you go silent for more than

a half minute, you're concocting plots and conspiracies. So, I want to know what I'm being suspected of." He looked at her directly, that gaze she couldn't hide from.

"All right," she said defensively. "All right. It was Harvey Hodge."

He looked truly disgusted. "Oh, my God, what did that self-important, self-serving little shi— shifter have to say about me?"

"Nothing. That's the problem."

"What's that supposed to mean?"

And she decided, *I'm just going to say it. Why not?*

"He came up to me and wondered what I was doing with George Clooney," she said. There. It was out. Straight-up.

Mick stared at her, bemused. "That's it?"

She was pointedly silent.

"And what does that translate to, in that devious little mind of yours?"

"He couldn't tell it was you in shift," she burst out. "Not only is he a *shifter,* it's his whole job to expose people, and he couldn't tell what was going on." It took her a moment of mental scrambling to even be able to voice the implications. "If you can do that, you really *are* good."

He held her eyes. "Oh, I am. *Very* good." And then he laughed. "Barrie, I did it to please you. Does everything have to be a conspiracy?"

"What makes you think George Clooney does anything for me?" she said without thinking.

"Oh, really?" he said with a spike of interest. "Not Clooney?" He looked her over speculatively, so intimately she felt herself blush from the soles of her feet to the crown of her head. "Who, then?"

"Well…"

"Oh, come on, tell. Is it a pirate you'd be wanting, me love?"

Suddenly she was looking at Johnny Depp, pirate accent and all.

"Or maybe you prefer someone a little more classic?"

It was Cary Grant in front of her now, that sculpted face, the quirky, bemused arch of his eyebrows…

As they walked, he continued to shift.

"Nope, nope, nope, doggone it, I've got it…." And there was Jimmy Stewart, with his unforgettable stammer.

"A little younger?" Leo DiCaprio looked out at her with the heartbreaking eyes of Jack in *Titanic*.

"A little rougher?" Now she was walking alongside Russell Crowe, striding with the sexy bulk of *L.A. Confidential*.

Marlon Brando. Paul Newman. Robert Redford.

She was bowled over by the transitions. She was walking with a pantheon of the most gorgeous men that Hollywood had ever produced.

"Stop. Stop." She was laughing, giddy, breathless.

Suddenly his hands were on her waist and he was looking down into her eyes. "What, then?" His voice was low and husky. "Tell me what you want."

And Barrie looked back at him. "I want to know who *you* are. I want you to be *you*."

He leaned down to her and kissed her, with all the color and neon of the Boulevard pulsing around them.

And as his lips feasted on hers, she felt all the sexy roughness of Russell Crowe, the dashing wildness of Johnny Depp, the innocent beauty of a young Leo Di-Caprio, and the aristocratic charm of Cary Grant, all rolled into one endlessly fascinating, endlessly desirable man.

Heat flooded through her, from her lips to the very core of her; she felt she'd just burst into flame. His tongue was inside her mouth, tasting, teasing…and then plunging, sliding so deep she lost her balance. But he caught her, lifted her up and set her on the low wall of a planter, arching her backward so he could crush her mouth open under his. Her back was against the brick of the building, and he was pulling her hips forward against his, then cupping her breasts in his hands. Her nipples strained through the beaded silk of her bodice, into his palms, and now he moaned and lifted his head to kiss down her neck, biting, sucking, turning her insides molten.

Her legs curled around his thighs, and the huge bulge of him was pulsing urgently against her. She gasped in delirium as he kissed her cleavage, his tongue slipping inside her bra to lick her nipples, and she could feel him throbbing against her core, half-inside her even through their clothes. She felt herself opening from within, feverish to feel him inside her.…

"God…oh, God…"

And suddenly he was pulling back, dragging her to her feet and holding her against him hard, but no longer kissing her. She could still feel the pulsing bulge of his sex against her thigh, but he'd ceased moving urgently against her, and she was reeling with desire and confusion. "What...?"

His fingers were strong on her back, and his voice was gruff and shaky, but resolved. "Our first time isn't going to be in an alley. I want you in silk sheets and a proper bed and completely to myself."

He held her close, and she stood pasted against him with her eyes closed as their racing hearts slowed... feeling his touch in every cell of her body as his fingers caressed her waist, and she breathed in the faint smell of cologne and the heady scent of pure male. He whispered her name against her ear, and she opened her eyes dreamily....

"Let's go home," he said huskily.

She turned in his arms—and froze.

Behind Mick, halfway down the block, a slim shadow was crouched down on the sidewalk. She stiffened against Mick and clutched at his arms. "Oh, my God..."

She broke away from him to run down the street, but in the few seconds she had taken to react, the figure had vanished.

She could hear Mick pounding down the sidewalk after her.

The mysterious shadow was gone, but there was a bouquet of flowers lying in the middle of the sidewalk. She stepped up to it slowly and looked down.

In a second Mick was by her side. "Barrie, what—" Then he fell silent, seeing what she saw.

They were looking down at Johnny Love's star. Someone had placed a bouquet of flowers on it.

"I thought I saw Tiger," she said to Mick softly. "But it couldn't have been."

She looked up and down the sidewalk. They were alone.

Chapter 13

For the first time in her life Barrie had species envy, wishing at least to be a different kind of Keeper, maybe an Elven Keeper like Sailor, so they could just teleport and be back at home, in bed. There were more kisses in the dark luxuriousness of the limo on the way home, deep, delicious, toe-curling kisses that set her ablaze again…but no matter how she teased and writhed and caressed, Mick kept deliberately moving her hands above his waist and concentrating his oh-so-skillful efforts on her throat and ears and mouth until she was nearly mad with desire.

"I hate you," she murmured into his ear with the last breath she had left, and he laughed into her hair, and said, "Oh, just wait."

As the limo pulled up toward the gate of the estate, Barrie somehow found the presence of mind to get the remote from her purse. As the limo headed up the drive, Mick suddenly rolled on top of Barrie, and for the first time since they'd gotten back in the car, he not only kissed her but let her feel the whole hot, hard length of him on top of her, bruising, demanding...until she was liquid in the seat...

And then he pulled back and opened the door to lift her out of the car, because she was too dazed to manage it on her own.

At the doorway he took the key from her, scooped her up in his arms and kicked open the door.

Low lights were on in the front hall, and they were reflected in the antique mirrors on the walls. He took a glance around at the art, the mirrors, the sculpture, and she could see he was pleased, but also that there were more important things on his mind.

"Bedroom..." he said huskily.

"Down the...hall to the left."

He was kissing her neck as he walked in, and all she could feel was fire rising from the very core of her, so she didn't understand why he stopped still in the doorway.

She opened her eyes in a dreamy haze, looking at the room through the romantic spill of moonlight through the French doors...and realized that there were piles of clothes all over her bedroom, including covering the bed, with the cat sleeping on top of the biggest mountain. She'd forgotten her dress crisis of the afternoon.

"No closets?" he asked her dryly, and she blushed from head to toe.

"I couldn't figure out what to wear."

He set her down and looked her over in the copper dress. "You did perfectly," he whispered.

And then she was on the bed, where he was unbuttoning her dress, and his fingers were tracing trails of fire down her bare back, up her thighs. Then the perfect dress was on the floor and Mick's hands were on her body, and she was lost.

She pulled his tux shirt out of his pants and slipped her hands into his shirt, finding smooth, warm skin and rippling muscles...breathing harder and harder as he kissed her mouth, her neck, her ears. Her hands were fumbling with buttons, zippers, needing him naked, needing him against her, inside her.

He lifted her onto the bed, and for a moment he was not touching her as he made the piles of clothes disappear, and those few seconds were the longest of her life until his hands were on her again and she was arching up with her whole body, so she could feel all of him against her.

Their bodies lifted, fitted together, and his lips on her throat practically made her burst into flame. Her hands were moving on his back, reaching down for him, when he took her wrists in a strong grip and pinned them above her head as he moved on top of her, opening her mouth under his, opening her legs with his hips to rock against her, rubbing the ramrod bulge of him against her, slow and teasing, as his right hand caressed her breasts until moans were coming out of her throat.

His hand was between her legs now, opening her, thumb and finger circling and teasing until she was slippery wet against his hand, and then somehow it was no longer his fingers but the huge head of his sex, velvet softness over steel hardness, the ridge of him exciting her into madness, and she moaned and arched her back, urging him inside her. "Please…"

"Barrie…" he muttered roughly. He plunged, and she cried out, and he plunged again with a low growl in his throat, and their bodies found that ancient, intoxicating rhythm, desire and longing and knowing.

Moonlight flooded the room, bright and blue on their skin, and their bodies were reflected over and over in the mirrors, a hundred thousand times, and it seemed to Barrie that she could feel the ecstasy of every version of herself as they moved together. It was better than dancing, better than flying, a tidal wave of pleasure rippling through every version of themselves until they were crying out together, a thousand lovers and just two, melding into one.

Chapter 14

Barrie woke slowly. Her room was flooded with after-noon light, and she felt deliciously sore—and not just from dancing. She could still smell Mick's aftershave on her pillow and on her skin, mixing with her own scent and the smell of passion, and she felt flames between her legs as fantasies of their lovemaking invaded her thoughts. No, not fantasies, *memories*. It had all really happened, every exotic detail. She sighed, rolled over and opened her eyes.

She was alone in bed.

But she saw a note and a rose on the pillow beside her.

She reached for the paper and read, and felt her breath stop. She dropped back on the pillow, delirious with sudden wanting, imagined his body rising up hard and naked over hers, to claim her again....

And then a sudden and unnerving thought.

I want him. Not just want him, like, now.... I want him. Always.

The heat in her face was no longer desire but confusion mixed with a little bit of terror.

Oh, my God. This is real.

The erotic afterglow disappeared in the overwhelming reality crashing in on her.

After all, where was he? Rose on the pillow and pornographic note aside, she was alone in bed, wasn't she? Except for the cat. Who was giving her a wide berth this morning, as she absolutely should be, given that her mistress had apparently *lost her mind.*

Focus, focus, focus, Barrie told herself with a touch of panic, or maybe that was hysteria. *You're investigating a murder—or two, or three. Do your job.*

She sat up and looked at the clock. Amazingly, still before eleven.

She knew she was in for a barrage of questions from her cousins, but she couldn't very well miss the Morning Report, so she jumped out of bed and headed straight into the shower to wash off the telltale traces of the night, absolutely *not* allowing herself to think of Mick in the shower and almost succeeding, and then pulled on a severe gray dress that was the closest thing she had to a nun's habit. She forced herself to slow down and walk what she hoped was nonchalantly over to the main house. It wasn't easy, given that her body felt both charged with electricity and lighter than air.

All pretense of nonchalance instantly vanished as she walked through the back door into the kitchen. Sailor and Rhiannon were there at the breakfast bar, and they both jumped up as she walked in.

"Tell tell tell!" demanded Sailor.

"Tell what?" Barrie said innocently. She closed the door behind her and tried to keep a straight face as she walked to the counter to pour herself coffee.

"A certain shifter departed the house at dawn in a limo," Rhiannon said mock-sternly. "And these came an hour ago." She indicated a huge spread of flowers displayed in a vase on the cutting board. "I had the deliveryman bring them here, because I think we have a right to know."

Barrie felt her breath quicken at the flowers, an absolutely breathtaking tropical arrangement. There was a card, but she certainly wasn't going to read it in front of her cousins.

Instead she took a casual swallow of coffee. "I had a nice time."

"Oh, a *nice* time," Sailor mimicked her. "You look like you swallowed a klieg light."

Barrie gave up on nonchalance and what was left of her mind as a rush of endorphins and exultation rushed through her. "All right, I had a fantastic time. A fabulous, mind-bending, once-in-a-lifetime time."

And all the cousins burst into giggles like teenagers.

"That's more like it." Sailor shoved her playfully. "The man is stunning. He could be a movie star."

"Oh, he was," Barrie said, and burst into giggles again. "He was about ten of them." This time Sailor and Rhiannon stared at her, mystified, and she got hold of herself enough to tell them about the little shifter show Mick had put on for her.

"Wow," Rhiannon said admiringly. "Not just gorgeous but *fun*. You may want to keep him."

"Shifters do have their uses," Sailor said.

"It wasn't all fun and games, you know," Barrie said, trying to get some control over the conversation. *Good luck with that,* she thought to herself. "I was working. And I got an interview with DJ."

"You're kidding!" Sailor was wide-eyed. "Barrie, that's fantastic."

"He wants me to come to his house today. Tonight. Well, at dusk."

"At dusk?" Rhiannon looked skeptical. "What kind of a lame vampire trope is that supposed to be? Vamps are just as capable of moving around in daylight as we are."

"Oh, I think he was just being edgy," Barrie said, but Rhiannon was on a roll.

"That's not edgy, that's perpetuating a damaging Hollywood-created stereotype."

Sailor rolled her eyes and held up a hand to stop her cousin. "Rhiannon, it's DJ. He's being a movie star."

Rhiannon wasn't placated. She turned to Barrie. "Is Mick going with you?"

Barrie hesitated. "DJ only asked me."

"I'm not sure I like that." Rhiannon frowned. "Is it going to be safe for you?"

Sailor chimed in, "Yeah, last we heard DJ was one of your suspects for Johnny Love's murder."

"*If* it was murder," Barrie corrected absently, but she knew her cousins had a point.

"*And* DJ is a vampire," Rhiannon reminded her. Rhiannon never let her cousins forget that vampires were potentially the most dangerous of the Others.

"I don't think you should go alone," Sailor said.

"That's two of us," Rhiannon said firmly.

"I'll go with you," Sailor said.

"We'll all go," Rhiannon corrected.

Barrie stood, raising her voice just to get a word in. "Wait a minute, wait a minute. What do you think he's going to do, murder me in his own house?"

"Mansion," Sailor said. "More like a palace. With lots of grounds to bury you on. In."

"He's a vampire," Rhiannon repeated. "And it's a murder case."

Barrie threw up her hands in frustration. "We can't show up en masse. I'll never be able to get anything out of him. I need to have a casual, personal, one-on-one chat with him, and I can't do that with you two hovering."

But she knew immediately from the stormy look on Rhiannon's face that that wasn't going to fly, so she reversed tacks. "I'll take Mick, then," she said quickly. "All right?"

Rhiannon and Sailor looked at each other, and after a moment they both nodded warily. "That should be all right," Rhiannon said.

"I guess," Sailor said.

Rhiannon added, "And you make *sure* he knows that plenty of people know you're there."

"I will," Barrie promised, although she intended no such thing. She wasn't going to scare off the best lead she'd had so far.

*   *   *

She came into the Cave with her arms full of the flowers Mick had sent, feeling light-headed from the sweet and heady fragrance. She wanted to call him to thank him, but found herself in that classic female dilemma: the man is supposed to call first or you look too eager, too clingy.

Screw that, she thought. She set the flowers down on a side table and reached for the phone, an old-Hollywood-style Sultan with a huge silver receiver and a big rotary dial. Then she hesitated, visions of Dorothy Parker floating unwanted in her head.

But he sent flowers, the eager part of her piped up. *He wouldn't have done that if he didn't want to see you again.*

Unless he wanted to let you down gracefully, the cynic replied.

That's not a let-down bouquet, her eager side argued, and she reached for the phone again.

Don't you dare, the cynic snarled.

Barrie pulled back her hand as if the handset had burned her. She bit a nail, looking at the phone, debating....

And it rang.

She caught her breath—and snatched up the receiver. "Hello?"

"Is this the staggeringly beautiful, breathtakingly sexy Barrie Gryffald?"

His voice absolutely turned her molten; she felt as if she were going to pass out.

Somehow she managed to sit on the plush chair by

the telephone table and smiled into the phone. "Never heard of her."

"Damn, I was afraid it was too good to be true."

"I got the flowers," she said, almost whispering, though there was no one but Sophie the cat to hear them. "They're gorgeous, thank you."

"The pleasure was all mine."

She laughed and blushed. "If that's what you think you weren't paying attention."

She could hear the smile in his voice. "I'll have to look again. What are you doing tonight?"

"What did you have in mind?"

"I plan to show you," he said, and she nearly swooned again. Then his voice got serious. "But first, we need to talk. I don't think you should see DJ alone."

Barrie came down from her dreamy cloud in a rush of irritation. Did everyone think she was going to be stupid about this? She *had* to see DJ alone; she was sure it was her best chance of having a real talk with him.

"My cousins beat you to it. They've already insisted I not go alone," she told him. It wasn't *really* lying. She didn't say that she'd agreed to take them.

Mick sounded relieved. "Good. Even if he weren't a possible suspect, DJ is unpredictable. A vampire *and* a substance abuser."

"And an actor," Barrie quipped, but Mick didn't seem to think it was funny.

"I want you three to be very careful."

Now he was sounding protective and possessive in a way that thrilled her as much as it pissed her off.

"Don't worry, Rhiannon has already given us the 'vampires are dangerous' lecture."

"All right, then. I want you in one piece tonight."

"Really?" she managed nonchalantly. "What for?"

And he proceeded to tell her. Which took up a very hot half hour.

As Barrie hung up the phone, it was more than clear to her that she was in real trouble with this man. And worse…she didn't care a bit.

What do you wear to a movie star's house?

If Barrie hadn't been so completely floating in afterglow, she might have had another full-fledged clothes panic. As it was, the aftermath of yesterday's clothes panic was still cycloned all over the room.

She smiled, remembering how Mick had joked about it—and then how he'd removed that perfect dress….

Okay, stop that, she told herself sternly, pulling herself out of her dreamy daze. *You need to have your mind squarely on this interview. No fantasizing, or flashing back, or any of that—stuff.*

She zapped on her bedroom TV to check the local news as she dressed. She started with her favorite La Perla lingerie. In her experience knowing that you were wearing the best, even if it went completely unseen, was a major confidence boost.

As she was hooking her lacy flowered bra, the entertainment report came on, and there was Harvey Hodge with a larger-than-life smirk, delivering his review of *Rocket Man.*

Of course H.H. made it sound as if the premiere had

been the party of the year, which in her state she was not about to argue. She got a big kick out of Harvey's run-down of the attending celebrities; by her count Mick's shifts accounted for half of the guest list. Laughter bubbled up in her, and she flung herself onto the bed, giggling into her pillow. After a moment there was a featherlight bounce on the bed as Sophie jumped up to see what was happening, and Barrie reached for the kitty and cuddled her....

Until something on the TV made her bolt upright.

Harvey had continued down the guest list and was now talking about Travis Branson. Barrie scooped Sophie up and stood, walking toward the TV to make sure she heard every word Harvey spoke.

"There's a rumor around town—and you *know* I don't spill it if I can't stand by it—that the remake of the cult classic *Otherworld* has a silent backer. So, it looks like those sexy, scary Others will be back, film fans, coming soon to a theater near you. This is Harvey Hodge, your Entertainment Connection, wishing you an entertaining evening. Stay tuned and stay hip."

The news cut to the latest high-speed car chase, and Barrie muted the TV, frowning in concern.

So, the remake was going through.

Her heart fluttered with apprehension.

What would that mean for everyone associated with the film…who was still alive?

DJ lived in Brentwood, where Sunset Boulevard turned into canyon and park as it began its winding descent toward the ocean.

When she'd looked at the map DJ's assistant had e-mailed her, Barrie had found it odd that DJ wasn't in some swank place on the beach in Malibu. But as she drove the winding roads up to his compound, she understood. It was the land. Even the biggest movie people and rock stars in Malibu sacrificed the American dream of a backyard for their beachfront properties; there was just no extra inch of sand to be had. In contrast, it looked like DJ had not just acres but miles of land: grassy, wooded hills, and total seclusion.

For whatever, Barrie thought morbidly, and immediately scolded herself. *Open mind, remember? Keep an open mind. Vampires are human, too. I mean—they're something, anyway.*

The gate was a set of tall metal doors in a thick concrete wall and there was a guardhouse. Barrie had to steady her voice to give her name, and the guard walked around the car, checking under it with a mirror on a long hooked pole like the ones guards used at airports and studio gates.

What is he expecting, a terrorist attack? she thought, unnerved. For the first time she wondered if maybe Mick and her cousins had been right about the "don't go alone" thing. Then the gates rolled open electronically, and she swallowed and drove forward.

There was a long, winding drive up to the house, and it felt like driving through several different countries; as far as Barrie could tell the grounds had not been landscaped with gardens but rather there were whole different, discrete ecosystems, just as you would find at museum-class botanical collections like the Huntington Gardens.

The money it must have cost to develop and maintain all this... she marveled, and then forgot all that as the house came into view. It was Tudor and huge, more like a European estate than an American one, towering against the setting sun like a Transylvanian castle.

Barrie parked the car in the circular drive, right in front of the massive front steps.

What the hell...?

For costuming, at the last minute she'd decided on the Audrey Hepburn look, a simple wine-shaded sheath that let her legs and coloring do all the work for her. After all, there was no way she could out-starlet the starlets DJ was used to having around. *Keep it simple and keep it professional, that's all.*

She checked her face in the mirror, decided she looked terrified and shouldn't have looked, and got out of the car to climb the grand sweep of steps up to the portico.

An assistant opened the door, a young male vampire with dark hair moussed to within an inch of its life. In Hollywood assistants did everything, from picking up dry cleaning to walking their employers' dogs to procuring drugs and prostitutes, so it was no great surprise to see this one doing double duty as a butler. And no surprise that he was a vampire, either. Others very often hired assistants, secretaries and coworkers of their own Kind so they could be free in their behavior instead of constantly guarding the secret of their Otherness.

"Barrie, hi!" the assistant said with manic enthusiasm. "I'm Brad! He's just finishing up another meeting! He'll be just a few minutes. Just come with me!"

Three "justs," four verbal exclamation points and no reason to refer to DJ by name, Barrie noted as she followed Brad! into the manor. He walked her into a high entry hall and through an archway…into an atrium that had to be bigger than a Vegas casino. But this one looked startlingly like an African jungle. There were groves of trees that didn't look as if they belonged in California, a small river—okay, *stream* was probably more accurate—with bridges at convenient places, landscaping as realistic as any movie set. The room was alive, and not just with plant life. Barrie could hear what she was sure were real monkeys chattering in the trees above her, and as she looked around her, wild colorful birds took flight from the undergrowth, up toward the light of the domed ceiling. Though it was going to be dark outside, in here it seemed like a sunny afternoon.

"This is the African Room!" Brad explained.

"Yes, it is," Barrie murmured. *Island of Lost Souls is more like it.* "Is there an Arctic Room?" she joked.

"Of course!" the assistant answered.

She had no idea if he was serious, but she wouldn't have been a bit surprised if there were any number of life-size dioramas in the manor. She stared into the luxuriant foliage, half expecting to see elephants—and then flinched back in shock. Gleaming eyes stared at her from the undergrowth, and she made out the gold-and-black fur of a huge cat, poised to spring.…

"Don't worry about Steve," the assistant said quickly,

but with a touch of amusement; Barrie got the distinct feeling he enjoyed this part of his job. "He's stuffed."

"Steve?" she gasped.

"He's the greeter. DJ likes to get people's blood flowing."

Vampire humor. Charming.

"This way." Brad took her along a path that crossed the river twice on different types of bridges. As she followed him, Barrie felt more and more as if she were in a dream—or a movie.

There were living spaces in this jungle: a cave with a collection of rocks vaguely shaped like furniture, a harem sort of tent with gauzy veils and low pillows, an enormous tree straight out of *Lord of the Rings,* but with a bar and conversation area carved into the hollow trunk. Throughout the room the temperature was higher than outside, a suggestion of warmth while still being perfectly comfortable. It was impossible to tell how big the space was, as the path and river took circuitous routes that made walking through it seem like a real journey, and the wall-size murals and scrims were *trompe l'oeil,* giving the impression of vast distances. No doubt it had all been put together by some Oscar-winning production designer. It never ceased to amaze Barrie how much talent was crammed into the city, and DJ had the money to pay for the absolute best.

She followed Brad around another curving rock and stopped. The path ended at a large canvas tent decked out with all the luxury items one would expect on a fantasy safari: a teak desk, carved teak chairs, along with wicker ones in intricate patterns, a zebra rug.

And then there were all the modern accoutrements: desktop computer, laptop, iPad, phone system. She assumed there were concealed speakers, as well.

"The office," Brad explained unnecessarily.

And beyond the tent there was an elephant. Life-size, and too realistic to be anything but the real thing, professionally taxidermied. Barrie felt a frisson of horror and anger at the sight of that magnificent creature, stuffed and displayed. *It's just not right.*

But social outrage was going to get her nowhere here. She stifled her human response and followed Brad into the tent.

He crossed to a wet bar in the corner and poured rosy, icy drinks from a chilled glass pitcher.

She took the glass warily. There was no obvious smell of blood, so she sipped, and found she was drinking a virgin version of a Cosmo.

"Expecting something just a bit stronger?" a familiar voice said behind her. Barrie jumped; the voice sounded as close as if someone had leaned in to whisper into her ear. But when she turned, DJ was standing several yards away, observing her with a hint of amusement. Words like *hypnotic, feral, mesmerizing, predatory* ran through her mind in a jumble, and she found herself as intimidated as she had been the night before. The actor's eyes were especially riveting—nearly black—and he never seemed to take those eyes off her.

Brad the assistant had disappeared, and Barrie was acutely aware that she was alone in a secluded, guarded manor with a volatile and possibly not entirely sane vampire who might well be out of the reach of all human law.

I am in such trouble, she thought. And then she got hold of herself.

"This is an amazing place," she said, to break the spell.

"Do you know Africa?" he asked.

"I've heard of it," she said dryly.

"It's bigger," DJ said. "You should go. The game alone..."

Barrie had no idea what to say to that. DJ walked the tent in a prowling circle that was more animal than human.

"So, Keeper," he said, and his voice was so sibilant it could have been the voice of a snake. "You are sworn to protect all Others."

"All Others who live by the Code," she said, and was amazed at how steady her voice sounded. But suddenly she was not a starstruck thirteen-year-old meeting a legendary movie star. She was a Keeper, as responsible for that movie star as she was for a teenage street urchin. She felt the power of her ancestral duty surge through her veins, and she faced DJ as an equal. She thanked her father in her heart.

"Ah, the Code," DJ said with irony. "How would we live without it?" He looked around them and then spread his hands theatrically. "Let's stroll, shall we?"

Barrie nodded and followed him into the jungle.

As DJ walked her through the trails of the African Room, Barrie understood what a feat of design the... *set? Diorama? Terrarium?*...actually was. She forgot that they were in an enclosed, designed space, because the sights and sounds and smells were so perfectly orchestrated to create the illusion of an African veldt. She gasped as they came across a perfectly poised lion.

"It's beautiful," she told the actor.

"It was delicious, too," he said. She looked at him, aghast, and he gave her a catlike smile. "Of course I killed it. I killed everything here. Not a single part goes to waste, as you see."

She had to force down her feelings of revulsion and focus herself to remember why she was there, but when she spoke it was with amazing calm.

"I came today because I'm investigating what I believe is a dual murder. And I think it's intimately connected with the death of Johnny Love and whatever happened on the set of *Otherworld*."

It was absolutely impossible to read the look on the actor's face. "You're talking about Solly, obviously. Are you saying he was offed because of the movie? Fifteen years later?" He sounded incredulous, skeptical and bored all in the same breath.

Barrie ignored his tone and kept on point. "I think it's a strong possibility."

DJ stopped on the path and looked at her. "This requires a drink." He headed toward the hollow tree with the bar. After a moment Barrie followed him. She was acutely aware that he had not asked her about the "dual" part of the murder, only about Mayo. *Does that mean he already knows about Tiger?*

Inside the tree, behind the bar, DJ was pouring a shot of some intensely red liquid from a decanter. "And you?" he asked her, gesturing to the well-stocked shelves.

"I'm fine, thanks," she said, and sat on one of the wicker barstools to wait while the star downed his drink.

He touched his fingers to his lips, dabbing away a drop of crimson. "Murder would be inconvenient, seeing as I've been in talks to star in the remake. Does that mean I'm in mortal danger?" He gave a mocking full-body shudder.

Barrie looked at him steadily. "I think it means that you need to take every precaution for your safety until we get to the bottom of these murders."

He dropped the comic posture, and his black eyes pierced hers. "As reassurance goes, that was an epic fail."

Again, he was not asking about the other murder, but as ominous as that was, she kept her voice calm and purposeful.

"It wasn't reassurance, it was a warning. I don't think you can be too careful right now."

"Grim, but honest." He moved out from behind the bar, circling her, studying her. In the enclosed space, it was hard for her to keep cool, but she steadied herself and held her ground. "So, what is it you want from me, Keeper?" he challenged her.

"I want to know what happened to Johnny Love," she said straight-out. She had not at all known that she was going to say it, but once it was out, she knew it was the only possible thing she could have said. He was going to talk to her or he wasn't; there was no small talk she could possibly make.

He half smiled, but his eyes were distant. "You and the entire world."

"But do you know?" She was amazed that her voice

sounded so firm. Inside she was shaking like a leaf. She felt on the precipice of some vast unknown.

DJ leaned suddenly forward on the bar. His voice was expansive and dangerous. "You mean, was I conscious enough to understand? To be able to give an accurate account?"

"Were you?" she asked back without flinching.

He straightened, lifted his hands. "So sorry. I don't remember," he said.

The tropical birds called exotically somewhere in the atrium, and DJ said nothing more. It could have been the truth, or a lie, or anything; she had no way of knowing. She tried a different tack.

"Were Johnny and Mayo..." she hesitated "...involved?"

He smiled a cat smile. "*Involved?* How delicate of you. You mean were they fucking? The better question is, who *wasn't* Johnny fucking? The boy was a whore."

Barrie bristled. "He was sixteen. He was still a child."

"There are no children on movie sets. You grow up... or you die."

She stared into his face. "Well, Johnny died."

"That *will* happen when you play with fire," he snapped.

"Tell me what you mean," she said quickly. She could see his eyes flare, but after a moment he spoke.

"Johnny would use anyone to get what he wanted. He was fucking Branson to get more scenes in the movie, he was fucking Mayo to get more promotional face time." DJ smiled again, slyly. "I learned a lot from him."

Barrie caught her breath. "So...you think he was killed because someone felt used? Mayo? Branson?"

"Or maybe because he and Travis were starting to talk big about making *Otherworld* a coming-out party. For Others."

"Oh, my gosh," she murmured. If they really *had* been talking about breaking the silence and revealing the existence of the Otherworld to humans, the suspect pool had just become millions.

She forced herself back to the conversation while still trying to avoid DJ's hypnotic black eyes. "Then...you think he was killed because someone thought he was going to break the silence?"

"I never said he was killed," DJ said maddeningly.

"But do you think so?" Barrie persisted.

He waved a finger at her and dropped into one of the club chairs in the hollow tree, gazing up at her. "You tell me what *you* think, and I'll tell you if you're hot or cold."

She hesitated, and thought of Mayo hiring a shifter of Johnny's age to play Johnny. "I think Mayo was obsessed with Johnny."

DJ dropped his head onto the back of his chair and laughed, then sat straight up, startling her. "*Everyone* was obsessed with Johnny. *You're* obsessed with Johnny."

Barrie realized he had a point.

DJ flung a leg over the arm of his chair and studied her. "Johnny cultivated obsession. It was a highly successful career strategy." He leaned forward abruptly, with the trick that vampires had of moving faster than light; it suddenly felt as if he was right in front of her face, and she had to bite back a scream. "This is old news, *Keeper.* What do you *really* know?"

Barrie took a breath to steady herself, and even so she struggled to keep her voice even. "I talked to a cast member from the original movie who said Johnny died on set. Before the film was finished shooting."

DJ looked honestly startled.

But he's an actor, she reminded herself grimly.

He looked away, then back at her. "Fascinating. But it rather begs the question of who I was acting with the final week. Granted, we were partying pretty hard by then. Still, even tripping my brains out I *think* I would have noticed if my costar had disappeared."

Barrie felt her stomach drop in disappointment. It was exactly the same thing that Darius had said. The biggest piece of the puzzle she'd found didn't seem to fit.

"So, why would anyone say it?" she asked.

He lifted his shoulders dramatically. "People say all sorts of things about the film behind closed doors. A lot of people had every interest in making Johnny's death legendary. It was good for the movie."

She stared at him, aghast. "You're not saying…that someone killed him to make the movie a success?"

He smiled at her as if she were a child. "Oh, now, you're acting as if the idea is some kind of surprise. I thought you grew up in this town."

And so I did, but I don't know who told you so, she thought.

"Are you in touch with Robbie Anderson?" she asked out of the blue.

He barked a laugh. "Robbie. What do you mean, through a Ouija board?"

"You think he's dead?"

"Dead, or living a quiet, normal, entirely uneventful life somewhere—what's the difference? Shifters often die young, you know."

Even if I didn't, you vampires keep pointing it out to me, she thought.

"You must know why he disappeared," she said impulsively. "Johnny dead, Robbie missing—I think you may be the only one in the world who knows why, really."

She knew she'd struck a chord, because for a moment he was completely silent and still.

"I would be the only person who knew...*if* I knew. Which I don't," he said.

She was getting tired of the Cheshire cat riddles. On impulse, she said, "I think maybe someone was threatening all three of you. Using you."

He flicked a hand. "Everyone was using everyone else."

"But you three were kids. Sixteen years old. It wasn't a level playing field."

He looked away from her, but she could feel something in him responding to what she was saying.

"You have so much power now. You could expose whoever was using Johnny, Robbie, you...all of you. You could heal a very old wound."

He exploded to his feet, lashing out with a rage that didn't just startle but frightened her. "Everyone involved with that film ended up dead or damned. Doesn't that mean anything to you?" He was so angry she could see red in the corners of his eyes and the beginning of fangs. He was on the brink of Changing, and that was not good.

She stood very still and kept her voice very quiet, and even knowing how dangerous the situation had suddenly gotten, she still had to ask, "Are you saying you think the film was cursed?"

He smiled ambiguously, and though the redness was fading from his eyes, he didn't look entirely human. "It made me what I am. What would *you* say?"

They stood silently, then he turned and stepped out of the tree, walking off down the trail until he disappeared into the trees.

She stood for a moment with her heart racing and the river rushing in her ears, then she started back along the winding path through the "jungle." Her thoughts were whirling as she tried to get some grip on what had just happened.

The leaves rustled right beside her and she whirled with her heart racing—to see Brad the assistant step out of the undergrowth.

"I'll see you out," he said neutrally, for once not an exclamation point in sight.

As they stepped outside onto the portico, she was startled to see that it was full dark; she'd forgotten the real time in the artificial light of the African Room. And even more startling, her car was gone.

"The guard moved it," Brad said behind her. "I'll have it brought around right away."

Okay, maybe it just wasn't nice enough to leave right

in front of the house. But I didn't give anyone my keys,
Barrie thought uneasily. Instead of saying it aloud, she
thanked him and walked down the stairs to the curb to
wait.

The door closed at the top of the stairs, and darkness
surrounded her. The estate was remarkably quiet; she
could hear the rustle of wind through eucalyptus leaves
and night bird sounds in the tops of trees, and there were
stars, actual stars, appearing in the sky, not something
anyone saw too often in the city.

She heard a flipping and splashing somewhere nearby,
and turned to look. Beside the roundabout of the drive
there was a large pond, apparently stocked with fish;
as she watched, she saw one leap, glimmering briefly
in the moonlight before it splashed back into the water.

She walked closer to the pond and looked down at the
moon on the water, and thought back over the strange
interview.

DJ's feelings toward Johnny could at best be de-
scribed as ambivalent; even fifteen years dead, Johnny
obviously still inspired some serious jealousy. It couldn't
be easy for an actor to still be trying to compete with a
tragically dead young star.

But could DJ have killed him? Would *he have?*

At the time of Johnny's death, DJ had been only sixteen years old himself. Sixteen-year-olds were capable
of murder; gang shootings proved that far too often. But
movie stars rarely killed other movie stars.

Most movie stars aren't vampires, either, she reminded herself. And just as she thought it, she felt the

brush of air against her face as something swooped by her.

Something huge.

Barrie stumbled and spun in a panic, her breath catching in her throat as she stared up into the dark night.

The stars glittered above and the wind was light and teasing, but her bloodstream was flooded with adrenaline, the ancient fight-or-flight instinct. She wasn't alone. She could feel someone watching, could feel eyes on her skin as if she were being watched from a high vantage point.

She turned to run back toward the house, but the invisible creature whooshed at her again, a large, live, breathing force, this time barely missing her.

Barrie didn't think, didn't scream, she just ran. She felt the push of air beside her again, this time accompanied by the warmth of breath on her neck, such a crawly feeling she would have screamed if she weren't so intent on fleeing.

Her winged attacker circled, forcing her away from the house, toward the eucalyptus grove.

She ran and threw a look over her shoulder, her heart plummeting as she saw her pursuer for the first time, a big winged thing, an enormous dark shadow like an ancient pterodactyl.

Vampire.

Barrie felt low desert scrub scratching at her bare legs, drawing blood as she ran.

So not good, she realized; the vampire would only be more aroused by the scent.

She ran harder, heels pounding in the sand, scanning the dark frantically for someplace to take refuge. To the right of her there was a gulch, an amazingly authentic desert ravine, with sandstone cliffs and a dry riverbed, saguaro cactus and the towering shadows of Joshua trees.

She knew she had to shift, to buy herself some time with camouflage, but it was hard enough to shift or even glamour when you were standing still, much less when you were running for your life.

Still, she forced herself to focus on her astral body, fixed the image of a moth in her mind, something small, insignificant to the huge creature pursuing her....

And as she was concentrating...she ran straight into someone who grabbed her with strong arms.

Mick.

He pulled her down against the nearest boulder, shielding her with his body.

Barrie could feel the warm sand under her legs and hands, and Mick's strong body tense beside her, protective and pissed.

She leaned into his shoulder, gasping for breath, and looked up into the sky, scanning for the vampire. The night was black and the stars were bright, and the wind flowed and whispered around them, but she could see nothing, hear nothing. Mick's arms were tight around her, and she could feel his heart racing against her back.

"I don't...see it," she whispered. He rested his chin on her head and said nothing.

But after a prolonged moment of silence, he unfolded himself to stand, pulling her up with him.

"Out of here. Now," he ordered. He pulled her along

the boulders in the direction of the front drive, keeping close to the shelter of the rocks.

"What are you *doing* here?" she whispered.

"It looks like I'm trying to keep you from being drained of blood," he said tensely as he stared up into the night sky.

"It's not like that," she began, even though she could still barely breathe through the wild pounding of her own heart.

"Oh, it's not. What *is* it like, then?" he said, still scanning the sky as he steered her up the incline toward the mansion.

"Well, sort of like being pursued by a vampire and rescued by a shape-shifter before any bloodshed or mayhem, something like that," she admitted, breathless. As they crested the slope, she saw the Bentley parked and waiting.

"Good, we're looking at the same picture, anyway. Get in the car," he said.

"I have my own—" she started.

"Philip will come and take your car back. You're coming with me."

It was hard to argue with someone who had a spare driver to toss around like that, so she shut up and got in, sinking into the comfort and safety of the car as Mick shut the door after her.

The Bentley wasn't as roomy as the limo, but it was more luxurious, in its way. There was even a bud vase on the dashboard, with a fresh rosebud. Barrie couldn't take her eyes off it. It helped steer her mind away from her brush with death.

"Nice touch," she said weakly, feeling her body go limp with the adrenaline crash.

"Don't talk to me," he said stonily as he started the car and steered down the drive.

"Why not?" she asked, startled.

"Because I am really, really angry with you right now."

Barrie was silenced. He did sound furious. She huddled meekly in her seat, and he said nothing more until the tall metal gates of the estate were shutting behind them in the dark.

"Your cousins insisted on coming with you, hmm?" he said in a voice that could have cut glass.

"Things…came up…." She knew she was busted, but the excuse bubbled up, anyway.

"Right. What came up was a vampire in full-attack mode."

"You saw it," she said in a small voice.

"Hard to miss," he said grimly, and took a bottle of water from the console, handed it to her. "Drink this. You're probably in shock."

She meekly took the water, and the second she tipped it up to her lips she realized she was practically dying of thirst. She drank almost the whole thing down, then sat back in the seat and sneaked a look at Mick, who was stiff and silent beside her as he drove. "Was it DJ?" she ventured.

He looked at her for a moment. "I don't know," he said, his voice flat. "It was a vampire."

Great, she thought. *That part I knew.*

"What happened in there?" he finally asked, his

hands tight on the steering wheel as he negotiated the curving and pitch-black canyon road.

"It was…amazing. He's got a whole environment going. Trees. Dead big game. A river." She was aware that she didn't sound entirely coherent, but she couldn't help herself. "Why *did* you come? What did you think was going to happen?" she asked on impulse.

"I came because I had a feeling you were lying to me," he answered, his voice flat. "I have no idea what I thought was going to happen. With DJ, he could be just playing—or not playing at all." And then, much more softly, he said, "Impossible."

"What do you mean?" she asked.

"With DJ…impossible to tell."

There was something in his voice that puzzled her. "How do you know him?" Because the way he was talking, it was obvious that he did.

He glanced at her in the dark, then away. "He's a major contributor to the Circle Foundation," he said with a hint of irony.

"Really," Barrie said.

"I'm not sure that he actually knows it," Mick added. "But the checks keep coming."

"Well. How nice for you," she said.

"It is," he agreed. "Very nice. His name looks good on the masthead. These things mean something. Money makes money."

She nodded, processing this.

"Did he say anything useful?" Mick asked in a voice that implied that he doubted it.

"I think so," Barrie said slowly, although she was

struggling to remember exactly what DJ *had* said that was in any way helpful.

"And?" Mick was waiting.

"He said that Johnny was on set until the movie wrapped," she said. "And he said…" To her own total surprise, she burst into tears.

"Hey," Mick said from the driver's seat, alarmed. He reached over and took her hand. "What?"

It was a minute before she could get enough of a hold on herself to control her sobs. "It seems like everyone was using Johnny. DJ said that Johnny was in control. But he was a kid, a *kid*. I don't care how famous or how rich or how gorgeous, they were all just kids, all three of them. They were being used—by *everyone*—and it destroyed all three of them."

Mick was completely silent in the driver's seat beside her, as if rendered speechless by her outburst. He looked out the window at the dark and winding road of the canyon, and he said nothing, but his fingers were warm and strong around hers as she cried it out.

Finally she swallowed and spoke. "You don't think so," she said dully.

"I don't think I'm in a position to judge," he said, without looking at her. "But you do know that you can't believe a word he says."

"I'm not stupid," she said defensively. "The fact is he may not remember anything that happened on that film all that clearly. There are probably whole parts of his life he doesn't remember."

"Exactly," Mick said, and looked slightly less tense. They rode in silence for what seemed like forever.

"What do you think?" he asked finally.

Barrie bit her lip, thinking of the past hour, of the past three days. "I think a lot of people wanted Johnny dead," she said.

When the Bentley drove through the gates of the House of the Rising Sun, Barrie saw that her own Peugeot was already parked in the drive. Mick pulled in beside it and stopped the car.

"Like teleporting," she murmured.

"What?" he asked. He had been silent in his seat for the last few miles.

"Nothing," she said, not knowing what else to say.

"Barrie," he said, and the intensity of his voice nearly made her heart stop.

"What?" she said, her mouth dry.

He turned to her, took her face in his hands and stroked her cheeks with his fingers. She caught her breath and looked into his eyes, willing him to kiss her, but he didn't. It seemed as if he was struggling with himself. "I want to stay…if you want me to." But before she could answer he added, "But there's something I need to do tonight. It can't wait."

And before she could react, he was opening his car door and shutting it again, and almost as suddenly he was opening her door to let her out.

She got out of the car, and he walked silently beside her to her porch where he took her by the shoulders, his fingers digging into her bare arms. "I want you to be very careful. I think you should stay with one of your cousins tonight, and none of you should go out at all."

Barrie was torn between longing…and a ripple of fear. "I have no plans," she finally managed. "I think I'll just make some popcorn and turn in."

"Good," he said. "Lock the door. Lock everything." And then he bent to her and kissed her so thoroughly she completely forgot to ask what was making him so serious and scary all of a sudden.

Finally he drew back slightly, resting his forehead against hers, and she could feel his pulse racing just as hers was, as his fingers moved at the back of her neck. "I'll see you as soon as I can," he said against her cheek.

And then he was moving away from her, and there was the sound of a car door and an engine starting and the Bentley was gone.

Chapter 15

In the hall, Barrie locked the door behind her as Sophie wound herself around Barrie's ankles, meowing authoritatively. "Hungry, yes, I understand," Barrie told her, and was aware that her own voice sounded dazed. "You're an animal."

It was a relief to focus on the cat's simple, immediate needs instead of her own ravenous hunger.

As she opened cat food in the kitchen, it occurred to her that she had not talked to Mick about the silent backer of the remake of *Otherworld*. She had no idea if he already knew.

Just as she was debating calling him, the doorbell rang, startling her.

Maybe he'd come back. Her pulse started racing just at the thought.

She hurried out into the front hall and pulled the curtain back from the small window beside the door...then stared in surprise. On her doorstep was a collection of Keepers: vampire Keeper, were Keeper, shifter Keeper, Elven Keeper. Even if she didn't know them vaguely from Council meetings, she would have known they were the Beverly Hills clan just from all the Armani.

Her heart sank. The last thing she needed right now was this haughty crew. And from the look of them, she was in trouble. Reluctantly, she opened the door.

"We need to speak with you," said the tallest female, cool and Nordic, an Elven. The replacement for the former Beverly Hills Elven Keeper, Arthur Whitehead, who had been exiled for his insidious part in the recent series of Elven deaths by an ancient blood disease.

Barrie stared around at them. "How did you get in?" Maybe it was rude of her to ask, but she hadn't heard the gate buzz, and if Sailor or Rhiannon had let anyone in, they would have called her.

"The gate was open," the werewolf Keeper said. He had a Schwarzenegger body under his three-thousand-dollar suit.

Barrie frowned at him. *I doubt that.* True, Mick had left just a moment before, but the gate shut automatically after each exit; these Keepers must have manipulated it somehow.

She shook her head. "I just got home and—"

"We're afraid this can't wait," the vampire Keeper said. Rhiannon was a vampire Keeper and she didn't look anything like one, but this Keeper had the sallow skin and dark hair of a classic movie vampire, which he'd no doubt carefully cultivated. A real vampire in

L.A. would be more likely to go the tanned route, as camouflage.

And what is this, the royal "we"? Barrie thought, with a twinge of annoyance under her nervousness. But she opened the door wider for the Keepers to come in.

She felt a little as if she were being called on by the Royal Court, and she had to force herself to stay calm. *I haven't done anything wrong,* she reminded herself. *This is politics, pure and simple.*

She ushered the Keepers past the antique mirrors of the hall into the living room, and was at least glad that she hadn't been home often enough in the past few days for the place to be a total wreck. And despite her irritation at the unannounced visit, her manners won out.

"May I get you some coffee? Or tea?" she offered.

The fourth Keeper, a shifter with the hooded look of a secret Valium addict, answered curtly, "We won't be here that long."

Good, Barrie thought, and indicated the chairs and sofas with her hand as she sat. The Keepers all took seats, facing her like a firing squad.

"It's come to our attention that you are investigating the death of Saul Mayo," the vampire Keeper said.

"I'm not actually in—" Barrie started.

The Elven Keeper interrupted. "You've been asking questions about him all over town."

"Including visiting DJ, who is clearly not in your Keep," the vampire Keeper added.

The Keepers spoke in one continuous sentence, as if they were robots running on the same software.

"You're very new to all this, Ms. Gryffald. You

clearly haven't absorbed how things work in the hierarchy," the werewolf Keeper said.

"DJ is not one of yours, and it is completely unacceptable for you to be harassing him," the shifter Keeper said.

"Harassing?" Barrie repeated incredulously, but the Keepers rolled on as if she hadn't spoken.

"Brentwood is far out of your territory, and it's a complete breach of protocol to enter that district without going through proper channels."

As he spoke, Barrie focused on the vampire Keeper, watching him closely. She was acutely aware that she had just been pursued and attacked by a vampire, and that Keepers often cultivated the characteristics of their charges, with varying degrees of skill. Rhiannon, for example, could fly short distances, and take on the strength—and fangs—of a vampire, although it took a great deal out of her to do it. Obviously this Keeper knew that Barrie had been at DJ's estate, and depending on his skill, it was entirely possible that he'd decided to scare her a bit. But Barrie was pretty sure her would-be attacker was a real vampire, not a Keeper. It was the sense of paralyzing fear she had felt during the attack that made her think so. There was an uncanniness about an Other that was hard for a Keeper to emulate, and fairly or unfairly, she had always been especially wary of vampires.

Felt like a vampire to me, she thought. *And Mick said so, too.*

The Elven Keeper was speaking now. "Not only is Mayo not in your territory, he isn't even Other. There is absolutely no call for you to be anywhere near that investigation."

Barrie felt ire rising, and fast. This was exactly what Mick had been talking about, the infighting and lack of cooperation between Keepers in Los Angeles. Here she was being strong-armed by people who had no authority except in their own little elite circle—and in their own heads.

"Well, since I'm not investigating Mayo, there really isn't a problem," she said again, and started to stand. "So, thanks for dropping by—"

"There's another thing," the shifter Keeper said. "This...relationship you have with Mick Townsend."

Barrie tensed up in disbelief. "Excuse me?"

"It's a small community, Ms. Gryffald," the Elven Keeper said. "You weren't exactly being discreet at the premiere the other night."

Barrie stared back at her. "I have nothing to hide."

"Townsend is a maverick," the werewolf Keeper said. "He refuses to play ball, and he refuses to stay out of what is patently Keeper business. You may want to re-think things."

Now Barrie *did* stand, facing them. "*You* may want to rethink coming to my home and telling me what to do."

The other Keepers glanced at each other, and then they all rose.

"I hope you'll consider your position. You have a lot to live up to, and many eyes are upon you." The Elven Keeper looked around the house meaningfully, and then they all moved toward the entry hall.

Barrie followed them and shut the front door behind

them harder than she needed to, but she was furious. "Stuck-up creeps," she muttered as she locked it and stomped back toward the living room, not even caring that some Keepers, like vampires, had supersensitive ears. "Trying to order me around."

She didn't have time to stew, though, because her phone was pinging to announce a text. She scrambled for her purse, pulled out her phone and looked at the screen. The text read: If you want to know more, Travis will see you at midnight. There was a Malibu address.

The sender was DJ, the same phone number that Brad the assistant had used to confirm their appointment.

"Travis Branson," Barrie murmured, startled. She felt a rush of excitement, and also doubt. "Is this for real?"

Of course the director would respond to a request by DJ, that part she could believe. *But DJ may have just tried to kill you,* she reminded herself. *So what if it's a trick?*

She walked the living room in a circle, debating. Now that the Keepers were gone, Sophie padded into the doorway to see what was going on.

"How can I not go?" Barrie asked the cat. *Even if DJ's just messing with me and didn't really set it up with Branson, if I go there and say that DJ sent me, I may be able to talk to him, anyway.*

As baffling as the puzzle pieces were, Barrie felt that she was getting more of the big picture with every piece, every encounter.

She grabbed her phone and quickly texted her cousins. She knew she should add the emergency code or, better yet, go over to their houses and wake them up directly, but she hesitated.

"I have time to make it to Malibu by midnight," she murmured to Sophie, by way of excuse. And she headed for her bedroom to change.

It might have been the sea air, or the cold light of the moon on the ocean, but Barrie regained her senses once she hit the Pacific Coast Highway. The unexpected visit and attempted strong-arming by the other Keepers had pissed her off, but now that she was calmer she was willing to admit that she should have company on this particular late-night visit. She fumbled on her Bluetooth to phone Mick. All she got was voice mail.

"Don't kill me!" she said into the headset impulsively. "But DJ talked to Travis Branson, and he wants to see me tonight. I'm headed there now." She recited the address and wanted to say more but felt too awkward, so she finished, "I…I'll call you later if I don't hear from you."

She wanted to say "Please come with me," but she didn't quite have the nerve.

Branson's house was on the beach, of course, that extremely rarified strip of land known as Point Dume. Barrie had only ever been there because Declan Wainwright lived there, too.

Declan, she thought, with a surge of hope. *He'll come in with me. If he's home…*

But she already knew he wasn't. Not on a Friday night. Not when he ran the most happening club on Sunset.

She used her phone and left a quick message for him, anyway. *Can't hurt to have everyone in the Otherworld know where I am, right?*

As she disconnected, she realized she had arrived. She parked on the access road and got out of the car, looking at the wall of luxury houses.

Branson's house was built like most on Point Dume: four stories high, the lowest carved right out of the cliff, most likely laundry and servant quarters, quite possibly a wine cellar or whatever a werewolf kept in his basement. The higher floors commanded the best views, and were saved for master bedroom, living room, office or studio space, depending on the priorities of the inhabitants.

And, like most houses in Malibu, the entrance was at the back of the house, off a side street, and was guarded by a high concrete wall covered in some kind of green creeper.

To Barrie's surprise, as she approached she saw the gate was open a crack and there was a Post-it note: *Come in.*

She felt another rush of unease, and stood in the dark, listening to the crash of the waves beyond the wall of homes.

Every house in Malibu can't have an automatic door, she rationalized. The thought was no big comfort, and she'd already had one scare today.

But even though she wasn't armed, she had a few tricks up her sleeve. So, she took a breath and walked through the gate.

The interior walkway led through a small, neat garden with a couple of very well-groomed citrus trees on one side and a drought-resistant assortment of flowers and bushes. She smelled lemon blossoms and night-blooming jasmine in the moist salt air.

The front door was open as well, and there was flickering light inside. Candles. Again she hesitated.

All right, now, Barrymore, this is not looking good. You need to walk out of here, and you need to call someone and not be a total idiot about it.

But the need to know was strong, and she also felt a certain urgency.

What if he's hurt? What if he needs help? I've called everyone I can possibly call already. What if I wait out here and that few minutes' delay is the difference between life and death?

Caught between fear and duty, she compromised: she glamoured herself.

Her father had taught her basic invisibility as soon as she'd been old enough to understand the principles of auric control. He told her, without trying to scare her, that there were times when it was important to be invisible, and he wanted her to be able to achieve and hold invisibility, especially under stressful conditions, so he'd made her practice when she was angry or sleepy or after exhausting herself with exercise.

When she was a little older, Barrie had realized it wasn't necessarily Others that her father had been worried about, not by a long shot. Invisibility could come in handy in all sorts of situations.

And it was definitely easier to achieve when she wasn't trying to run from a vampire attack. She pulled on invisibility now, and stepped through the door into the darkness of the house.

The door to her left was closed, and when she oh-so-carefully turned the knob, one millimeter at a time, she found it was locked, leaving the only option moving forward up a staircase on her right, which led up to the next level of the house. She was glad to see it was carpeted, so she could move relatively noiselessly.

Her heart was pounding, and she focused on her breathing to keep it even and silent as she ascended the stairs and made the turn to go up the next half of the flight.

The stairs opened up into a huge living space, bathed in the blue of the moonlit night. Barrie had to prevent herself from gasping at the view; she was facing an entire wall of glass with what seemed like the entire ocean outside it, a dark silhouette of cliff and shimmering water extending to what seemed like infinity, white surf gently rolling onto the pale sand outside the house.

But when she pulled her gaze away from the window and turned to survey the rest of the room, the stifled gasp turned into a scream.

Because hung on the towering stone chimney of the fireplace was a body.

A werewolf body.

It wasn't the first time she'd screamed at this exact sight. She'd seen it on-screen, just a few nights before.

It was a recreation of the werewolf crucifixion from *Otherworld*.

And the body was Travis Branson's.

Barrie stumbled backward in shock and panic. One

part of her was reeling at the death. The other part was realizing something was very wrong. Weres didn't hold their beast form in death.

He's still alive, she thought in horror. *Oh, God, I have to get him down.*

But all the blood… His body was drenched, the fireplace was drenched….

How could anyone lose that much blood and live?

She forced herself forward, staring up at the gruesome sight. And from a closer angle she could see that Branson's flesh was human; there was no fur. His hands were human; his chest was human. The were visage was false, a furred mask.

And that was when Barrie fled. She ran, holding on to invisibility, and she thought she maintained it but wasn't sure, and she sure as hell wasn't going to stop and find a mirror to find out. She ran down the stairs, out the door. She ran through the garden. She ran across the street to her car, and only then did she let invisibility slip as she scrambled inside the Peugeot and locked the doors, and sat gasping and shaking and freaked, just trying to catch her breath and her sanity.

Killed. Killed and displayed. Someone is killing the Otherworld *people.*

She clutched the steering wheel just to have a hold of something real, and a few rational thoughts later she realized that there was a more immediate issue. Branson was a were, and even though weres did not hold their beast form when they died, the killer was obviously pointing to the fact he was a werewolf.

The regular police couldn't be called.
Mick. I need Mick.

Barrie waited in her car, shivering but watching the house intently. She'd called...everyone. Brodie, Rhiannon, Sailor and even Declan again. And Mick, who was her first call, and the only one who didn't pick up. Everyone was angry with her—and too relieved to be *too* angry.

And they all knew they had work to do.

The true nature of the crime was going to have to be covered up, and a logical explanation—method, motive, means—would have to be presented as the official story of the death. It was a prime example of why it was vital to have Others working at every level of law enforcement and related professions to keep up the wall that separated the Otherworld from the human world. And Brodie was perfectly placed on the Robbery Homicide division to handle a celebrity murder like this.

Barrie had never been at an actual crime scene before, and she was beyond grateful that she had such trustworthy connections to call on with this one. Not just Brodie, but his supervisor, Captain Riley, who was not an Other but an active sympathizer, the son of a Wiccan, and was committed to keeping the silence ab—

There was a sharp rap on the window right next to her, and she nearly jumped out of her skin.

Mick was looking in at her through the glass.

Barrie gasped in relief and scrambled for the door handle. He didn't say a word, just pulled her out of the car and into his arms.

She leaned against him, her heart pounding not just with the surprise but with a rush of desire. Which she immediately had to force down—everyone she knew was going to be converging on them any second now.

"Thanks for coming," she said.

"Don't be an idiot," he said roughly, and then he was kissing her, and she forgot all about anyone else coming. She only wanted him to keep holding her, to feel the rightness of being against him, feeling the beat of his heart in her own pulse....

He pulled back from her and shook her. "What the hell did you think you were doing?"

When she could focus enough to breathe again, she answered meekly, "I'm sorry. I should have waited. I won't do it again." She found herself suddenly shaking all over. "It's horrible. I never want to see anything like that again, ever."

He looked down at her with a mixture of anger and relief, and then he shook his head. "Show me."

She took him through the garden, into the house, up the steep and dark stairs, and then they stood at the entrance of the living room with the ocean beyond and the bloody werewolf hanging on the stone wall.

Mick stared for the longest time in silence. He seemed even more stunned than she had been. "Exactly like the film," he finally said. "It's a warning."

"It worked." Barrie looked around the blue moonlit room and shivered. "We should get out of here and wait for everyone outside. Brodie's mad enough at me already." She winced, remembering his voice on the phone.

"Brodie McKay? The Elven cop?" Mick sounded tense.

"Yes, he's—well, he's family now. He tends to be protective. He's coming with Tony Brandt. They're going to camouflage the murder."

"A cleanup crew. That's convenient," Mick said, as if from far away.

"Come on." She tugged at his arm, and he finally turned from the dead werewolf and left with her.

Rhiannon's Volvo and Brodie's ATV were just pulling up as Mick and Barrie came out through the gate onto the street. Barrie's cousins piled out of the Volvo; Brodie and Brandt got out of the Explorer.

Rhiannon and Sailor rushed forward, whether to hug Barrie or kill her was not entirely clear, but Brodie said sharply and quietly, "Save it. Everyone inside the gate. We can't be attracting any attention."

In the garden, after Barrie had endured the requisite hugging and reprimanding, she introduced Mick to Brodie, and they looked each other over with alpha-male wariness, then to Brandt, who also looked at Mick sharply and thoughtfully. She found herself feeling defensive, as if Mick was somehow being judged and found wanting. She reached for his hand, and he closed his fingers over hers absently.

"Let's take a look," Brodie said to Brandt, and then glanced at the cousins and Mick. "The rest of you stay here inside the gate."

Brodie and Brandt disappeared into the house.

"It's awful. Staged," Barrie said to her cousins, as

they all took seats on the planters around the fountain. "Like the killer was sending a warning."

"It's more than that," Mick said, slipping an arm around Barrie as he looked up at the house. She leaned into him as he spoke. "In the film that scene was about the were being made an example of for trying to break the Code of Silence."

Barrie glanced up at him, frowning.

He elaborated. "The vampires talked about it in the scene before the murder."

Barrie's mind was racing as she scrambled to remember. "I don't think that was in the scene."

She could see Rhiannon and Sailor thinking, too.

"No," Sailor said. "We just saw the movie. That wasn't in the scene."

An odd look flashed across Mick's face in the dark. Then he shrugged. "It's been a while since I've seen it. I could be wrong."

Barrie bit her nails as she looked up at the house. The bloody scene inside was imprinted in her mind, probably forever. The sweet fragrances of jasmine and lemon blossoms that surrounded them just seemed painful in the circumstances.

"I don't see how we're going to be able to keep things under wraps anymore," she said aloud. "Two Hollywood players on that level dying so close together?"

"And both connected to *Otherworld*," Rhiannon brooded.

"People aren't necessarily going to see it that way," Sailor pointed out. "They've both worked on so many other films, Mayo especially. He's green-lit dozens of movies just at WIP. We're seeing it as related to *Otherworld* because Barrie made the connection. And you know how everyone in town expects people to die in threes. No one ever thinks that the deaths are related, they just know that death comes in threes."

It was true. When a major celebrity died it always set the gossip mill speculating over who would be next.

"That's sort of brilliant, Sailor," Rhiannon said. "Maybe we can even encourage that kind of talk."

"No," Barrie said violently, startling the others, who looked at her in shock. "It's too close to what might really happen." The thought was actually terrifying, because she realized she was fully expecting more people—and Others—to die. But before she could say that, there was the sound of footsteps, and everyone turned toward the house as Brodie and Brandt came out into the garden. The cousins all stood, anxious to hear.

"He died from blood loss, caused by a spear through the throat," Brandt reported in a low voice. "Severed the carotid and jugular. Exsanguination was almost instantaneous, occurring within a minute. You can see the blood spray curtained all over the walls. Then the body was moved, but not far. He was speared through the throat and died in front of the fireplace, then hung up on the chimney soon after. Core body temperature indicates he's been dead only a few hours." He turned to Barrie. "You must have found him very shortly after the killer left."

Rhiannon and Sailor eyed Barrie with a combination of relief and accusation.

"I know, I know," she muttered.

"The killer might have been right there in the house with you!" Rhiannon exploded.

"I was invisible. And I'm fine," Barrie defended herself.

Before her cousins could jump on her, Brodie stepped forward to stop the onslaught. "You three can argue about it later." That quiet tone of authority—coming from a six-foot-five-inch Elven homicide detective—silenced the cousins. "Right now we're going to have to move the body again. We can restage the scene as a home invasion and process it that way for the official record, release it to the press. It will scare the hell out of Malibu residents, but it won't hurt people to take a little more care with security, and it's a story that fits the appearance of the scene."

"Can I help?" Mick asked tensely.

Brodie turned to look at him, and again Barrie had the uneasy feeling that he was evaluating Mick, judging him. "We could use the help," he admitted finally, but Barrie felt he wasn't thrilled with the prospect. Then Brodie turned to the cousins. "And I want the three of you to go home," he told them. "Take care of Barrie. Stay in each others' sight. I'll be over as soon as I can."

After they'd all nodded, he stepped closer to Rhiannon, and they spoke together in low tones.

At the same time Mick moved to Barrie's side and took her hand as he leaned into her. "I'll come over after we've finished here. If you want me to," he said in a voice so low and hungry she could have fainted right there.

"I want you to," she said softly.

He squeezed her hand hard and then stepped back from her. "Be careful," he said, holding her eyes.

"Be careful," Rhiannon said to Brodie and Brandt.

And they all parted uneasily.

Chapter 16

Sailor drove Barrie's car home, claiming she shouldn't drive "in her state," and Rhiannon drove her own Volvo. They arrived at the House of the Rising Sun within seconds of each other and got out of the cars to stand in the drive, in the jasmine-scented moonlight beside the pool. The dogs, Sailor's Jonquil and Rhiannon's Wizard, bounded up joyfully to greet their mistresses.

"Thank God that's over," Sailor said as she wrestled Jonquil onto the pavement.

Barrie shook her head. "It's not over. It was a warning."

"But to whom?" Rhiannon asked, as she fended off her enormous Wizard. The three cousins and the dogs drifted toward the pool, which glowed aquamarine under the towering shadows of palm trees.

Wired as she was, Barrie found her legs were shaky.

All those adrenaline crashes tonight, it's a wonder I'm still conscious. She sat on a poolside divan to think over Rhiannon's question. "A warning to anyone connected to *Otherworld*," she finally answered. "Anyone who may have been in a position to expose things that the killer didn't want exposed. Or anyone nosing around about it," she added reluctantly, realizing she was talking about herself.

"That does it," Rhiannon muttered. "I'm not letting you out of my sight until this *is* over."

Barrie kept going; she couldn't help herself. "The question is, what did Branson know?"

"To deserve to die like that…" Sailor shuddered.

"Exactly," Barrie said. "Someone *really* doesn't want the movie made. Branson was killed after his anonymous financial backing was announced, just this afternoon. Now there's no director. No director, no movie. At least for now."

"So, it's a cursed movie again," Rhiannon said.

"It sure is looking that way," Sailor said. And despite the warmth of the soft night breeze, all three of them shivered.

Barrie stared into the depths of the pool. "It's not a curse, it's *someone*." It was all too easy for her to call up the vision of the bloodbath inside the beach house, the director's body, splayed and displayed. "Someone who has no fear, and no remorse, about killing…horribly."

"It's also someone strong enough to overpower a were," Rhiannon pointed out.

"Or someone clever enough to take him by surprise," Barrie said. "Whoever it was, there were no signs of forced entry, and no signs of a struggle on the first floor or the stairs. Which looks like Branson knew his killer, or felt safe with him or her. Enough to let them in, anyway."

"What in the world were you doing there, anyway?" Sailor demanded.

"I got a text from DJ that Branson had agreed to see me and was at home tonight."

"So, it was a setup," Rhiannon said, anger flaring.

"No," Barrie said. "I mean, I don't think so. I mentioned to DJ earlier this evening that I wanted to talk to Branson about *Otherworld*. I think he was—well, it seemed like he was following up on that and had arranged an interview for me." *That was just a few hours ago,* she marveled. It seemed like weeks. She added very reluctantly, "I guess I should tell you—I was attacked at DJ's estate this evening."

"What?"

"Attacked?"

It was like having a stereophonic parental explosion. Her cousins' voices ran together, topping each other in outrage.

"You didn't tell us?"

"And you came here anyway?"

"Was it DJ who attacked you?"

"I'm not sure," Barrie said in a small voice. "But… it was a vampire."

Rhiannon's gasp chilled Barrie's blood.

"A vampire would have the strength to spear a were and lift him up to hang him on that fireplace," Rhiannon said. "It makes sense."

"*And* he knows the scene from the movie. DJ, of all people," Sailor said, incensed. "Did he *seem* guilty? When you saw him this afternoon?"

Barrie paused to think about that. "He seemed like... not like anyone I've ever met. It's hard to tell what he's thinking...or anything about him, really."

"Vampire," Rhiannon said.

"Actor," Sailor said darkly.

"Whatever this is, it's gone far enough," Rhiannon said. "Barrie, you can't just go off investigating on your own like this. People *and* Others are being killed, and it looks to me as if you were meant to find Branson's body the way you did. A warning."

"I agree," Sailor said. "Someone knows you know things they don't want you to know."

"But if I am being warned, then I'm getting close," Barrie said. Her cousins drew themselves up as if they were about to kill her, and she added quickly, "Yes, all right. I'm *not* going to do anything alone again. But if that was a warning, then someone is going to a lot of trouble that they wouldn't be going to unless I'm close to the truth."

"What truth is that?" Rhiannon asked.

"That Johnny Love was murdered on the set of *Otherworld,* and the killer is willing to kill anyone who knows about it to keep that secret, and maybe other secrets, from coming out. Anyone, including Mayo and Tiger and Branson."

Her cousins were silent for a moment, processing that.

"Well, what did DJ tell you?" Sailor demanded.

Barrie paced in the moonlight, frustrated. "I don't

know, that's the problem. He talks in more riddles than the Mad Hatter. Except that—he did say Johnny *and* Branson were talking about using the movie to break the silence and make the existence of Others generally known."

Her cousins stared at her. "That's pretty big," Sailor said.

"You mean, you think Johnny's death—and Branson's—were political?" Rhiannon asked.

Barrie considered this. *Do I think it's political?*

She was shaking her head before she even had a conscious thought. "No. I think it's personal. It *feels* personal."

"Why?" Rhiannon said, and her voice was soft, supportive and encouraging.

Barrie frowned, and let herself answer again without thinking. "Because everything about Johnny Love was personal. I don't know about Branson. But Johnny? People had personal reactions to him, not political ones. People got obsessed with him, for heaven's sake. He made people *feel,* not think." She pounded her fist on the pillar of a trellis. "Johnny is the *key. He's* the one I need to talk to."

And then she lifted her head. "Johnny's the one I need to talk to," she repeated dazedly.

She stood straight. "Merlin!"

Chapter 17

Barrie ran straight through the main house to Merlin's room and skidded to a stop on the polished hardwood floor of the back hall, then reached out to pound on the door. It wasn't very polite, but things had progressed far beyond polite. She was sure Merlin would understand.

Sailor and Rhiannon were at her heels almost instantly, mystified.

Merlin opened the door, and his kind face lit up when he saw the cousins gathered in the hall.

"My, my, all three of you! To what do I owe this happy…" Then he frowned, looking more closely at them. "But you don't look happy. Is something wrong?"

Barrie could barely speak; her words were tripping over each other. "Merlin, I know you weren't able to find Johnny Love in the afterworld. But is there any chance of reaching him if we tried to *call* him? Call him to come here?"

"You mean a séance?" Sailor asked, startled.

"A summoning," Merlin corrected her gently.

Barrie had never done either before, and she didn't care what it was called as long as there was a chance it might work. "Either. Both. Whatever might get us in touch with Johnny. I think it's the only way we're ever going to get to the truth."

Merlin's sky-blue eyes clouded as he considered. "Of course, my dear. It may not be the only way, but it is almost certainly the most direct way." He paced, thinking. "For this, I think we need the library. But bring the oval mirror from your hallway, Barrie. I find that a particularly easy passageway myself."

Barrie and Rhiannon ran and got the mirror, and Merlin directed them to set up the library of Castle House in a configuration that was remarkably like the kind of séance they'd all seen a hundred times in movies and on TV: a round table placed in the center with a cloth over it, candles lit in every corner of the room, the standing mirror set up near the table, a bell, a Bible and a candle placed on top of it.

Merlin directed them, "Now, we all sit at the table and join hands."

The cousins looked at him.

"I feel like I'm in sixth grade again," Sailor admitted, as they extended and clasped their hands.

"You can't argue with a thousand years of results, my dear," Merlin told her.

But once he began to speak, that grade school feeling disappeared entirely. It was partly his gravitas, the utter commitment he had to the mission and the ritual.

Well, if anyone would know how ghosts like to be summoned... Barrie thought.

"Now, you three must visualize this young man, as you most clearly remember him. Close your eyes...."

They obeyed him, letting his voice guide them.

"And now concentrate on his essence, the thing that made his soul most uniquely himself." He let them sit for a while in the cool silence of the room.

Barrie could see the flickering of the candles on her eyelids as she pictured Johnny, that beautiful, golden, mesmerizing star.

And then Merlin's voice spoke out, rich and strong. "We are gathered together in the name of the Unknowable Unknown, to request a communion with the departed. We seek the immortal soul of Johnny Love."

The candles wavered in the darkness.

The antique clock began to strike, and Barrie nearly screamed aloud with the shock of it. She could feel her cousins jump in the chairs next to hers. The clock struck three times, and she shivered. The dead hour, it was called. 3:00 a.m. They had started just in time to catch that powerfully psychic time. From Rhiannon's worried look Barrie knew that her cousin remembered the significance of the hour, as well.

Suddenly all the candles except for one at the far end of the room were snuffed out. All three cousins gasped at the sudden blackness.

Merlin said gently, "We welcome you. You are safe here. We welcome you."

They all sat in suspended silence, their anticipation vibrating in the darkness. Barrie stared toward the mirror. It was hard to make out, but she thought—*thought*—she could see something moving in the mirror, the outlines of a human form, lit by the reflection of the faraway candle.

And then there was no question as a ghostly shape began to materialize in the mirror.

"Oh…my…God," Sailor said so softly Barrie wasn't even sure she'd spoken aloud.

In a backwash of light, they could now see a luminous figure: the unmistakable pale skin, blond hair and blue eyes of an Elven, silky blond strands falling in his face, the long golden smoothness of teenage muscles. The figure was hazy, but he didn't seem to be wearing any clothes at all, and he was as beautiful as an angel. And so familiar…

"Johnny," Barrie breathed. Her heart was beating a mile a minute.

"You called," he said. His voice was faraway, not quite on this plane, but that mocking, teasing inflection was unmistakable. The image in the mirror rippled.

"We did. We wanted to talk to you…." Barrie suddenly found she was crying. "I'm sorry. I'm so, so sorry."

"Ah, that's sweet of you, love," Johnny said in that rich and ever-so-slightly Irish voice. "It's not so bad, really. Might even be getting used to it."

"We—" Barrie started, and then she realized she had no idea at all how she was supposed to address a ghost.

"Johnny, we miss you here. We want you to be happy. We want you to be at peace. But your—" she groped for the right word "—your passing was so hard, for so many people. We want to make it right, on this side."

"I don't understand," the beautiful image in the mirror said dreamily, then wavered. For a moment Barrie was afraid he would disappear. But the image shimmered and clarified, and his blue eyes looked out from the mirror again.

"Johnny, were you murdered? Did someone kill you?"

The image in the mirror shook his golden hair in confusion. "Did someone kill me?" he repeated.

"You don't know?" Barrie asked, equally confused. She could feel her cousins stir uneasily on either side of her; it was all so puzzling.

"How I got here?" He shimmered again, liquid gorgeousness, and his exquisite face turned haunted. "It's so hard…so long ago…so dark…so much chaos…"

Barrie could barely see through her tears, but she could feel Sailor trembling by her side and saw tears running down her cousin's face. And when she looked to Rhiannon, it was to see that she was fighting sobs, as well. The feeling she and her cousins shared galvanized her. She blinked through the water in her eyes, and she made her voice soft and strong.

"Johnny, I don't know if you can see us. But we loved you. We *love* you. So many, many people loved you. We want you to be at peace."

Barrie could feel Sailor and Rhiannon on both sides of her, their hands tightly squeezing hers. They were nodding, aligned with her.

"We do, Johnny."

"We want to make it right."

"We all do," Barrie said. "Please, if you can, tell us… tell us what you know of your passing so we can make it right."

Merlin said softly, "He may not know. He may not be able to say. That's often the way in death by trauma."

Maybe it was wrong, but Barrie had to know. She had to push. She leaned forward, looking into the mirror. "Johnny, did someone hurt you? Did someone kill you?"

"How very many ways there are to kill…." the golden reflection mused. "I can't tell you, love. I would if I could." And the beautiful, ethereal being stared out of the mirror, his presence so intense, so real, that Barrie froze and forgot that she was looking at a ghost, just a reflection of a ghost.

And he was looking back at her just as intensely, and suddenly a strange and knowing look crossed his face.

"But someone can. Oh, someone so close to you. Someone who was there. *Ask Robbie,*" the beautiful specter whispered.

"Robbie?" Barrie stammered.

Sailor and Rhiannon were frozen at her sides, their hands clenching hers.

"How can I ask Robbie?" Barrie asked, bewildered. "Robbie is dead."

Across the table from her, Merlin said softly, "I think perhaps not, my dear."

"Oh, you know Robbie. You *know* Robbie," the beautiful ghost said. And the second repetition carried an inflection so carnal that Barrie understood what Johnny was saying.

Robbie.

Mick.

Mick *was* Robbie.

She felt herself losing her grip, even losing consciousness. The room around her no longer felt substantial.

"Ask Robbie," said the ghost of Johnny Love. "Ask Robbie what happened."

And everything went black.

Chapter 18

Barrie blinked her eyes open…and found herself on a sofa in the dim great room of Castle House. Rhiannon was sitting on a footstool beside the couch; she held a cool, wet washcloth pressed to Barrie's forehead. Sailor was pacing in the shadows of the room but started forward in relief as Barrie moved.

Barrie's first instinct was to sit up, but Rhiannon put a hand on her shoulder, gently keeping her still.

"Hold on, hon. Just lie back."

Barrie's head was pounding, but it wasn't from fainting. "He said…"

"I know, sweetie."

"But it can't be, it can't be." Even as Barrie was denying it, she felt the sick sense of truth in her gut. All the mystery. Mick's uncanny knowledge of the movie, his strange asides about the film, about Johnny, about DJ, his knowing just who to talk to to get the information they needed. He knew too much. She had always been aware that he just knew too much.

Mick was the long-lost Robbie Anderson.

She struggled to get up again, and this time Rhiannon let her, but she was looking concerned. "Sweetie, I think you're in shock. Why don't you just sleep here tonight?"

"You can just crawl in with me," Sailor encouraged. "We can all sort this out in the morning. Everything's always easier in the morning."

Their loving concern made Barrie want to weep; it felt as if someone had scraped off all her skin, and she didn't want anyone looking at her.

"I want Sophie," Barrie said, and stood shakily. "I want my own bed." Sometimes a cat was the best comfort you could hope for. But she also knew that Mick was coming over, and she wanted to be alone to confront him, although she wasn't about to tell the other two that.

Her cousins exchanged a glance, and Barrie flared up. "I'm fine. I'll be fine. Look in on me all you want to but just let me sleep." And she didn't look at them, so she wouldn't have to see in their faces how *not* fine she was.

She was in bed with the cat, in that half sleep where things were happening that could only happen in dreams but you were still half-awake and you couldn't tell the real from the dream. Johnny Love was in her room, but there were no walls. She was in the werewolf murder scene from *Otherworld,* only the werewolf hanging on the stone wall was alive, growling and writhing and powerful enough to spring—

A door opened somewhere, and Barrie was shocked into full reality; it was her own bedroom door.

And Robbie walked in.

She hadn't given him a key, she hadn't left her door open, but of course none of that mattered to a talented shifter. He could turn into an ant, a mite, and get in pretty much however and wherever he wanted. Certainly he'd gotten into her, she thought bitterly.

He just stood at the foot of the bed, as if waiting for her to give him permission to come forward, and he was reflected in all the mirrors of the room, illusion on top of illusion. She was silent as she just looked at his face, really looked at him. He didn't look like Robbie Anderson. He had copper hair and green eyes, unlike Robbie Anderson's gold-brown hair and golden gaze. His features were different. It was only the surreal beauty of him that gave him away.

He looked at her in the bed, and she felt the familiar fire in her body. It wasn't fair.

"I've been calling," he said, his voice low. "You haven't picked up for hours. I was worried."

He moved closer, and she knew she had to say something then, to stop him, because in the next second it wouldn't matter who he was or what he intended to do to her, it could be anything, as long as he touched her again.

"I know who you are," she said, her mouth dry and her heart pounding off the charts.

He didn't stop in his tracks, exactly, but he was suddenly very still.

"Johnny told me. He couldn't say if you killed him,

but he did say you would know what happened." She picked up the cat then and hugged her close to her chest.

"*Johnny* told you? What did you do, have a séance?" He stopped, and Barrie could tell he understood. To his credit, he didn't try to pretend he didn't know what she was talking about. And in a million years she couldn't have interpreted the look on his face.

"How is he?" Mick asked abruptly, and if she hadn't been so completely confused about everything, she would have said his voice was longing.

She shook her head and felt tears close by. "He's... *lost*. Unresolved. He doesn't actually know what happened to him."

"I didn't kill him, Barrie," Mick said, and as he shook his head, the mirrors in her bedroom reflected him, hundreds of images.

"I don't even know who you're trying to be!" she cried out. "How can I believe you?"

"Just let me explain," he said. She waited, and he paced the room, his reflections pacing with him, and it was a long time before he stopped and spoke.

"You have to understand. I don't think of myself as Robbie Anderson. Ever. I left him behind fifteen years ago."

"But how could you just disappear? You were so famous."

The moonlight through the French doors caught his face, and for a moment he looked as ghostly as Johnny had. "I shifted. I shifted into someone else permanently. Someone different. Someone I could actually *want* to be."

Barrie was silent, just looking at him.

"I was afraid what happened to Johnny would happen to me."

She stared at him. "You thought someone would kill you?"

"That and...other things." He began to pace again, laughed without humor. "I thought I could lose my soul. I know that sounds dramatic." He shook his head. "I told you I used people. When you're as famous as we were, the three of us, so young, you have a lot of people lining up to be used. It was like...realizing I was hooked on a drug and I needed to quit, go cold turkey, before someone really got hurt. Like me. And about a dozen other people."

His voice lowered, became raw, painful. "Johnny had *just* died. No one said it was murder, just that he'd OD'd. DJ was so coked out, speeded out, whatever else he was doing, I couldn't even talk to him anymore. I didn't know what I wanted or who I could trust, all I knew was that everyone was wanting something different from me and it was going to destroy me just as surely as it had destroyed my friends. So, I just—disappeared."

"Where did you go?" she asked in spite of herself. She was wary, but fascinated.

"It's not like I had an actual plan," he said wryly. "I just got in the car and drove. I went north. I don't know, I was thinking Yosemite, the redwoods, anything. Which turned out to be good thinking, if there had been any thought behind it at all, because a few people remembered seeing me on the coast road, a gas station guy and someone in a diner, and when people started looking for me and couldn't find me some people assumed I'd been in a car accident, that I went off a cliff or something, only they couldn't find the car or me.

"When I got myself together enough to read the papers, I realized that's what they thought and that I could use it. So, I drove the car back down the coast and pushed it off a cliff. I had the windows open and a door open, and I figured people would find it and think my body washed away. But no one ever found the car. It's still there, I guess, off Highway One, somewhere near Santa Cruz."

He had his hands on the windowsill and was leaning on it, and Barrie thought it looked as if he were looking out over that cliff. He smiled thinly. "But crashing the car that night was like burying myself. I never went back to that person."

"Then what?" she asked reluctantly, but compelled.

"I had some time before people started looking for me. Since no one found the car, no one knew for sure I was gone until I didn't show up for my first day of shooting on the new movie Darius had lined up for me. I feel terrible about that now, how disruptive it must have been for everyone involved, but back then I didn't think anything of it at all. It was like none of it had anything to do with me anymore, like Robbie was another person already.

"Anyway, I had time—I had all this time to clean out my bank accounts. I was emancipated from my father, who never did give a damn about anything but the money he could make off me, anyway. I was only renting a place in the Hollywood Hills, had no possessions that really meant anything to me." His smile twisted.

"I did, however, have a pile of money. Darius had gotten me top dollar for my last couple of roles. So, I was set, as far as that goes. I had plenty of time to figure out what to do with myself. I ended up out in the desert, in Joshua Tree." He gave her a faint smile. "I always was a U-2 fan. I rented a cabin, did some hiking, but mostly sat looking out at the desert and the stars—that's the *real* stars—and practicing holding a shift for hours, days, weeks...until I could just *be* that person full-time without even thinking about it."

It was such a fascinating story that Barrie was forgetting to be angry. It was a remarkable thing to have done at sixteen. Desperate and lifesaving and crazy and eminently sane, all at the same time.

"There are a lot of Others out in the desert, the ones who can't take city life—or don't want to. I met an old guy, werewolf, who ran a whole slate of recovery groups that served a whole lot of little towns around the national park, and that's when I started thinking that I could use all that money I'd piled up to do some good for other Others."

"How long have you been back in L.A.?" she said, too curious not to ask.

"Oh, a while. Eight or nine years. I went to Europe first, there was a lot of capital there for a long time, and a lot of private interest in foundations for Others. That's where I started to build a base of endowments. But I missed California, and I finally had enough time and distance to come back."

He turned from the window and looked at her. She was still sitting up in bed, holding the cat, watching him.

"And that's it." He looked drained, as if he had relived every moment as he was telling her about it.

"That's a lot," Barrie said.

He moved toward the bed, but then stopped. "Barrie, I didn't kill Johnny. He was my best friend, the closest thing to a brother I've ever had. It nearly killed me when he died."

She pressed her back against the headboard of the bed. "But you knew that someone *did* kill him."

He hesitated. "I *thought* so. But not until I'd killed myself off—at least as far as the real world was concerned—and had time to think about it. It took me months to even be able to look at the whole thing."

He'd been sixteen. Barrie's heart ached for him.

"But I don't know who killed him, I swear. By the time I'd worked it out that someone might have, it was too late to look into it. I didn't exist anymore, anyway."

And finally he was silent.

Barrie's mind was whirling; she didn't know what she was feeling or thinking. And evidently she was squeezing the cat just a little too hard, because Sophie meowed in protest and pulled away from her, jumping off the bed in a huff. Deserted, Barrie looked at Mick. "Were you ever going to tell me?" she asked in a small voice.

He looked at her. "I'm not sure," he admitted.

She felt as if he'd knifed her in the heart. "That's honest, I guess," she managed.

"Barrie, please understand. Robbie died when Johnny died. I buried him so long ago."

"But I can't..." She struggled with what she was trying to say. "We can't be anything together unless you tell me everything. I need to know you. *All* of you."

"I *want* you to know all of me." He moved slowly closer to the bed and sat on the edge of it without touching her. "Can we start over, one step at a time?"

Barrie was roiling with emotion and confusion. She knew she should be remembering that no matter what he said, Robbie Anderson could be Johnny's killer. And if he *was* Johnny's killer, he could have killed Saul Mayo and Tiger, and Travis Branson, too.

But she didn't believe it. At least, she didn't believe he'd killed Johnny.

It was a little easier to believe that he might have killed Mayo. Certainly there were things Mick, or Robbie, wanted to stay hidden: his whole new identity and life, for example. And the plans for a remake of the movie might have threatened that. But would he go so far as to kill to protect his anonymity?

His whole life seemed to be about helping others— and Others. As much as Barrie knew that she needed to be careful, she just couldn't believe he was a killer.

But maybe he had devoted his life to helping others to make up for having killed Johnny.

It was all so much to take in, and she wasn't doing very well at it. Especially because the only thing she wanted to do was reach out for him, to hold and comfort the haunted man who had been that haunted boy, and who was looking at her now, asking her to love him. . . .

"No," she said. She threw back the covers to get out of bed, and he stood with her.

"Barrie..."

"No."

She tried to push past him, but he caught her hand and she froze. He stood still in the dark, looking down at her hand in his. Then he bent his head, and his lips were on her wrist, kissing her palm, and she could feel tears on his face. She reached with her other hand, touching his bowed head, feeling the softness of his hair, and he sank to his knees as if he could no longer stand. She stood there as he twined his arms around her legs and pressed his head against her waist, and the feeling was so sensual and so desperate that her own knees buckled and she swayed against him. He caught her, held her.... She looked down at him...

...and he drew her down, into his lap, into his arms, and his mouth crushed down on hers and she was lost.

Chapter 19

She was making love with Mick, and then he was Robbie, and then he was Johnny. As he moved on top of her, inside her, he was constantly changing, shifting, and every different shift was reflected multiple times in the mirrors, like hundreds of movie screens projecting them.

Barrie looked into the mirrors, at the muscles rippling in his back as he moved inside her, and she saw the trident tattoo there, and with every shift only the tattoo stayed the same....

Barrie started awake. It was still night, and Mick was sleeping at her side, his arm flung over her in a strong and protective embrace. As she regained full consciousness she was all too aware of the length of his body against hers, the intoxicating feeling of his bare skin covering hers....

She forced herself to shut off the sensations that flooded instantly through her and eased out from under his arm. She sat up carefully, an inch at a time, so as not to wake him.

And then she leaned over him to look at his back. The trident tattoo from her dream was there on his left shoulder blade.

But that's not right, she thought with a shiver. And her dream danced in her head.

She rose slowly from the bed and crept out of the room.

Outside in the hall, she eased the bedroom door closed and moved noiselessly into the living room.

She went to the entertainment console and grabbed the *Otherworld* DVD from its shelf, then hurried to the computer she had set up on her desk in the corner.

She slid the DVD into the disk drive and used the remote to click through the movie until she came to a scene that was etched in her memory, as it doubtless was etched in the memory of millions of teenage—and not-so-teenage—fans: the three young stars bathing nude in a hot spring. Barrie bit her nails as she watched through the scene, focusing intently on Johnny and Robbie. Especially on the lingering shots of their naked backs.

Then she suddenly leaned forward and skipped through to the end of the film, the final confrontation in the mirrored throne room of the Avalon Ballroom. She leaned forward and paused on a shot that showed a glimpse of Johnny Love's bare back, so brief it took her several attempts to freeze the specific frame. When she finally did, it was there: a trident tattoo, just like the one on Robbie's back.

But in the hot springs scene, *only Robbie had the tattoo.*

"What are you doing?"

The voice came from behind her, and she spun to face Mick, standing shirtless in the arch of the doorway.

He looked from her face to the frozen image on the computer screen. And she could see a million things on his face, none of which she could interpret.

Her voice was shaking as she spoke. "Johnny didn't have a tattoo like that. Only in this last scene."

Mick was silent.

"I guess you're going to say you all got matching tattoos some time during the movie, between the hot springs scene and the last scenes." She turned to the computer screen and pointed to the trident on Johnny's shoulder. "But that's not a fresh tattoo. The colors are faded. It's yours. That's not Johnny, that's *you*. You forgot to change it when you shifted."

She turned back to face him and spoke softly. "And I know you could do it. If anyone in the world could shift into Johnny and make everyone believe it, it was you."

He looked at her in the dark. "Yes. It's me. I was playing him. That's why the set was closed."

Barrie felt a dull pain in her heart. "He *did* die on set."

Mick looked away. "Yes."

"How?"

"They told me he OD'd. It wasn't hard to believe, not the way he and DJ—well, all of us—had been partying. Mayo and Branson came to me and said that Johnny was dead and the film was dead, too, if we didn't figure out a way to shoot the last scenes."

His face crumpled; he looked haunted and terribly young. "I was a kid. I was crazy with…loss, grief, fear, a million things that I couldn't even put into words. And I was an actor." Now his face was bitter. "It's hard for anyone outside the business to grasp the mind-set. Your every move is orchestrated by other people. My whole life was based on doing what directors and producers told me to do."

He swallowed. "They said I should do it for Johnny, that it would make everyone remember him, his last role. Of course the only thing they cared about was getting the film in the can, but I believed them."

Mick closed his eyes briefly and then opened them. "I shifted," he said. "I shifted and I played him. The last scenes are all me. If you look at the editing, we're never on-screen together. They had a stand-in on set with me for two-shots, and a stand-in playing me when I was playing Johnny."

"That's why he seems so different at the end," Barrie murmured, without realizing she was speaking until she heard her own words.

"But I don't know who killed him. By the time I'd worked it out that someone might have, it was too late to look into it. I didn't exist anymore, anyway."

"And when were you going to tell me all that? Or were you?"

It was as if she'd stabbed him in the heart. "Barrie. I was." He put his hands to his head and paced. "I'm not used to telling that truth to *anyone*. Please believe me. It's not that I don't want to. It's just that it's going to take time."

He looked at her pleadingly, but she shook her head, slowly at first and then violently. "I don't know. I can't think!" she exploded. She sat on a couch and instantly sprang up again. "I have to think. I think you should go."

He flinched as if she'd slapped him, but he nodded. "Then I will."

She felt her heart breaking as she watched him walk out. She stood without moving until she'd heard the front door close.

Something brushed her leg, and she nearly jumped out of her skin, then realized Sophie was at her feet.

Barrie picked up the cat…and burst into tears.

Chapter 20

Barrie wasn't sure how long she was curled up on the couch, crying. She might have slept. She might have dreamed. It felt like her whole life was over and the only thing that was keeping her breathing was the warm, furry presence of the little cat nestled on top of her.

When her phone buzzed she thought through her dull gray haze that it was the alarm clock, and she couldn't for the life of her remember any appointment she had, or anything in the outside world to live for, for that matter.

Then she reached out and felt the phone. The screen read Blocked Caller. It wasn't Mick, then, so she answered it, a dry-mouthed hello.

"Is this the Keeper?"

The voice on the other end was familiar, but so hoarse she could barely make it out.

"Yes…who is—"

"He came to me tonight."

Barrie realized with a jolt that it was DJ on the other end of the line. His voice was slurred, and there was a strange intensity behind it.

"Who did?" she managed.

"Johnny. I woke up, and he was standing in my room."

She was awake now, trying to process what she was hearing. *A dream? Or a ghost? Or could it possibly have been Mick?* She was reeling, not knowing what to think.

"You have to help me." DJ was babbling now. He sounded terrified. "What does he want? What do I do?"

Barrie sat up and tried to focus herself and him. "What did he do? What did he say to you?"

"He said I was next."

She felt a cold chill run through her whole body.

"He said Travis is dead. Murdered. Hung up like the werewolf from *Otherworld.*"

Barrie's mind was racing. The only way DJ could have known that was if Johnny really had come to him. Or if DJ had been there to see Travis Branson dead. Or killed him himself…

Or if Mick was there impersonating Johnny, a voice she didn't want to hear said inside her head.

The actor was speaking on the line. "And he said—he said he talked to you and you could explain."

All right, there was no way DJ could have known they'd had a séance and talked to Johnny. That made his story much more plausible. Beyond that…DJ was a movie star and a vampire, but at the moment he sounded like a terrified teenager.

Things were so weird already, it was entirely possible that Johnny *had* visited DJ. She felt responsible, as if she'd opened a door.

And then that implacable voice inside her said, *But Mick could have done it, too. He's the only one besides Sailor and Rhiannon who knows we had a séance tonight.*

She squeezed her eyes closed to shut out the voice. "Are you alone?" she asked the actor.

"I can't find Brad," he said, and his voice was shaking. "He's not in his room."

Not that Brad would be much good, anyway, Barrie thought.

"I'm calling the police now," she told him. "A detective who's an Other, Brodie McKay. You can trust him. But right now you need to lock yourself away somewhere with a weapon, do you understand?"

The actor didn't answer.

"DJ?" she said sharply into the phone.

The line had gone dead.

Barrie redialed frantically, but the call went straight to voice mail. She stood with the phone in her hand, paralyzed, then she spoke firmly and authoritatively, for anyone who might listen to the call. "Do what I told you. We're coming right now. The police will be there any minute."

She punched off and hit Brodie's number, praying he would pick up. She was elated to hear his golden Elven voice. "Barrie. Is something wrong?"

"I just got a call from DJ," she said in a rush. "We have to get over there right now. He thinks someone is in his house and coming after him, and I just lost phone contact with him."

There was a short silence. "Are you sure this is for real?" he asked warily.

She thought of DJ's terrified voice…and reminded herself that he was an award-winning actor.

"Brodie, I'm not sure of anything," she said desperately. "But he did say that Johnny's ghost had come to him to warn him, and he knew that we'd had a séance and summoned Johnny. I think it's for real."

Brodie's voice was tense but calm. "I'm teleporting straight there, then. *Do not* go there, Barrie, do you hear me?"

"Yes, I hear you," she said automatically.

"Good," he said. "I'll call you from the house as soon as I arrive."

"Brodie, be careful," she said, but he'd already hung up.

Barrie jumped up from the couch in a frenzy of anxiety and confusion. What was going on? Had the ghost of Johnny really visited DJ to warn him of danger? Was the killer about to try to kill one of the few remaining witnesses to Johnny Love's murder?

Or was DJ trying to lure her back to his place to finish the job he'd started that afternoon? In which case, had she just put Brodie in mortal danger by sending him to the lair of a killer vampire?

She felt a jolt of adrenaline and fear at the thought. Elven could teleport and reach a location within seconds; it was one of their innate skills. The great danger was that teleporting weakened them. Once he'd teleported, Brodie would be in no shape to confront a crazed vampire.

And there was another horrifying possibility, the one that inner voice kept nudging her toward. Was Mick once again playing Johnny, appearing to DJ as Johnny for nefarious purposes of his own?

All the various possibilities were almost too much for her to bear. But at least she knew she wasn't thinking entirely rationally.

I need help. I need Rhiannon and Sailor.

She grabbed her phone to call Rhiannon—and saw that she had recent texts from both her cousins, both marked with their code for "urgent." She hadn't been answering her phone for hours while she was with Mick.

She quickly read through the texts in increasing disbelief.

There had been an emergency Keeper call, a report of an Elven and a vampire in an armed standoff with human hostages. Both Rhiannon and Sailor had been summoned in response to the crisis.

"What the hell is happening tonight?" Barrie muttered. "It's not even a full moon." Then she read carefully through the texts again with increasing suspicion. What really were the chances that there would be a joint Elven/vampire emergency happening tonight along with everything else? There was something fishy about it. In fact, the whole situation smelled.

She punched Rhiannon's number and got routed straight to voice mail.

"It's me," she blurted into the phone. "Where are you?

I think that crisis call you two got was a trick. *Be careful,* and call me as soon as you get this."

She called Sailor and got her voice mail, too, and left the same message. Then she checked her own messages and was dismayed to see that Brodie hadn't called her yet.

But he said he'd call as soon as he was at the house. What's happening?

She called Brodie herself, but again got nothing but voice mail.

She threw the phone down on the couch and paced the living room, biting her nails.

Okay. Okay. I'm going to get in the car, and I'm going to drive toward Brentwood. Then at least I'll be close by if Brodie needs help.

She couldn't just sit there waiting to see what was happening. At least driving was doing *something.*

She picked up the phone again and ran for her bedroom to dress.

She wasn't speeding—exactly—but it was after 3:00 a.m., and she made pretty good time on the 101 to the 405 toward Brentwood. Every minute that ticked by made her more nervous. It had been almost a half hour since she'd talked to Brodie, and he still hadn't called her back. Teleporting was instant, that was the whole point, so he must have been at DJ's house for all that time.

"What's happening?" she muttered aloud.

And she couldn't keep her mind off the really worrisome thing: that teleporting left an Elven very weak.

What if he'd been ambushed?

They were dealing with a killer of three people, possibly four.

Barrie grew increasingly agitated as she thought about it. Rhiannon would never forgive her if anything happened to Brodie. No, that wasn't true, but Rhiannon would never *recover* if anything happened to Brodie, which was even worse.

The phone trilled on the seat, and she snatched it up, answering without regard to the California Safe Driving Act.

"Brodie!" she said breathlessly.

There was a slight silence, and then Mick's voice. "Not exactly."

"Oh," she said, conflicted. "I'm sorry, I really do need some time—"

"Barrie, listen. I'm at DJ's estate, but there's something wrong. The house is empty, the gate and the front door are standing wide open and—"

"What are you doing there?" she demanded, feeling another spike of adrenaline. Things were moving too fast, and she didn't understand what it all meant.

"I came to talk to DJ. After what you said…I realized that he—that the two of us may be the only ones besides the killer who really know anything about what happened to Johnny. And that it's time for us to talk it through, all of it—and figure out exactly what *did* happen, before someone else gets killed. Only now I'm afraid I might be too late."

She felt a wave of fear for him. "You have to get out of there."

"I can't do that. Something's obviously going down. DJ might be in trouble...."

"Mick, no...." she said desperately.

"Barrie, I have to. What else can I do?"

"No! Wait—"

But he'd already disconnected.

"Damn it." She threw the phone back on the seat beside her and pressed her foot to the gas. She was going to kill him. Unless someone else did it first.

Mick was right. As Barrie drove up the winding road toward DJ's estate, the huge metal gates were standing open, an eerie sight in the moonlight, and the guardhouse was empty.

Even more alarming, the house was completely dark as she drove up the circular drive. Mick's Bentley was in front of the stairs. There was no sign of Brodie.

And at the top of the sweep of steps the front door was standing wide open, a black hole into the house.

"This is so not good," she murmured as she stared up at it through the windshield. She stopped the car and just looked. The mansion was imposing enough during the day. At night, under the moon, it was Vlad's castle for sure.

A man...no, two men she loved might be inside, possibly in great danger. Brodie... She'd admired him, and respected him, but in the past twenty minutes she'd realized that she loved him. He was going to be family, and that was how she thought of him. He would come to her rescue in any circumstance, and she was fully ready to come to his.

And Mick…Mick was more complicated. As intimate as they'd been, she still didn't know him at all. She had a sense she could be more intimate with him than with anyone she'd ever known, the kind of intimate she'd barely dared to dream about.

And if he turned out to be a killer, she was in real trouble, because she loved him. She loved him. And that meant she had to go in.

She looked up at the Gothic, towering front of the house, biting her nails.

She knew it would be lethal to try entering without camouflage, and she wavered between invisibility and some other form. Either way she would be vulnerable to detection by an Other but safer than if she did nothing.

She decided on invisibility because it was easier for her to hold for longer. She killed the overhead light in the car and opened the door, then sat in the dark and breathed, focusing her awareness on her astral body, the energetic field that surrounded every living creature, and brought it into focus so that spirit force field concealed her physical body. She breathed in and out for prolonged minutes and then looked down at herself and saw nothing.

It's showtime, she thought grimly.

Chapter 21

Walking into the house was like walking into a jungle. She could hear the night cries of the birds in the African Room, and the rush of the artificial river. As she walked silently, carefully past the archway, her pulse spiked as she caught the gleam of eyes in the darkness. *Steve,* she thought to herself, remembering the massive stuffed tiger. *It's just Steve.*

And now that it was dark she was startled to see that the arch of the ceiling was dotted with thousands of glowing stars, or lights masquerading as stars, and arranged in perfect perspective. She could pick out constellations, Orion, Cassiopeia, the Pleiades, just like in a real night sky.

But she didn't move into the African Room; it felt like too public a place, too much of a display, for real business to be conducted there. Wherever DJ and the others were, she was sure it wasn't here.

In the enormous entry hall there was a huge spiraling staircase leading upward. But she knew there had to be a downstairs, as well; vampires liked the underground, craved it. She was willing to bet there was an extensive lower level to the house. And instinctively she felt that this would be where DJ's private rooms were, the ones he kept for himself and his intimates.

A central column beside the stairway housed an elevator, which no doubt would get her where she needed to go, but using it was out of the question; she couldn't risk the noise of the machinery.

But through an arched doorway she found a tiled hall leading to a stairway leading downward.

She stopped at the top of the steps, staring into the ominous opening, feeling a chill that had nothing to do with the slight draft coming from the stairwell. She had to struggle to hold on to her glamour as she looked down the steep descent.

There were candles flickering in candelabra mounted on the stone walls, an eerie and live trail of light straight out of a Gothic horror movie.

Naturally the whole house is production designed, Barrie told herself. *This is no different from the African Room.*

But an African jungle by day had an entirely different feeling than a vampire's cellar at night.

She forced down a wave of fear, took a breath and started down the stairs, stepping carefully to keep her descent as soundless as possible.

The stairway spiraled downward, and every ten or twelve steps there was some alcove in the wall housing a disturbing tableau: a bleached white skeleton dressed in a priest's vestments, a suit of armor with glowing, inhuman eyes behind the visor, what looked like a genuine Francis Bacon painting of a grotesque pope on a throne, a mirror with a moving shadow inside it, eerily insubstantial.

It's the Haunted Mansion, okay? she told herself. *Illusion. Nothing to get excited about.*

The real danger was coming.

Her unease mounted as she continued downward; the stairs seemed to go on forever, and she felt her pulse rising with each step.

This is unreal. How far underground does it go?

At last she hit the bottom of the stairs, which opened into a dim vestibule with an arched door on the far side. Barrie took another breath and moved silently across the small, round room to the doorway.

And stepped into a dream.

She had to fight to get her bearings as she looked around in astonishment.

She was standing inside the climax of *Otherworld*. It was the huge circular ballroom from the film, with mirrors set in the velvet-draped walls and archways leading off into what in the movie had been balconies overlooking the ocean, but here, underground, she had no idea what could be beyond those pillars and arches.

The ballroom before her was not merely a vast empty space. In the film the location had been being used by the three young Others as a sort of living space and throne room; it was divided into multiple galleries where there were canopied beds, an area with a long plank table for feasting, statues and suits of armor, and arches and mirrors, installations of mannequins in sexually compromising positions, cages with collections of elaborate costumes, and toys from all eras of civilization, even a full-size carnival carousel. In the exact center of the room was an open space that looked like a throne room, only circular, with three ornate thrones facing each other. There were standing wrought-iron candelabra and candles in wall holders, creating a live wash of flickering light.

As she gazed around in wonder and dismay, it occurred to her that perhaps this actually *was* the set, disassembled and reassembled right here.

Her heart was racing so fast she could hardly focus on her own thoughts. *This is craziness. DJ must be completely obsessed with the film. And if he's this obsessed, he could very well be the killer.*

She was beginning to see the very big flaw in her plan. The house was enormous; there were a million places where Mick could be, where Brodie or DJ could be—and where the killer could be. There had been no sign of anyone yet, and she couldn't call out for fear of drawing the attention of the wrong person.

The underground hall that she was now in was as huge as the African Room, perhaps bigger, as there seemed to be passageways leading off in all different directions.

But as she looked around her, she realized that was the least of her problems.

Just as in the movie, the curved walls of the ballroom were lined with mirrors.

And the trouble with a glamour is that it tricks the eye but not a mirror or camera.

So, anytime she was in the line of sight of a mirror, *she* was in sight. In the relatively uncluttered place where she was standing now, she was surrounded by hundreds of her own reflections.

She stared at herself across the room and instantly dropped to her knees beside a statue to get out of the mirrors' range.

Now what? she asked herself with a touch of hysteria as she hugged the floor. *Crawl across the floor to the staircase? Find the elevator and take a chance on that? Turn into a spider and hide until this is over?*

And then suddenly her heart leaped with terror…as she felt hands on her shoulders, pulling her up.

Chapter 22

Barrie felt a scream rising in her throat, and then a hand was clamped tightly around her mouth and she stared into the black and fathomless gaze...of DJ.

He put a finger to his lips and stared into her eyes to see if she was going to cooperate. She nodded, shaking, and he released her.

He must have seen me in the mirrors, she realized.

"What's happening?" she whispered. "Are you all right?"

"We're not alone," he mouthed.

"Who?" she choked out.

He raised his hands to silently indicate *I don't know.*

"Have you seen Brodie? Or Mick?"

He frowned, even as his eyes were darting around them in the dark, searching for anyone hidden in the shadows. "Who are they?"

She didn't have time to explain who. She was too busy wondering *where* they were.

"You haven't seen anyone?" she whispered.

"I *feel* someone," DJ answered ominously.

You're a vampire, she thought. *Turn into mist or something.*

But that wasn't fair. He was also a troubled soul, psychologically fixated at the age of sixteen in a haunted past.

I need to get him out of here, she thought. *We can look for Brodie and Mick just as well on the way out, and it's better than staying here.*

"Come on," she whispered. "We're getting out of here."

The actor shook his head wildly. "I can't leave. I've tried. Someone's put up a wall. There are hexed crosses up at every exit. I'm locked in."

Barrie's heart dropped in dismay. *This is a planned attack, then, an ambush. And by someone who knows the rules of the Otherworld.*

The clink and rattling of chains echoed from somewhere in the vast, silent room, and she and DJ both froze. They *weren't* alone.

Then DJ put a finger to his lips and held up a hand, indicating she should stay hidden.

He stepped forward toward the sound, into the circular space that held the three thrones. "Who's there?" he called out in an impressively menacing voice.

He is *an actor,* Barrie thought from her position crouched below him. But then, as she looked up, she saw a look flicker across DJ's face: confusion, recognition, wariness, disbelief.

"Who are you?" he said to someone Barrie couldn't see.

Another voice came from the darkness. "Come on, Deej, we don't have time for this. You know who I am."

From her hiding place, Barrie felt a profound shock. It was Mick's voice, but he sounded like a different person, a younger person.

She crawled closer to a standing screen so she could peer out through the cutouts to see what was going on. She nearly gave herself away; she had to bite back a gasp. She was looking out not at Mick Townsend but at Robbie Anderson. Golden-haired, golden-eyed, those incredible cheekbones, that lithe body. Not a teenager anymore, but he didn't look much older, either.

"Rob?" DJ said hoarsely. He sounded dazed, all posturing gone. He sounded like a child. "It can't be."

"It is," Mick said. "For tonight, anyway. Just like old times," he added, looking across the throne circle at DJ. He glanced around at the room, the thrones, the whole setup from *Otherworld.* "Just exactly like old times." To Barrie his voice sounded dangerous, uninterpretable.

"All the ghosts are walking tonight," DJ muttered. "Where have you been? All this time... Damn, Robbie—"

"It doesn't matter now. Time is what we don't have. People are dying, and we have to stop it."

"Oh, I'm going to stop it. I'm going to stop *you.*"

Suddenly DJ lunged and grabbed Barrie, hauling her up off the floor. His arm was hooked around her neck, and she could feel that incredible vampire strength; she was completely immobilized and knew he could crush her throat in an instant.

Mick/Robbie stood completely still, but in the wavering light of the candles she could read terror on his strange, beautiful face. "Let her go," he said slowly and carefully. "She's got nothing to do with this."

DJ's grip tightened on Barrie's throat. "But you're the one who brought her into it. What were you looking for, a cover story?"

"I don't know what you're talking about," Mick said. He looked at Barrie's face, and she could feel him willing her to stay still.

"I know you killed Johnny," the actor lashed out. "Was Mayo going to spill it after all this time? Maybe some publicity scheme he was cooking up for the remake?"

Barrie felt the rage in him, vibrating through the arms that held her captive, and she felt light-headed. *It can't be.*

Mick shook his head. "Now you're saying I killed Johnny, Mayo—and Branson? Come on, Deej, *why?* Saul—anyone would want him dead, and you know I'm not grieving for Travis. But Johnny? You think I could kill Johnny?"

DJ stared across the circle at him, and the actor's face looked like a Greek sculpture of Dionysus, and no older than when the two boys had been in the movie. "I *know* you did, pal."

Barrie's heart dropped to her shoes. He absolutely meant it; she could feel it in his body against hers.

DJ looked around them at the set, the scene of the

movie. "You think I didn't know? I was fucked up to the moon, but you think I couldn't tell you from Johnny?"

His black eyes bored into Mick's golden ones. "Oh, I knew. I even understood. Hell, we all wanted to kill Johnny at some point. You just got to it first." He laughed, a hollow sound. "Those last scenes, they kept talking about camera angles and reflections, and yeah, I could barely stand, but I knew. You were shifting your little heart out those last two days. Playing yourself and Johnny. I don't know how you kept it straight."

Mick closed his eyes briefly. "I was *playing* him. I didn't kill him."

Barrie swallowed through the choke hold and looked at Mick, and she saw a teenager. A heartbreakingly open, gorgeous, vulnerable teenager.

"They told me if I didn't the movie was dead," Mick went on.

"So, you did it for all of us," DJ said, in a voice so mocking it cut Barrie to the core.

"I did what I was told," Mick—or Robbie—said softly. "Didn't we all?"

For a moment DJ was silent, with Mick's words hanging in the air between them. And Barrie, tight in his grip, could feel him thinking, weighing what Mick had said.

"No," DJ said savagely. "You lie. If you hadn't killed him, you wouldn't have left." His voice hitched. "You left me alone. You, Johnny…you left me alone with all of *them*."

Mick took a careful step forward, and DJ's grip instantly tightened on Barrie's throat. Mick stopped in his tracks. "I'm so sorry for that, Deej. I had to get out. I wasn't thinking about anything but getting out, getting away." He spread his hands. "What chance did we have? Three kids against the whole machine?"

There was silence in the cold and candlelit throne room, and then Barrie felt DJ shaking his head.

"You're good. You're very good. But you're lying."

"I think so, too," another voice said, cutting through the darkness, young, clear, male. DJ's grip loosened on Barrie, and she turned toward the sound. And out of the shadows appeared Johnny Love, as pale skinned and golden as when he had manifested at the séance. Only this time he had a gun. Again Barrie had to fight to keep from gasping aloud.

Mick and DJ stared at Johnny, and for the moment reality rippled; they were impossibly but unmistakably in the movie now, the three actors reunited.

"Johnny?" DJ whispered.

"No," Mick said. "Not Johnny." He stepped forward carefully. "You're Tiger's friend, aren't you?" he asked the specter. "Phoenix." Barrie was shocked to realize that he was right. When she focused on the image of Johnny, she could see the telltale shimmer around the edges. Phoenix was a better shifter than she'd thought. Or perhaps anger and grief and determination had made him stronger.

"Right in one," Phoenix said. The gun never wavered.

"I'm so sorry about Tiger," Mick said.

"We're all sorry," Phoenix said. His eyes were fixed on the two older men. "But sorry isn't going to bring Tiger back. It isn't going to bring Johnny back. Somebody needs to pay." He leveled the gun at Mick.

Barrie pushed away from DJ, freeing herself, and called out, "Phoenix, wait!"

All three spun around, and reality rippled again. She was facing all three of the actors from *Otherworld,* on the set from the movie. She had to shake her head to clear the dreamlike feeling of déjà vu, to focus on the desperate situation in front of her.

Phoenix stared at her, confused.

"Let her go," Mick said, his voice taut. "She's got nothing to do with any of this. Barrie, *go,* let us handle it. Please."

She shook her head slightly and kept her focus on Phoenix, who was now holding the gun on all three of them. "I think there's more to this, Phoenix. If we all talk it through, I think we can get to what really happened."

Phoenix didn't answer her, but he was silent, watching her. She could almost feel his ragged breathing from across the room.

"You killed Mayo, didn't you?" she asked him softly. "You and Tiger."

"Mayo killed Johnny Love!" Phoenix cried out. "He killed him!"

Mick, DJ and Barrie stood in the triangle of thrones and looked at each other, with the trembling teenager in the center of them.

"He deserved to die," Phoenix finished with tears in his eyes. "For Johnny."

"How do you know Mayo killed Johnny?" Barrie asked softly.

"It was Tiger who found out," Phoenix said, swiping at his eyes with his left sleeve, never lowering the gun.

"Mayo heard Tiger could do Johnny Love. He started coming around, buying dates. He wanted Tiger to do things. He'd have a script, you know, make Tiger say things."

"What kinds of things?" Mick asked. Barrie thought he looked as pale as a ghost himself.

"Lame-ass things." Phoenix's voice changed, became mocking, mimicking. "'I belong to you, I'll always belong to you, you're the only one.' Me 'n' Tiger would just about die laughing after." His face hardened. "But one night Mayo was making Tiger do the whole bit as Johnny—'I'm yours, you're the only one'—and Tiger broke up. He laughed, you know? I mean, who wouldn't?" Phoenix looked around at the three adults defiantly. "And Mayo flipped. Started choking Tiger, calling him things. 'You little shit, I made you, you're nothing without me.' Like that. But Tiger was smart. He shifted. Suddenly old Mayo's holdin' Jim Morrison. Shocked him enough that he let go of Tiger and he got away."

Barrie was mesmerized. She could see the whole scene playing out, the young prostitute mouthing off to the mogul who was used to having the entire world bow to him, the mogul's fit of rage, the shock of Tiger's shift.

Phoenix was nodding to himself. "But that's how we knew he killed Johnny. It had to be, see it? Just exactly the same way. Johnny laughed at him and Mayo killed him." The boy's eyes were gleaming, determined. "So, we decided he had to die. For Johnny."

"Oh, Phoenix," Barrie said softly, her heart breaking.

"So, Tiger calls Mayo up again and says he misses

him, wants to see him, he'll be good this time, all that. They make a date, and Tiger takes the drugs with him. The same stuff that killed Johnny, right? That's the way it had to be."

Phoenix was shaking, his eyes far away as he remembered. "And there I am, waitin', and waitin'...but Tiger doesn't come back. Next thing I know I'm hearin' they're both dead." He looked around in anguish.

"So, who killed them?" Mick asked tensely.

Phoenix swung toward Mick, leveling the gun at him. "You did."

Barrie's heart dropped all the way through her chest to the ground. "No..." she whispered.

"Or you did." Phoenix swung toward DJ. "Silver bullets, in case you were wonderin'," he added, lifting the gun slightly. And then his eyes went from Mick to DJ. "One of you, or both of you. But someone's going to pay."

"You're wrong, Phoenix," Mick said softly.

"It doesn't make sense, Phoenix," Barrie said just as softly. "Why would *they* kill Mayo and Tiger?"

"Because Mayo killed Johnny," Phoenix said. "So, they killed Mayo. They were avenging Johnny. That's fine, all on its own, but they killed Tiger because he was there." His face crumpled again. "That's how people treat us. Like we're nothing. Like we don't count at all. Like they can just use us and throw us away...."

"That's how Mayo treated *us,* too, Phoenix," Mick said. "Mayo, and Branson, too—we were just props to them." He looked to DJ through the flickering candlelight. "But *we* wouldn't kill Tiger. That would be like

killing Johnny. We're the same, you and Tiger and us.
You think we can't see that?"

DJ nodded slowly, transfixed. "We're the same," he
said.

Phoenix looked from DJ to Mick, and Barrie could
see he was wavering. Mick took a tentative step toward
him.

"No!" Phoenix shouted, brandishing the gun. "You're
just trying to save your asses. How do I know you didn't
kill Johnny?"

Mick took another step. "I didn't kill Johnny, and
neither did DJ. We loved him. He was a part of us. Our
lives have never been the same since he died. You kill
us and the people who killed him win. Not just Mayo,
but everyone. Everyone who used Johnny and sucked
things out of him and wasn't there to protect him when
he needed it. The whole system."

Barrie knew there was something they were overlooking, and it suddenly flashed on her like blinding light.
"You didn't kill Travis Branson, did you, Phoenix?"

The teenager glanced toward her, startled. He looked
confused. "No. Why would I?"

Barrie looked to Mick. "So, who did?"

Mick looked back at her and nodded slowly, processing the information. "This isn't making sense. If Mayo
killed Johnny, and Tiger killed Mayo, then who killed
Tiger and Branson?"

"See?" Phoenix said. He looked wildly from Mick to
DJ. "It's one of them."

"No," Mick said. His eyes went to DJ. "You know
who."

The two men looked at each other across the circle, in the wavering candlelight.

"Damn," DJ said softly. "Darius. It has to be." And Mick slowly nodded.

Darius, the agent, Sailor's godfather? "Why?" she said in shock.

There was a sudden disturbance in the air, a cycloning spiral that would have looked like special effects if not for the sheer power of the vacuum that the air current created. And once again reality and film merged…as a figure appeared in the dark spiral, powerful, winged, lethal.

Darius Simonides.

The air calmed to a breeze, and the vampire settled on the floor, looked around at the assembled others.

"Enter the Wicked Witch of the West," DJ said.

"Shut up, Dennis," Darius snapped. "And stay where you are. Heroics don't suit you. I'll take that," he suddenly said to Phoenix, who had lifted the gun in his hand to fire. But suddenly Darius was no longer standing in front of him; he'd completely vanished. And then, before anyone could move a muscle, he had appeared again behind Phoenix and snatched the gun away, shoving the boy savagely to the floor, pinning him with a booted foot to the chest.

Barrie gasped and started toward him; Darius turned on her faster than her eye could follow, leveling the gun at her. She froze in her tracks. "That's good. Not one move. Do not make the mistake of thinking that I am joking."

Now that he had the floor, he held the gun almost casually, as if he didn't really need it to keep them all in check. He turned to Mick, and looked him over.

"Well, Robbie. You managed to fool all of us, didn't you? You've elevated 'hiding in plain sight' to an art form."

"I didn't do it to fool anyone," Mick said casually, but Barrie could hear the tension in his voice. "I did it to leave one life behind and start a new one that was actually mine."

Darius shook his head as if he were wounded. "We made you famous, Mayo, Branson and I."

Robbie—Mick—looked almost sick with contempt. "Whatever you did, you did for yourselves. You created us, the three of us, as a moneymaking machine."

Darius looked genuinely surprised. "We weren't just making money. We were making stars."

"Did you kill Johnny?" Barrie asked. She couldn't help herself.

"Of course not," Darius snapped. "That was Mayo and his exotic appetites. He was obsessed with the boy. When Johnny switched his...allegiance to Branson, Mayo killed him in a jealous rage, just as this young one—" he nodded to Phoenix, who was still huddled on the floor "—and his unfortunate friend deduced."

"And you knew it?" Barrie accused, disbelief and outrage warring inside her. "You never said anything? You let him get away with it? Why?"

Mick answered for Darius. "Power. You knew Mayo was going to have plenty of it, and keeping his secret meant you had something over him for life."

"Of course," Darius acknowledged. He sounded

bored. "He'd taken away my biggest client." His eyes went from Mick to DJ with a ghost of a smile. "If you'll both forgive my saying so." He shrugged. "I had to consolidate my losses. Of course, no one could replace Johnny—or you, really." His eyes went again to Mick, and lingered. "But I can't say I've done badly, over the years, with Mayo in my pocket and DJ in my stable."

DJ moved angrily, but Darius snapped his head around to look at him, and DJ froze in his spot and said nothing. Barrie shivered; she was close enough to feel the pure fear emanating from him.

"So, why did you kill him?" Mick demanded.

"I didn't," Darius said, glancing casually back to Mick. "Again, this young shifter was telling the truth. It was his shifter friend who killed Mayo, with that exotic cocktail. Mayo called me as he was dying. He was high as a kite, of course, didn't even know he was done for. Rambling on with his last breath, some bright idea that this young shifter should play Johnny's role in the remake."

Phoenix lifted his head at that, and Barrie felt a pang. *So, Tiger did have his moment of thinking he'd gotten a lucky break. At least he had that.*

"I could sense disaster brewing, and I flew to the Marmont to try to avert it. I was too late to save Mayo, but in time to have quite an interesting conversation with the young shifter, who was valiantly ready to send me along the way Mayo had gone." He smiled. "It seems Mayo, Branson and I are the root of all evil, corrupters of youth, exploiters of talent—"

"He got that right," Mick said evenly.

"And he was unfortunately correct about the manner of Johnny's demise, as well. Unfortunately for him—as that insight necessitated his own dispatch. I administered the second cocktail, not without a slight...struggle."

"That's why there were no footprints and no witnesses," Barrie said. "You flew, and left Tiger's body there."

Darius shrugged elegantly. "And that should have been the end of it. There was no reason for anyone to have connected that boy to Mayo." His gaze rested on Barrie for a moment. "And I could hardly have anticipated that you would take his death so seriously. He was a little nothing, a nobody—"

Phoenix gave a sob of rage from the floor. "He *was* somebody. He *was*."

"Yes, he was," Barrie said. "He was somebody."

"But hardly worth dying for, my dear," Darius said softly, and Barrie felt a chill.

"Then what about Travis?" Mick demanded.

Mick was keeping him talking, Barrie realized, but she had been thinking the exact same thing: *Why did the director end up dead?*

Darius shook his head in disgust. "Travis couldn't leave well enough alone. I'd cleaned up Mayo's death, we could have gone on without anyone asking any questions about Johnny or the movie...but then, even with Mayo dead, Travis wanted to continue with the remake. Ridiculous idea. He's too old to do it justice, anyway. A film like that needs a young edge."

Barrie couldn't believe he was even bringing up

the point; he sounded as if he were in a development meeting.

"But he even went so far to find independent financing. And that was just too much. A desperate move, anyway. He thought it would revive his career, and he was willing to risk all of those skeletons being dug up again. Perhaps you've heard the saying—'Three can keep a secret—if two are dead'? I realized the wisdom of it, and dispatched Branson. With Branson dead, the financing goes away, and the curse on the film is alive and well. I don't think I'll have to worry about anyone else attempting a remake for a long, long time. We can all go back to business."

He looked around at the four of them, and his voice dropped.

"If only you'd left it alone. We could have done all this with so much less bloodshed. As it is, I'm afraid there's going to be an unfortunate accident that kills four people tonight."

He glanced around at the enormous stage set. "And I couldn't have asked for a more appropriate setting. You have such a flair for the dramatic, Dennis, but this time it's going to kill you." His eyes swept down the line of candelabra, and he tutted reproachfully. "How many fire codes are you breaking, do we think? This is the problem with thinking you're immortal. Sooner or later the premise is tested."

"You wouldn't kill me," DJ said. "I'm worth too much to you."

"You may be right," Darius said. "And, touching as it is to see you and Robbie together again, I can't imag-

ine your loyalties stretch so far as to include dying for
your friends, old or new. As one vampire to another, I'm
willing to offer you a reprieve—with certain conditions,
of course. Your silence being paramount."

The two vampires looked at each other, and Barrie
had a horrible sinking feeling that DJ might cave.

"You'll never get away with it," she told Darius
quickly, trying to break the spell. "Do you think Rhiannon and Sailor won't hunt down my killer?"

Darius turned toward her and regarded her contem-
platively. "The vampire council won't let them near this
one. I'll see to that. Too many celebrities involved for the
brand-new Canyon Keepers to merit the case. Besides,
my dear, did you think I came here without establishing
an alibi? Right at this moment I am at a screening with
four hundred other people. I have any number of shifter
friends who were happy to do it for me."

Barrie's heart sank.

"It won't work, Darius," Mick said. "There are too
many of us, plus Mayo and Tiger and Branson. You'll
never explain all these bodies. There has to be a killer."

"And that's where you come in, dear boy," Darius
said, and Barrie was struck by the mesmerizing power
he had. It was no wonder at all that he'd been able to manipulate the three teenage boys that the Pack had been,
not to mention half of the rest of Hollywood. "As my
assistant and several colleagues will testify, I've had a
message from the long-lost Robbie Anderson, who con-
tacted me out of the blue and wanted to see me and DJ
here tonight. Apparently you're a crazed killer. You've

already killed off Mayo and Branson, and even the unfortunate boy who got in the way."

Mick shook his head in disbelief. "Why would I do that? Why would anyone believe you?"

"Because you killed Johnny. You confessed to DJ just before you tried to kill him. DJ escaped, the Keeper and the boy did not. It will be an Oscar-worthy performance from an Oscar winner."

Darius's black eyes slid to Barrie's face. "And tell me that your cousins won't believe it. This man has lied to you from the start."

Barrie looked to Mick, and their eyes locked.

"I won't do it," DJ announced.

Everyone whipped around to look at him. The candles wavered in the wrought-iron candelabra around them.

Darius rolled his eyes. "Don't tell me you're developing a conscience at this late stage."

"Maybe I am," the actor said in a voice that shook only slightly.

A small smile spread across Darius's face. "Suit yourself. Another body isn't going to make that much difference at this stage. I made you, I can make another to replace you."

Barrie felt her veins turn to ice at the unbridled arrogance. But they had bigger problems.

Darius looked around at all of them. "Have a seat, Robbie." He jerked the gun slightly at the triangle of thrones.

Mick stared back at him. "You think I would ever do anything you say again?"

Darius's black eyes shone. "Oh, I think you will." He turned and leveled the gun directly at Barrie's head.

Mick flinched. He looked at her, and, keeping his eyes on hers, he lowered himself to the throne. They gazed at each other, barely breathing.

"And you, Dennis," he said to DJ, who walked carelessly to another throne and dropped into it, flinging a leg over the armrest like a petulant crowned prince.

Barrie felt a wave of déjà vu; it was so exactly from the last scene of the movie.

Darius must have felt the same thing, because he looked at the two actors—present and former—with an expression of nostalgia on his face. "What a waste, really. Ashes to ashes. At least you can comfort yourselves in the thought that you are immortal…on film, anyway."

He stepped to a candelabra, picked it up as if it weighed no more than a feather and tossed it against the drapery. Flames instantly licked up the velvet-covered walls; the circle of mirrors reflected the dancing light.

Darius looked to the empty throne with real regret. "If only Johnny were here to complete the circle. I'd like to see that one last time."

And suddenly Barrie knew what she had to do.

She shifted.

She hadn't had practice in holding a full shift for long, but then, she didn't need to do it for long. Johnny's look was engraved in her consciousness. She'd spoken to his ghost, he'd even come to her in her dreams. So, she held his look and his essence in her heart, and she breathed into her astral body and became him.

"You have your wish!" she called out in Johnny's

voice, and Darius turned to her, startled, and then drew
back in shock.

Just as Tiger had saved himself—once—from Mayo
by taking him off guard, Darius was now so startled at
the sight of Johnny Love that he relaxed his bead on DJ
and simply stared at Johnny.

And in that split second Mick leaped from the throne
and tackled Darius.

They struggled with the gun. And as they fought,
Darius Changed. His eyes turned from black to red as
fangs sprouted from the roots where his canine teeth
were grounded, and he suddenly seemed twice his size
as the supernatural strength flowed into his limbs.

But on the other throne, DJ was Changing, too. The
animal ferocity that was always just below the surface of
his performances now was fully realized. He was a creature, a vampire, and there was no hesitation or laxness
in the way he flew at Darius with the full strength and
fury of his kind. The two otherworldly beings grappled
with each other in a tangle of fangs and leathery wings.

Mick grabbed Phoenix up from the floor and hustled
him over to Barrie. "Take him. Get him out of here."

She knew he was playing on her maternal instincts
to get her out of the fray, and she was having none of it.
"I'm not leaving. We have to put Darius down."

"Let me help," a voice said behind them, an ethereal
sound, but Barrie felt the resonance in her soul. She and
Mick turned as one…and she gasped.

The real Johnny Love stood in front of them, insubstantial but large as life. "He's not immortal and we

are," he told Robbie. Mick. Whoever the shifter was, other than the man Barrie loved.

To her shock, Mick grinned at the ghost of Johnny with a careless, adolescent, fuck-you smile. "Hell, yeah," he told Johnny. "Let's do it."

They turned as one and called out, "Deej! Let's off this bastard!"

DJ pulled himself away from the fight, and for a split second, the three Others looked at each other. In the candlelight they seemed caught between adulthood and adolescence, a trio of supernatural beauty the likes of which had never been seen in the fever dream that is Hollywood before or since.

"Get him!" Johnny called.

And the three of them converged on the vampire with all the idealism of youth and the strength of manhood and the supernatural power of their Otherworldly nature.

Invincible.

For a split second Darius seemed stopped in his tracks at the sight of them. Then he drew himself up, bared his fangs and crouched on his haunches to spring. As the fire raged around them, DJ tackled him with all his vampire power, pinning him to the floor. Mick picked up a chair and smashed it against the floor, then grabbed one of the splintered wooden legs: a perfect stake. DJ held Darius and Mick held the stake and Johnny used invisible strength to drive it home, piercing the vampire's flesh, cracking through ribs.

Blood spurted from Darius's chest as he arched and hissed and writhed in his death throes.

At that final moment it didn't feel like a movie to Barrie, but horribly, tragically real.

Darius spasmed in death, blood still fountaining, and then went still on the floor, pinioned through his heart.

And as the fire raged, a blistering heat, Barrie grabbed Phoenix and Mick grabbed Barrie and DJ grabbed Mick...but then they all looked back at the beautiful, golden ghost of Johnny Love, surrounded by mirrors and flames.

"Go!" Johnny shouted at them. "Go!"

And still they hesitated, until Johnny Love smiled, that heartbreaking, unforgettable smile.

"I'm fine," he told them. "I'll be fine now."

As he faded away, the others all ran for the stairs, ran for their lives, as the fire ate through the dying, curling, burning images of *Otherworld*.

Chapter 23

As it turned out, DJ had not been breaking as many fire codes as Darius had suggested. The basement room was completely fireproofed relative to the rest of the house. While the basement burned itself clean, the rest of the house was untouched; the blaze never even raised an alarm with the County Fire Department.

"I may be a junkie, but I'm not stupid," DJ huffed.

It was the height of Hollywood absurdity, but strangely fitting.

Barrie brought Phoenix back to the House of the Rising Sun, and after she had tucked the exhausted boy into a guest room, the Keepers convened in the great room with Mick, DJ, Brodie, Declan and Merlin in attendance. Rhiannon circulated through the room, pressing pastries and coffee and tea on everyone who would take them.

"Darius is dead," Barrie told them. "Staked through the heart with the help of Johnny Love. There's going to be nothing left of him in that inferno."

Sailor was crying; Darius had been her mentor, her godfather. She wasn't blind to or even surprised by his villainy; in fact, Sailor and Rhiannon had deduced that someone had lured them away from Barrie with the fake call about the Elven-vampire standoff. Brodie in turn had never made it to DJ's house, because he'd received texts apparently from both Rhiannon and Sailor calling for help at their own crisis, and of course he'd rushed to their aid. It was obvious in retrospect that Darius had been the one to orchestrate all those diversions.

So, surprised, no—but it was still a brutal blow to Sailor, and indeed to them all.

The biggest shock of all was the cold-bloodedness of the vampire's kills. Mayo had killed Johnny out of lust and jealousy. Tiger had killed Mayo out of empathy and revenge. But Darius had killed Tiger and Travis Branson, and covered up Mayo's crime, and attempted to kill Barrie and Mick and DJ and Phoenix, all for business. Nothing but business. And power.

"I don't know if I ever want to act again," Sailor sniffled. "What's the point, when people can do such horrible things to each other for money and for fame?" Declan pulled her close against him on the couch, soothing her.

"There's a nightmare side to the business, no doubt," Barrie said. "But remember, at its best Hollywood still creates dreams for everyone in the world. We need the good people to keep dreaming for us."

"Hear, hear," Mick said softly, and slipped his arm around her.

Brodie was on his feet, thinking through the real-life consequences of the situation. "We're going to need to account for Darius's death."

"Nobody can trace him to DJ's house," Mick pointed out. "He covered his own tracks by sending a shifter to some banquet in his place to create an airtight alibi. Whoever that shifter is, he's going to keep quiet so as not to be implicated in Darius's disappearance himself."

"So, we just say nothing?" Rhiannon asked.

"Could be the best course of action," Brodie admitted.

"And if that doesn't work, well, all that's left of him is a pile of ashes, and wildfire season is coming up," Sailor said.

Everyone looked at her in shock.

"So cute, and yet so devious," Declan said dryly, and hugged her.

Finally they turned to the real issue at hand: the teenager sleeping in the guest bedroom. Though Tiger was the one who had actually killed Mayo, Phoenix had been in on the planning of it.

Not a single adult in the group had any thought other than that Mayo had gotten exactly what was coming to him. He was a pedophile and a murderer who had cut short the life of one of the most talented Others ever to walk the planet, and he had gone scot-free for fifteen years, not to mention that he'd enjoyed a life of unprecedented power and fortune for every one of those years. Tiger was only one of a long line of young people—and young Others—Mayo had exploited, sexually and otherwise.

"But we can't have Others executing people—or conspiring to execute people—without trial simply because they deserve it. That would be anarchy and chaos," Rhiannon said.

"So, we put him on probation," Barrie said. "Phoenix is only sixteen. We can't handle him as if he were an adult, but we can't leave him alone. He's our responsibility now."

"That's right," said Mick. "I'd be willing to mentor him. And Deej will, too."

"Me?" DJ did a comic double take. "What do I know about kids?" he protested.

"Everything," Mick shot back at him. "You never grew up. I have a feeling it would be even better for you than it would be for him."

Even DJ had nothing to say to that. Mick looked at Barrie. "We'll be checking up on you. Both of you."

She felt emotions welling up in her, so strong she could only squeeze Mick's hand.

Rhiannon stepped up to Mick and looked at him steadily. "Thank you for keeping her safe."

He met her gaze. "It was good practice. I plan to be doing a lot of it in the future."

Rhiannon smiled. "I was getting that picture."

"So, what do we call you?" Sailor demanded. "Robbie? Mick? Michael?"

"Just don't call me late to dinner," Mick said, and everyone groaned good-naturedly. Then he looked serious. "Robbie was a onetime guest appearance. He's retired for good now."

"Johnny Love, Robbie Anderson and DJ reunited to defeat evil," Sailor sighed. "You know what's sad is— the best parts of this story can never be told."

"That's sort of the story of our lives," Rhiannon said.

"What's important is *we* know it," Barrie said, and threaded her fingers through Mick's.

There were hugs and kisses all around, and finally Mick and Barrie walked out the back door and across the patio, past the pool, which rippled enticingly in the moonlight.

"That water looks pretty fine," he said thoughtfully, and the tone of his voice made her blush all over. "What time do you think...?"

"They should be asleep in an hour or so," she said, and felt a shivery thrill of anticipation.

"We'll have to think of something to do until then," he said, and drew her under an arch of jasmine to kiss her. The fragrance surrounded them, and she sank into the bliss of his touch, his lips, his body against hers, his arms enclosing her.

"Do you know I fell in love with you when I was thirteen?" she said dreamily as he kissed her ear, the nape of her neck.

"And I've been trying to find you ever since," he said into her skin, and she felt fire race through her.

"City of dreams," she said, and stretched up against him.

"It is," he said, and then she was lost in his embrace.

* * * * *

A sneaky peek at next month...

NOCTURNE™

BEYOND DARKNESS...BEYOND DESIRE

My wish list for next month's titles...

In stores from 19th July 2013:

❏ Phantom Wolf – Bonnie Vanak

❏ Daysider – Susan Krinard

In stores from 2nd August 2013:

❏ Dark Rival – Brenda Joyce

Available at WHSmith, Tesco, Asda, Eason, Amazon and Apple

Just can't wait?

0713/

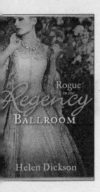

Join the Mills & Boon Book Club

Subscribe to **Nocturne**™ today for 3, 6 or 12 months and you could **save over £50!**

We'll also treat you to these fabulous extras:

- 🌹 **FREE L'Occitane gift set worth £10**

- 🌹 **FREE home delivery**

- 🌹 **Rewards scheme, exclusive offers…and much more!**

Subscribe now and save over £50
www.millsandboon.co.uk/subscribeme